MAGICAL CREATURES ACADEMY

LION SHIFTER

LUCÍA ASHTA

LION SHIFTER

Magical Creatures Academy: Book Two

LUCÍA ASHTA

Lion Shifter

Magical Creatures Academy: Book Two

Cover design by Sanja Balan of Sanja's Covers

Editing by Lee Burton

Additional editing by Elsa Crites

ISBN 978-1-0972-3126-3

Version 2019.06.10

Ghostly Return
Transformations
Castle's Curse
Spirited Escape
Dragon's Fury
Magic Ignites
Powers Unleashed

The Witching World
Magic Awakens
The Five-Petal Knot
The Merqueen
The Ginger Cat
The Scarlet Dragon
Mermagic
Spirit of the Spell

The Light Warriors
Beyond Sedona
Beyond Prophecy
Beyond Amber
Beyond Arnaka

PLANET ORIGINS UNIVERSE

Dragon Force
Invisible Born
Invisible Bound
Invisible Rider

Planet Origins

For Leia Stone.
Thanks for being a wonderful friend.

LION SHIFTER

MAGICAL CREATURES ACADEMY

Rina Nelle Mont

Second term student ~ Class schedule

9:00 AM – 10:45 AM Monday – Friday	Defensive Creature Magic 101	Prof. Marcy June Marsh
	Irele Hall	Illumination Room
11:00 AM – 12:45 PM Monday – Friday	Basic Shifting 201	Prof. Conan McGinty
	Irele Hall	Enchantment Room
2:15 PM – 3:45 PM Monday – Friday	Beginning Creature History 201	Prof. Wendell Whittle
	Irele Hall	Auditorium

I HURRIED TO EMERGE FROM THE PORTAL THAT bridged the fae's Golden Forest and Sedona, that city of red mountains nestled in the southwestern desert. Though the fae-created portal was the only way for a shifter like me to travel to the alternate dimension that served as home to all the fae, I couldn't stand another moment of the circular tube of flashing lights. It reminded me of one of those rickety amusement park rides that spun and flashed until my vision and stomach swirled with their particular brand of sensory overload.

I stepped onto pavement and stumbled out of the way of the ragtag group of fae prancing through the portal behind me.

Yeah, they pranced, I stumbled. Life wasn't fair.

I bent over, hands on knees, breathing hard as if I'd run the distance between the fae's Golden Forest and Sedona. The sun was bright and hot already even though it was early morning. Most of all, it was gloriously steady, as was the asphalt beneath my Converse.

"Oh, thank God," I wheezed, begging my stomach to keep its contents down. Puking was not the way I wished to start my second term at the Magical Creatures Academy. And I especially didn't want to throw up in front of Leander Verion, prince of the elves, not after the summer we'd shared together.

My brother Ky plodded over next to me, where he proceeded to bend over in perfect imitation of my elegant pose. "You okay, Rina?" he breathed in between pants.

I chuffed. "As well as you, I think."

He groaned. "How the hell do the fae do it? They're just as cheery as usual. Well, Leo isn't usually cheery…"

No, he wasn't. The elfin prince was as mercurial as they came, a fact that shouldn't have endeared me more to him—it really shouldn't have.

"Boone," my brother grunted, as the large werewolf plopped down onto his butt next to us, clutching his knees against his chest. "Y'all right?"

"Mmm," Boone replied noncommittally, then focused on pulling deep breaths in through his nose, out through his mouth. "I hope I never have to do that again."

I nodded, my long golden hair sliding around my down-turned face. "I hear ya. That sucked."

"It totally did," Boone said. "At least it's over." He sighed loudly—then his breath caught in his throat.

"What is it?" Ky asked. He and I turned around to

figure out what had made Boone go rigid. But all I could make out were the multi-colored sparkling lights of Leander's portal. They were as bright as the sun overhead, and obscured everything beyond them.

Boone rocketed to his feet, wobbled a bit, then tramped toward the others with heavy, lumbering foot-falls. Ky looked at me with wide eyes before lurching off after his friend. I remained where I was. I didn't see anything out of the ordinary—well, beyond a couple dozen fae of all types and sizes. The fae we'd traveled with spanned between a foot tall to the size of Leander, who was six-feet-two-inches of solid, yummy man ... er, elf. All of the fae had pointy ears, and most of them had wings, though not all did. Adalia, who'd become a close friend during my stay with the fae over the summer, was wingless. I was still learning the many different pedigrees and types of fae. Their race was the most varied among all magical creatures.

"Stand down!"

Boone's booming voice rang through the parking lot that should have been empty except for us. 6:30 AM was a little too early for the rest of the students of the Menagerie to begin arriving for the start of the new school term.

"Stand down, or we'll make you!" Boone was next in line to inherit the alpha rule of the Northwestern Werewolf Pack; his thunderous voice already possessed a ring of authority. I wanted to obey him, and he wasn't even talking to me.

I scrambled toward the others, ignoring how unsteady I was on my feet.

3

Some words, barked in response, filtered through my awareness, but I couldn't quite make them out. Leander's portal sparked and sputtered loudly as it faded from sight.

The moment it did, my heart took off in a thunderous beat.

Four men and one woman, all large and bulky with bulging muscles, were staring Boone, Leander, and my brother down, our motley crew of fae forming a loose half circle behind them.

Shifters, they had to be, unless a group of body builders had decided to show up at the trailhead for a random showdown—yeah, not freaking likely.

"What do you want?" Leander challenged, his voice a level mixture of authority and power.

The woman took a step forward and began to prowl in front of the four men at her back, her face turned toward us. Her shoulders bunched as she hunched into them, rounding her back and reminding me of a hyena. The frizzy chin-length hair that puffed out around her face and stood up around her crown only contributed to the image.

She bared her teeth in a sinister sneer. "You know what I want, and if you're smart, you'll hand them over without causing problems for yourself and your little friends."

Leander laughed, hollow and mocking. "You actually think we'll hand over two of our own? Then you don't know much about us. You especially don't know anything about me."

"Oh I know everything about you, Leander

Verion, Prince of the Elves." Her lip curled as if she smelled a particularly foul odor. "I also know everything about your father, Dillmon Erion, King of the Elves."

The way she said it, I half expected her to use air quotes around the king's title.

"You talk a good game, but we all know there are holes the size of craters in the infrastructure of the elves. Your father is king of a weak race."

Boone growled and took a step toward the woman with the striped and over-dyed hair.

Leander held the wolf back with a hand on his shoulder. "Whatever misguided opinions you have of my father, me, or our people, is not my concern. You'll retreat immediately and allow all of us to progress without interference."

"Or what?"

"Or we'll make you." Boone's words were barely comprehensible over the snarl that colored every syllable.

Dye Job glared at Boone, then Leander, and finally Ky. When she moved on to pick me out of the crowd, her thin lips spread into a menacing smile. The men behind her jeered, reminding me once more of a pack of hyenas.

"Oh, I don't think we'll do that. We take what we want, don't we, boys?"

The men whooped and grunted their agreement.

"Exactly," Dye Job continued. "So hand over Kylan and Rina Mont, or pay the price of shielding them." Her smile widened. "Trust me, the price of defying us is steep. We leave no survivors, do we, boys?"

"Not a one!" hollered one of the men, whose shoulders were twice as wide as mine.

Dye Job beamed while scrunching her brows low around her eyes, making her appear deranged enough to attempt to wipe out twenty-some creatures all to get to Ky and me.

I shifted from foot to foot. Should I just hand myself over? It had been one thing to allow Leander's father to protect Ky and me over the summer. He had the resources to do so without placing undue pressure on him or his people—or at least I thought he did. But the fae and werewolves that surrounded my brother and me weren't soldiers. They were students, still coming into their magical potential.

Before I could speak, Ky stepped forward. Leander lunged for him, but my brother swept his hand away.

My brother moved halfway between the two opposing forces and rose to his full height. As tall as Boone and Leander, strength radiated off him. Shoulders straight and strong, back tense, and biceps bulging as he flexed his muscles, he was every bit as formidable as Boone or Leander.

"If I turn myself over to you, will you leave here peacefully without harming anyone else?" he asked.

"No," I gasped as Leander and Boone took several steps toward him.

He put a hand up, halting their further approach.

"You'll leave my sister alone and leave here and never come back."

"Suuuure," Dye Job said. "That sounds exactly like something we'd do."

The men at her back erupted in wheezing cackles —like a band of octogenarians with a lifelong two-pack-a-day habit. That ratcheted up my unease.

By the way Boone bent his knees and cracked his neck to either side, he also realized these creatures had no intention of leaving here without a fight. Leander didn't visibly react, but over the summer I'd discovered that the prince rarely revealed his thoughts.

Adalia moved to my side and offered me a nervous half-smile. I returned the gesture, my own half-smile twice as nervous as hers. There was no way I could allow Ky to sacrifice himself for me.

"So you'd rather risk the death of your entire team instead of taking me up on my offer?" Ky asked. "It's a really good deal. You should take it. My friends and I will tear you to pieces if you don't."

"Is that why you're making the offer, then? Because you don't want to hurt us? That's so considerate of you." She spread mockery thick across her words. "Let me tell you how this is going to go down. My boys and I are going to take you and your sister, and we're going to kill anyone who tries to prevent us from doing our jobs. Is that clear enough for you?"

"Clear as it needs to be," Boone snarled as he stalked toward Dye Job.

Ky lunged forward and made a desperate grab for Boone, catching hold of him by the shoulder. "Last chance," my brother announced. "Take me and you all leave in one piece."

"No can do, buddy boy," Dye Job said. "Rage wants both of you, and we give Rage what he wants."

A few seconds passed during which Dye Job stared at Ky, Boone, and Leander, and the three guys stared right back, scooting closer together to form a wall to separate the rest of us from Dye Job and her cronies.

Dye Job leaned around the guys to flick a final look at me before calling over her shoulder, "Let's git 'er done, boys."

A chorus of growls and snarls erupted on both sides, before the crunching and snapping of bones and cartilage silenced the four "boys." They hunched further in on themselves, their features distorting with pain, as the mottled fur of a hyena rippled across the exposed flesh of their arms, necks, and faces—I'd been right.

The outlines of Boone and Ky's bodies blurred. Their entire forms vibrated so hard their teeth clattered for a few seconds before their bodies began to flicker in and out of focus.

The flickering was the final stage of their shifts. Their bodies solidified and ceased moving, revealing a glorious mountain lion and a wolf with thick, dappled gray fur, the same height as my brother's lion.

Ky and Boone completed their shifts while the "boys" were still halfway through theirs. The larger-than-normal wolf and the golden, desert-colored lion lunged toward the half-shifted creatures. Ky swiped a massive paw at one of the hyenas, slicing him open along the gut. Blood gushed from the wound as the creature whimpered and retreated from my brother.

The wolf pounced on a second, clamping lethal teeth around the neck of the one-third man, two-thirds hyena. His eyes glazed as Boone crunched down on fur and flesh.

I risked a glance at Dye Job; her eyes were wide. Obviously she hadn't expected Ky and Boone to complete their shifts faster than her boys. The stronger the magic within the shifter, the more seamless the shift, and the Menagerie only invited the most magical shifters in the world. She should have realized.

From a baldric draped across her back, Dye Job drew a sword that must have weighed a good forty pounds and rushed to intervene. Leander ran forward too, and several of the fae among us moved to aid their prince. The rest of the fae were too small and delicate to offer much help, though Adalia, who was approximately my size and unable to shift into any fierce animal—that I was aware of anyway—pressed herself against me in a fairy shield. I appreciated the intention, but I wasn't going to let a friend sacrifice herself for me, so I gently slid her to my side.

The two remaining hyenas completed their shifts and met Ky and Boone's attacks head-on. Leander cut off Dye Job's intervention, facing off with her without a single visible weapon of his own.

My breath caught in my chest. I reached for Adalia's arm without looking away from the show-down in front of us. I squeezed her hard; she squeezed back with equal ferocity. She adored her prince. I adored him too … for entirely different reasons. Still, I wasn't prepared to admit it to anyone yet, especially not Leander.

Dye Job wrapped both hands around the hilt of her massive broadsword and swung it at Leander. He whipped both hands forward to pulse a flash of silvery power at her. The arc of her attack didn't stop, but it did slow. Her cheeks scrunched toward her eyes, and she pressed her mouth into a tight grimace as she put all her strength into the swing of her sword.

Leander spread both palms open as he pulsed more magic the color of moonlight. Dye Job waded through the fog of his power as if she were waging her attack through a vat of thick molasses. Her sword finally aimed for Leander's head when he sidestepped the blade—and released his hold on his magic.

Her sword sank toward the ground with unexpected momentum, throwing her off balance when the sharp tip clanked heavily against the asphalt. Leander rounded behind her as the three human-sized fae who'd moved to his defense drew up at his back.

He had her—for the time being at least.

I cut my attention to Ky and Boone, my pulse leaping in my throat. Adalia clutched at my arm as Boone and Ky faced off with the two uninjured hyenas. They circled each other, teeth bared, a constant snarl rumbling from their throats.

The two remaining hyenas were unusually large, as some shifter animals were. Though the same in appearance as a regular hyena, they were fifty percent bigger, which meant they were a head taller than the mountain lion and wolf.

My breath hiccupped in my chest when Ky swiped a paw, claws extended, at one of the hyenas. The animal dodged the attack, squealing repeatedly in that disturbing way hyenas did—like a deranged man laughing up a storm in a psych ward.

The wolf and second hyena growled viciously and charged at each other, maws wide and paws smacking at each other in an attempt to clamp onto flesh before the other. I stopped breathing while I waited to see which of the two would overcome the other.

My heart couldn't take this shit.

Ky leapt onto the other hyena, knocking him to the ground, where the two rolled on the pavement, swiping and baring teeth in a desperate attempt to land on top.

A gunshot rang out into the morning.

My heart missed a beat entirely as Adalia shrieked and pulled me into a full embrace, clutching at my upper arms while she craned her neck to see who else had shown up to threaten us.

"Jacinda, order your crew to stand down right this second or I'll mow them all down."

"I MEAN IT," THE MAN SAID EVENLY, POINTING THE semi-automatic rifle he held in steady hands at Dye Job—Jacinda. He was a mixture between Mad Max and Captain Jack Sparrow, if either had ebony skin, waist-long dreadlocks, and wore ripped jeans and a faded Guns N' Roses t-shirt.

I hoped with desperation he was on our side and not here to claim Ky and me in Jacinda's place. His warm chocolate eyes glinted with competence. If he wanted to take us, he would. Besides, he was the only one with a big-ass scary gun.

"You know I'll follow through," he said casually, while the lone woman with him stepped to his side.

She was of average height and build, but like her companion she oozed competence and expediency. With her dirty blond hair and pretty but unremarkable face, she could have blended easily into a crowd. However, there was no chance of that. I wasn't sure what it was about her—certainly not her Smurfette t-shirt—but I was certain she was as dangerous as the big man with the big gun.

Jacinda flicked nervous eyes across the pair, and the two of her crew left standing positioned themselves so they could keep watch of Ky, Boone, and the newcomers at the same time. Their felled cronies panted shallowly atop the pavement. Their injuries were severe, the gashes upon their bodies deep and gaping, but perhaps their super shifter healing could still rescue them.

Jacinda appeared undecided for a few moments before finally pasting across her face what I thought was supposed to be a placating smile. "There's no need for extreme measures here, Damon. You can put the gun down and we can talk this through."

"It's good of you to point out what I *can* do," Damon said, "even though you know I won't."

"We can talk about this like friends, can't we?" She waved her hands in front of her in feigned innocence.

Smurfette barked out a harsh laugh. "Friends. As if."

"We haven't been friends in a very long time," Damon said. "In fact, I'm pretty sure we never were. I tend not to like people who try to stab me in the back."

Smurfette narrowed her eyes at Jacinda, perhaps remembering the traitorous event. When she crossed her arms over her chest, I noticed she wore a wicked curved blade along both hips.

"Excuse me," Leander said, "but who are you? And what are your intentions?"

Good! I needed to know. Every muscle in my body was clenched, and Adalia was gripping me so hard I might bruise.

Damon kept the barrel of his semi-automatic pointed at Jacinda, but flicked his gaze to Leander, and then over to the rest of us. Smurfette continued to glare at Jacinda, who hadn't once glanced at her fallen comrades since the two of them had arrived on the scene.

"We're Enforcers," Damon said, and my breath hitched as it ping-ponged through my chest. I hadn't thought any of them had survived the Voice's attack at the end of last term. I'd believed all seven-hundred or so of them dead.

"You're cockroaches, is what you are," Jacinda grumbled. "You're supposed to be dead with the rest of them."

Smurfette took several menacing steps toward Jacinda, stalking around the trajectory of Damon's gun. "Say that again, bitch," she snarled.

I took half a step backward, dragging the terrified-looking Adalia with me, before realizing I'd done so. Smurfette was *fierce*. If Jacinda wasn't scared of her, then she was crazy.

"You wouldn't back off," Jacinda spit out the words. "So you forced us to deal with you however we had to. You should've listened. You were fools."

Jacinda was definitely cray-cray. Certifiable.

Smurfette spluttered in rage before finally managing to get the words out. "Deal with us? *Deal with us*? Is that what you call slaughtering us in the middle of the night while we slept?"

Jacinda shrugged. "Hey, we did what we had to. You left us no choice."

Smurfette growled so viciously that everyone surrounding her, with the exception of Damon, took a step away from her as she stalked a few feet closer to Jacinda, who held her ground. I didn't think the Enforcer could formulate words anymore. Had she been in a cartoon, smoke would've been whistling out of her ears.

"You have no honor," Damon told Jacinda as he towered behind Smurfette.

Jacinda shrugged, her frizzy mop of hair brushing her over-developed shoulders. "Honor's for the weak and struggling. We're survivors."

"Don't go making this about something it's not. You're power-hungry fuckers, the whole lot of you, nothing more."

"You have no right to police our every move! You can't—"

"We can. And we will." He waved his gun between her and her hyenas. "Now, what's it gonna be? Are you going to surrender or should I sic Sadie on you?"

Smurfette—Sadie, I guess—snarled as convincingly as any animal while a flash of orange magic rippled across her bare arms. What was that? I swiveled to face Adalia, whose eyes were wide with shock. So she'd never seen anything quite like it before either … not from a shifter. Magic like that was supposed to be reserved for mages, and for exceptional creatures like Leander … and maybe me.

Jacinda finally snuck a glance over her shoulder to take in the hyenas. The breathing of one of the fallen ones had slowed to the occasional shallow inhale, suggesting his wounds were too grave for his shifter healing. The other struggled, a thick thread of saliva hanging from his mouth as he panted without reprieve.

Ky and Boone hadn't backed off from the other two, and Leander and the three fae behind him were positioned within striking distance of Jacinda.

Her shoulders drooped by a fraction of an inch, though she schooled her facial features into impassivity. "We won't surrender"—Damon raised his gun by an inch so its barrel pointed at her chest—"but I'm open to talking terms," she rushed to say.

"Terms?" Sadie barked without mirth. "Are you out of your fucking mind? You *murdered* our friends in their sleep. I'm gonna rip you to pieces so tiny no one's gonna know it's you once I'm done."

"Sadie," Damon warned. "Alive would be better."

"Not for this trash."

"We'll take her to Thane. He'll get answers out of her. Finding out about what the Voice and the Shifter Alliance intend to do is more important than killing her."

Sadie growled.

"It's how we'll prevent another attack like the one that took out our friends," Damon pressed.

She growled again, more softly this time, resigned.

Damon nodded once, his heavy dreadlocks thudding against the back of his black t-shirt. "Come now, Jacinda, and maybe we'll even get some medical help for your minions."

"I'm not going anywhere if you're planning to hand us over to Thane," Jacinda said.

Damon smiled coldly. "It's either that or kill you on the spot. Your choice. As you can see, Sadie would rather see you dead. That one there will probably die within the hour if he doesn't get help."

"He might die anyway." The slightest hint of concern vibrated through her voice.

"Yeah, he might, and he'd deserve it. But if you come with us, he'll have a chance of not bleeding out right here, right now."

Police sirens wailed in the distance, undoubtedly heading our way. Surely someone had called in the gunshot that was so out of place in the small town.

"You have ten seconds and then I'm deciding for you," Damon said. "We all need to be gone before the human cops get here."

Sadie prowled closer to Jacinda, and Leander and the three human-sized fae closed the gap behind her. Boone and Ky stalked nearer to the two standing hyenas.

"Fine," Jacinda said tightly. "I'll let you take us, but you get help for my men. If you renege on that promise, so help you…"

"No," Sadie said a little too happily. "So help *you*. Thane's been waiting to get his hands on any of you.

You assholes killed his wife." She grinned maniacally and Adalia squeezed my arms.

Jacinda visibly gulped. Who the hell was this Thane?

"Unlike you, we keep our word," Damon said. "Come on. We're moving." With the barrel of his gun, he ushered her in the direction they'd come from.

Jacinda hesitated for a second before following his direction. The two standing hyenas edged around Boone, and Ky and fell into line.

"You got the others?" Damon called over his shoulder to Sadie as he pressed the other three ahead.

"No problem," Sadie said. "I can handle this scum." She flicked each hand in the direction of one of the fallen hyenas, mumbled something unintelligible under her breath, and hovered them into the air with a glow of orange light.

"Wow," I whispered.

"See ya later, kids," she called back to us while floating the creatures further across the parking lot, in the opposite direction of the small residential street that bordered the trailhead of Thunder Mountain. Blood dripped from both bodies, marking out a consistent trail. I hoped they had a plan, or the police would follow the blood splatters straight to them.

Ky, Boone, Leander, the rest of the fae, and I watched the two enforcers and their prisoners until they took a sharp left turn … that led to nowhere in particular.

"Where are they going?" I asked.

"I don't know," Leander said, "but we'd better get

the hell out of here ourselves before the police find a bunch of supes standing next to pools of blood."

"Right. Absolutely. That's a very good idea. We should go."

I rambled when I got nervous. This was most definitely not the smooth beginning to the new school year I'd hoped for.

Leander moved to my side, his silver eyes scanning me from top to bottom. I flushed at his attention, and Adalia, always observant, released the death grip she had on my arm and stepped away to allow Leander to take her place.

He placed a hand on my shoulder, squeezing gently. "Are you all right?"

No, definitely not. Ky and Boone just killed two hyenas!

"Yeah, I'm fine."

But the way compassion brimmed in his gaze suggested he didn't believe me. "You'll let me know if I can help in any way, won't you?"

I nodded a bit too abruptly. "Absolutely. Of course. I'm sure I'll be fine soon." Then I shut up because I'd basically admitted I wasn't okay in the first place.

I sighed in relief when Boone and Ky set off in the same direction Damon had taken, leading us toward the massive, towering, impenetrable mountain—that wasn't as impenetrable as we once thought. Leander's stare, which seemed to penetrate my exterior, remained on me while the wolf and lion skimmed the base of the reddish mountain, and when we passed the point where Damon had veered left, they continued circling around to the right. When we'd walked for at least five minutes, avoiding prickly shrubs, the gnarled, exposed roots of Juniper trees, and more cactus plants than I cared to count, the police sirens stopped, meaning the cruisers had likely arrived at the scene.

Ky and Boone began sniffing the ground. Like that, they led us further around the base, until Ky stalled, sniffing in one spot. But Boone continued on.

"What is it, Ky?" I asked. He looked up, and if a mountain lion could smile, he did. His majestic face lit up and an almost wistful air settled around him, making him seem … entirely magical. He hesitated with whatever he was experiencing, then trotted after Boone.

When they both stopped at the same location, I knew they must have found the entrance to the school. Completely unmarked, no one without magic would be able to sense the point of access. A sprawling campus of higher magical learning was contained in the middle of Sedona, and none of its residents realized a thing.

In unison, Ky's and Boone's bodies blurred, their edges losing all definition. They quickly cycled through the phase where their animal forms vibrated, and when their bodies began to flicker rapidly, as if they were illuminated by a strobe light, the rest of us crowded them in preparation to move through the mountain. If the cops were at the trailhead, there was a chance they might spot us and find such a large group of people suspicious after a random gunshot.

Ky and Boone popped back into their human bodies. Boone nodded at Leander and about-faced toward the mountain … and disappeared inside it.

A trail of fae, including Adalia, followed right behind him.

Leander and my brother were the last. My brother moved to my side.

"What happened back there?" I asked. "What made you stop?"

He smiled, once more a wistful air settling across his features. "I caught the scent of a true mountain lion."

"Oh." I hadn't expected that. "That's pretty amazing."

"Incredible." He stared pensively off into the distance before snapping himself out of it.

"Ready?" Leander asked both of us.

"Of course," Ky said, but I didn't bother. Was I ready for another wild term at a crazy-ass school for magical creatures? I wasn't entirely sure.

Ky pulled past Leander, and the elfin prince winked at me.

Okay. Twist my arm. I'd follow the sexy prince anywhere, even if his father had gone to great lengths to ensure I realized he forbade the two of us being together—apparently, I was the wrong race; I lacked the requisite pointy ears.

With a foot inside the mountain, Ky extended his hand to me.

Was I embarrassed to take my big brother's hand in front of Leander? Yes, absolutely. Was I embarrassed enough to refuse his offer? Hell no. Walking through solid rock in the pitch dark was creepy; I didn't imagine I'd ever get used to it.

I clasped Ky's hand and allowed him to pull me inside Thunder Mountain. Leander stepped right behind me. His presence prickled along my back as I reeled from the absence of most every other sensation I was supposed to feel.

The air was too thin, too insubstantial, the darkness too thick, the ground too tenuous. I shuffled my feet along in the wake of Ky's momentum and forced my panic down. Now that I knew what was on the other side of this wall of rock, a little discomfort was worth it.

There was no place else like the Magical Creatures Academy on this Earth. It gave *bizarre* a whole new definition.

I sucked in the rich air of the Menagerie with greedy gulps. I wasn't entirely certain it was real air—after all, the entire campus was housed within a mountain that shouldn't contain it—but my body seemed to think so.

Ky released my hand, and he, Leander, and I meandered up the pebbled path lined with flowers of nearly every color, some of them containing multicolored petals within one blossom. The scent of their perfume and the azure of the cloudless sky lifted my spirits. The wily willows, scattered across the entirety of the campus, leaned in our direction as we passed, as if to extend a jovial welcome. I swore one of the trees was actually waving at us, its branches swaying in a distinct back and forth motion.

The sunshine glinted off Leander's shoulder-length hair, making it glow like the moon itself. His wings were as white as new-fallen snow, tipped with a silver sheen that matched the rest of him. Dressed in jeans and a t-shirt like my brother, I could make out the lines of his firm shoulders and back beneath the thin fabric. He filled out his jeans like a cowboy dream, just the distraction I needed to help me shake the unease of Jacinda and her minions trying to take Ky and me by force.

My step faltered, and Ky and Leander turned toward me.

"What is it?" Ky asked while Leander took in my shocked expression before scanning the length of my body, up and down, taking his time. The prince took a step closer to rest a hand on my forearm, concern scrunching his brow.

I lifted a trembling arm to point. "Th-there."

"Boone and the rest of the fae?" Ky said.

I shook my head, my loose hair bouncing everywhere as I worked not to freak out. "Not them, Ky. Obviously not them. R-rasper the Rabbit is back from the dead."

"What?" Ky and Leander spluttered in unison, narrowing their eyes to see beyond our friends.

"How's that possible?" Ky whispered.

"It isn't." Leander's full mouth settled into a straight, grim line. "I mean, theoretically it is, but Sir Lancelot would never allow it. The magic required to bring someone back to life is the darkest there is. He'd never permit something like that on campus. When the person—or rabbit—comes back, they're dark, right down to their souls. And Rasper the Rabbit wasn't exactly happy-go-lucky to begin with."

A shiver racked the entire length of my body.

Rasper the Rabbit had been downright terrifying, and that was before he'd died and come back to life. I gulped and willed my feet to continue moving forward.

"Come on, squirt," Ky said gently. "The sooner we pass Rasper's inspection, the sooner we can put it behind us."

I nodded fervently, but my legs still wouldn't move.

"I won't let him intimidate you, Rina," Leander said, squeezing my arm reassuringly. "I promise."

Again I nodded as if in a dream—more like a nightmare.

It wasn't like I'd been happy the poor rabbit had died. To boot, he'd died a gruesome death while defending us, fighting the shifters who'd invaded the school until his last breath. I'd grieved his death in my own way, realizing it wasn't his fault he'd been so freaking scary—or maybe it had been his choice to be so frightening—but it was still easier to forgive his gnarly disposition when he was no longer around.

Ky took my hand again and tugged me gently in the direction of the academy's humongous gates. "No point putting off the inevitable."

I nodded absently and allowed him to guide me forward … toward the scariest creature on the entire campus.

After several paces I gasped, choked on my own saliva, and ground to a halt.

Ky stopped on the pebbled path, dropped my hand, and turned to face me, hands akimbo. "Come on, Rina. I get that you're scared, but get over it, will ya. This is getting ridiculous."

I didn't even bother resenting my brother for calling me scared in front of Leander. I lifted the same shaky arm and pointed toward the gate again.

Ky scoffed loudly. "Enough with the theatrics. We have——"

"What the...?" Leander trailed off, squinting in the direction of the gate.

My brother swiveled toward the entrance to the school and his jaw dropped for a moment before he snapped it shut. "What the fuck is going on?"

"There are two of them," the prince of elves said.

"No," I squeaked. "There are three of them. You can barely see the third one behind the pillar. See him now?"

Leander's only response was to press his lips more tightly together. Up ahead, Adalia and the rest of the fae also hesitated, their heads canted toward each other as they presumably discussed the three Raspers.

"Come on." Ky grabbed hold of my arm and pulled. I allowed him to lead me toward the group of fae. Better to face the triple terror in a horde.

I figured we'd talk about it together before advancing, but neither Ky nor Leander slowed once we reached the rest of the fae, who immediately fell into step behind their prince.

Adalia found her way to my other side when Leander drew up to the gates, at least twenty vertical feet of splendor. Its precious metals, resplendent gold in white, yellow, and rose tones, woven into braided patterns across the tall bars, shone in the early morning light. Its precious gems glittered, the bright blues, greens, and reds of sapphires, emeralds, and rubies beaming colored rays across the ground as if we were at a rave.

Even so, I barely noticed the gate. I was too busy previewing what my nightmares would look like for the foreseeable future.

Leander stopped in front of the gate and two of the rabbits squared off with him, the third rounding the pillar that had partially concealed him to join the others. When Ky united with Leander in facing the rabbits, I cowered behind him, and Adalia cowered behind me.

"Good morning," Leander said, using his regal voice. "I am Prince Leander Verion, prince of the elves. And you are?"

The three rabbits lined up next to each other and straightened to their full height, which made them exactly as tall as Leander and my brother—before taking into account their erect jackrabbit ears, which put them over seven feet tall.

"We're Rasper's brothers," the one in the middle said, his voice like sandpaper. "We're here to exact vengeance for Rasper's death."

I swallowed dryly, infinitely grateful their wrath wasn't directed at me. Their black beady eyes studied the crowd as they crossed their arms over their chests in three identical movements.

"We're also here to protect all of you," the one to

the left said. "If Rasper believed it was an important mission, so do we."

His two brothers growled at that, making me wonder whether they weren't in agreement with the importance of Rasper's mission, or if they simply wanted to eat us or something equally horrible. With the rabbits, it was difficult to tell.

The three of them were identical to Rasper in every way, down to the way they were dressed. The brothers wore the same white button-down shirts, and only differed in how many buttons were clasped. Left had all but the top button closed, whereas Middle and Right wore their shirts half unbuttoned, revealing a lot of chest that would've been cute on a cotton-tailed bunny. On them, it was eerily disturbing—it gave them a *Miami Vice* look that was entirely out of place on a killer rabbit. With plain black slacks that displayed a sizable, lumpy bulge, bare feet that revealed claws better reserved for predators in the wild, and sharp, needle-pointed teeth, my nightmare was complete.

"We won't allow admission to anyone who doesn't pass our test," Left said.

"And there are a fucking whole lot of you," Right said, "so you'd better get to cooperating before we cut you."

"We don't cut the students," Left admonished. "We only frighten them when necessary." His tone was actually peppy, and here I'd been thinking that Left was the more reasonable of the three.

"We have a schedule to keep," Right rasped, "so

enough with the fucking around."

Adalia clutched my arm a little too tightly as I attempted to shrink out of sight of the rabbit mafia.

"We're not 'fucking around,' as you so elegantly put it," Leander said. "We're waiting to hear your names so we can proceed with admission to the school."

Right grunted, Middle picked his teeth with a claw on his paw, and Left glowered at Leander. A few beats passed where I was pretty sure all of us standing behind Leander and Ky were praying the earth would swallow us before we could become rabbit stew, in the twisted sense.

Finally, Left took half a step in front of his brothers, his big floppy feet smacking against the pebbles, scattering them. "I'm Rammer. This is Raider"—he pointed to Middle—"and that's Raker." Right inclined his head toward us, scowling.

"We're pleased to meet you," Leander said. Even though what he said wasn't true in my case, I was glad he was speaking for all of us. "We offer our condolences for Rasper the Rabbit's death. We were all very sorry to learn of his passing."

The tension across the rabbits' faces ebbed a bit. Raider nodded tightly.

"We also thank you for coming to help protect the school and its students. These are troubling times, and we honor your contribution."

Whoa. Leander was working it, all right. And his diplomacy was effective. The rabbits' tension eased by another fraction.

"We're ready to begin the admission process, if you please." Leander closed the distance between him and the rabbits, Ky shadowing him, perhaps unwilling to allow Leander too close to the killer rabbits without him.

I didn't follow. There was no way I was getting any closer to the rabbits until I had to.

"State your full name for the record," Rammer said, though Leander had already offered it.

"I'm Leander Verion, prince of the elves."

"And you?"

"I'm Kylan Bond Mont."

"Your arm," Rammer said, while Raider and Raker circled around them. Raker pulled the glass straw-looking thing from a holster on his hip while Raider proffered the compass-compact-mirror apparatus that magically confirmed our identities.

Leander offered Rammer the crook of his elbow and my pulse began hammering in my head. I realized that Leander wasn't as vulnerable as he appeared, offering the vicious rabbit the soft flesh of his inner arm, but I couldn't help but be nervous for him.

Rammer brought the tip of the straw device to Leander's arm, but instead of resting it against his flesh as Rasper had done, he punctured his arm with the blunt tip of the element, the diameter of which was almost as wide as my pinky finger.

Leander grimaced, and Ky hissed, "You're not supposed to cut him with it. You're only supposed to *rest* the tip of the sanguinator *on top* of his skin."

"Oh," Rammer said, pulling out the straw thingy

—a sanguinator, apparently—not appearing the least bit concerned that he'd created a gouging hole in the elf's arm. "That's probably enough blood," he said to his brothers.

"Ya think?" said Ky, sarcasm on full display.

Rammer ignored him, but Raider and Raker pinned Ky with matching rabbit death glares. Ky bared his teeth at them before Leander said, "It's fine, Ky. Let it go."

Ky growled, as did Raider and Raker. This wasn't going well at all...

When Rammer finally placed the tip of the sanguinator against the compass-mirror thingy, it took only ten seconds for the apparatus to whir and flash like a boiling kettle with confirmation that the prince of the elves was precisely who he said he was.

"You can go in," Rammer said, but neither he nor his brothers moved out of the way.

"Thanks, but I'll wait for all of my people to be approved before entering," Leander said while he flicked a backward glance at me.

"Whatever. Next!"

Ky bared his arm and walked to the rabbit, and I could barely stand still from the nerves. I leaned into Adalia, comforted by the fact that we were both in this together. This time, Rammer only pressed the tip of the sanguinator against my brother's arm, and thirty seconds after he'd deposited Ky's blood in the compass-mirror thingy, he received his approval.

"In ya go," Rammer announced.

"I'll wait for my sister, to enter with her please."

My brother hardly ever said *please*.

"Which one's your sister?" Raider said, the roughness of his voice making me squirm. At my slight movement, his gaze landed on me like a laser beam. He sneered with a little too much pleasure, as if he were preparing to feast on my fear. "Ah, that tasty one."

"Tasty?" I squeaked, and then wished I hadn't.

Raider grinned. "Tasty."

I shot an alarmed look at Ky, who moved to my side. Leander took up a protective position on my other side, moving Adalia out of the way. The prince was squinting at the mobster rabbit, displeasure etched across every one of his beautiful features.

"I'll be meeting with the headmaster as soon as I get inside," Leander said, diplomacy absent, the tacit threat of his words vibrating across them. "It won't be good if I have to tell Sir Lancelot that your behavior toward the students is inappropriate. The headmaster values etiquette and respect above all else."

Raider waggled his beige furry jaw, petite bunny nose twitching. "State your name for the record, girl."

"My name is Rina Nelle Mont," I said in a rush. With a thick swallow, I stepped from between Ky and Leander and toward Rammer, offering him my arm. I clenched my eyes shut while he pressed the sanguinator to my skin. I didn't open them again until I heard his pronouncement.

"You may enter the Magical Creatures Academy. Your identity has been confirmed," Rammer said.

The breath I hadn't even realized I'd been holding

left my body in a whoosh. I snatched my arm back when I realized Rammer was still holding it and scampered out of the way. I circumvented the rabbits and had to refrain from running toward the closed gate.

"Open the gate!" Raker said, his voice like the exhaust of a dirty diesel engine.

Both doors of the gate swung open inward, though nothing visible caused the motion; it had to be one of the many magical spells that governed the functioning of the academy. The precious metals and gems glittered, but I was in no mood to appreciate their beauty. I hustled through the gate as a trumpet blared some fanfare above my head. Once I was on the other side of the gate—and away from the monster triplets—I glanced upward.

The same foot-tall fairy from last term was there, but his heart just wasn't in it. Where his *too-too-do-doooo* blare had been crisp and joyful in January, now it was limp and deflated. Seated atop one of the gate's massive pillars, his tiny trumpet hung dejectedly by his side. His sigh was so heavy, I could make out the rise and fall of his chest from where I stood, twenty or so feet below.

Poor little guy. The rabbits were probably scaring the crap out of him too. The bunny mob had likely threatened to eat him and pick their teeth clean with his bones or something.

When Ky waltzed through the gate after me, the fairy brought his trumpet to his lips, but only emitted a single *toot* before allowing his brass instrument to plop against his lap.

I feel ya, little guy.

"Let's go," Ky said. "You're acting weird."

I was acting weird? "Are you serious right now, Ky? Did you see them?"

"Yeah, and they're just terrifying enough that maybe we'll be safe at school this term."

That was uncomfortably sobering...

I insisted on waiting for Adalia, but the moment she ran through the gate to a wheezing *toooo* that sounded like a deflating balloon, we booked it out of there. We didn't stop walking until we reached the administration offices inside Acquaine Hall, which I knew from experience held its own breed of unsettling creatures.

"Welcome to the Magical Creatures Academy," I muttered to myself as I yanked open the double doors and slid into the building's cool interior. Adalia and Ky followed me in as my sneakers squeaked across the marble floor.

"I don't need you to tell me how to do my job," a deep voice growled from the open door to the admin office. "Someone oughta teach you some manners. We're not slaves of the Menagerie. We're employees."

I sighed. Pygmy trolls. Ornery, ugly-enough-to-be-cute-if-they-weren't-so-mean pygmy trolls.

Better to get it over with. Surely they'd be better than the triplet rabbit mobsters. I steeled myself for their colorful fro-hawks and round, tiny butts, and walked inside.

❦ 4 ❦

Check-in went surprisingly smoothly, probably because Adalia and I did everything Pink Fro-Hawk told us to do, offering our acquiescence via monosyllabic responses that suited the troll just fine. Also, compared to the rabid rabbit triplets, the ornery pygmy troll didn't seem quite as bad as usual. It was easier to ignore the perma-frown that etched lines into his little-old-man face when I wasn't afraid he'd kill me on the spot.

Even Ky was unusually quiet, and I wondered if he would have preferred to wait with Leander and Boone. After all, they were his best friends; I was just his "squirt" of a sister. Since the Shifter Alliance had attacked the school at the end of last term, he'd rarely left my side. We'd spent more time with each other recently than we had since he hit puberty.

But we met up with Leander, Boone, and the rest of the fae soon enough, sprawling out on the open rectangular quad enclosed by the campus' buildings. There was little to do but wait since we'd been assigned the same dorm rooms and roommates as the term before, and the school provided for most of our needs. After last term, I knew to expect that my spare uniforms and course materials would already be in my room when I arrived. I suspected pygmy trolls were the ones who kept the dorm rooms up, but I didn't linger on the thought. I didn't think I could handle the idea of mostly naked pygmy trolls rifling through my drawers.

Time rolled by slowly, which suited me just fine. Life was about to get extremely busy, and the magical springtime sunshine was bliss on the bare skin of my arms and legs now that I was back in my crisp uniform.

"Those rabbits were freaky," Adalia said, not for the first time since we'd claimed seats on the grass. I'd mostly managed to forget about Rammer, Raider, and Raker, but Adalia and many of the smaller fae still appeared rattled.

"At least we only really have to see them at the start and end of term," I mumbled, leaning into my hands behind me and stretching out my legs and crossing them at the ankles. I closed my eyes, sighing. While the fae's Golden Forest had been magical in its own way, I'd missed the Menagerie—the good bits of it at least. Bright sunbeams snaked down between the thick tree trunks of the campus' wily willows and other trees old and tall enough to defy logic. Then again, most everything within the Magical Creatures

Academy defied logic. When magical spells controlled much of the school's functioning, nearly anything was possible.

"I'm sorry for what that rabbit said to you."

I didn't need to open my eyes to attach the voice to its owner. My heart began to thump noticeably in my chest.

"My prince," Adalia said as I slid my eyes open to linger on Leander.

"Would you mind leaving us for a few minutes?" Leander said.

Before he'd completed his request, Adalia was jumping to her feet. "Of course, My Prince." She bowed low, swiveled on her heel, and moved to join the other fairies.

Unreasonably nervous, I stared at him. Though we'd spent an entire summer in proximity to each other, there'd been far too little of the closeness I'd hoped for. Leander's father had proven remarkably skilled in orchestrating interference. I suspected even Ky had worked to keep the two of us apart, but whether because of his own reasons or the king's orders, I didn't know.

"He shouldn't have said that you're tasty," Leander said, taking a seat beside me on the grass, and I blinked a few times to remember what he was referring to. Right. The rabid rabbits.

"It's okay," I said with a shrug.

"Is it?" The elfin prince's silver eyes pinned me in their stare and I resisted the urge to fidget.

"I mean, no, it's not okay, actually. I just said that

without thinking. It's just"—I shrugged again —"there's nothing I can do about it. I'm used to it, I guess. Guys always say crap like that."

He stared at me without blinking for a full thirty seconds. "If that's what men say to you, then they shouldn't."

An inexplicable wave of emotion rose within me, and I fought to tamp it down. He'd obviously never been in Berry Bramble High, or any comparable high school across the United States, where inappropriate behavior was an everyday occurrence.

He tilted his head and trailed his attention across my face. I sensed the trajectory of his gaze like a caress. "Though I suspect that you must be tasty."

My cheeks instantly heated and I hurriedly looked away. When I couldn't resist any longer, I peeked back at Leander. My breath hitched. His eyes were illuminated like bright full moons, and they were pinned on me ... as if nothing else existed. My own gaze dipped to his full lips, the ones I'd pictured against mine more times than I'd admit to anyone.

"I'm sorry we didn't get to spend much time together while we were at my home," he said. "I'd hoped there would be time for us to get to know each other."

I smiled gently. "That would have been nice."

So damn nice.

"Maybe while we're here we can—"

"Hey, Leander, we should go chat with Sir Lancelot," my brother called, moving toward us, his eyes narrowed, jumping from Leander to me and back again. "You know the owl, he doesn't like to wait for his updates."

"Fine. I'll be right there," Leander called over his shoulder, not turning to look at my brother. He stared at me for several unblinking beats. "I guess this will have to wait."

But as he stood, I wasn't sure what "this" was or what any of it meant. I kept thinking—maybe hoping—that Leander was interested in me. But he hadn't said or done anything that made it explicitly clear what he was thinking. Okay, maybe saying I looked tasty was something, but what was it exactly? I wished I knew!

The elfin prince stuffed his hands in his pockets, tucked his feathery wings firmly against his back, and smiled. "I'll catch ya later, Rina."

"Sure. Yeah. Sounds good. Great," I rambled.

His smile broadened, and I flushed. I watched him walk away, allowing my gaze to travel the length of his body, lingering anywhere I wanted ... until I noticed that Ky was glaring at me. Oops. I softened my eyes and mouth until I projected innocence, but Ky only scowled and fell into step with Leander, Boone right behind them.

"What was that all about?" Adalia asked as she settled on the ground next to me once more.

"I'm not really sure, to be honest."

"You like Leander Verion." It wasn't a question, and I wasn't surprised. Adalia didn't miss much, despite her happy-go-lucky, upbeat attitude.

I sighed heavily, resigning myself to the conversation. There was little point in denying what she'd already deduced. "Is it that obvious?"

"Yes."

Ouch.

"You realize you two can never be together though, right? Not even for a casual fling on campus?"

"I hadn't really thought of it." I ran a hand across blades of grass, sensing the fairy's opalescent eyes on me.

"Prince Leander Verion will marry another fae, a princess from one of the stronger clans. King Dillmon Erion will be mindful of alliances now more than ever. The first prince has been committed since birth, as is common for the heirs to the throne. The only reason Prince Leander Verion hasn't been promised yet is because the king has been keeping his options open, seeking to ally us with the strongest available fae tribe."

"Hmm, I see." I couldn't compose a more appropriate response in time. Why hadn't anyone told me this before? I'd realized Leander was off limits; I couldn't help but notice with how his father worked to keep us apart, always sending us in opposite directions of the Golden Forest. But hearing that he was a bargaining chip to be married away … well, it would have been good to know.

"I wasn't planning on marrying him," I said defensively, mostly because I was annoyed with myself for not realizing what everyone else but me apparently had.

"I know," she said gently. "And I know that my

prince is intriguing … you'll just have to find someone else to crush on."

I scowled, allowing myself to be fully petulant for a few moments before caring what Adalia thought of my reaction. "I wasn't *crushing* on him. I just … I don't know, I just thought there might be something there. Obviously I was wrong."

"Oh, I'm not so sure. I see how the prince looks at you, especially when he thinks no one's watching. But he knows better than anyone what he can and can't have. The king won't budge on this. He can't."

I nodded too quickly, allowing my long hair to slide across my face, affording some privacy for my disappointment. I couldn't have Leander. All right, I'd deal. It wasn't like there weren't far more pressing issues to worry about anyway. With Rage and Fury after Ky and me, my focus had to be on survival— nothing more. The shifter brothers had the support of the entire rebel faction of the Voice behind them.

"What's up, bitches?"

Another voice I recognized instantly. I hurried to blink my moodiness away and found Jas arriving with Wren and Dave in tow. A wave of relief spread through me at seeing Dave. He'd been afraid the Academy Spell would kick him out over the summer break, but I'd been relatively certain he'd be back. Despite his many botched shifts, he wasn't a quitter— an attitude I suspected the academy rewarded—and he possessed enough power to keep Melinda busy healing him of his varied magical mishaps.

"Does Jas always have to be so crude?" Adalia

asked before our friends entered hearing range. "There's no need to call me a 'bitch.' That's just uncalled for."

"I agree," I said. "But I have the feeling you'll make her pay for it throughout the term."

Adalia blinked at me with big, innocent, doe eyes. "Why, whatever do you mean?"

I threw my head back and laughed. "You're brilliant, you know that? She has no idea that you're messing with her."

She grinned. "Don't ruin my secret."

"Never. It's way too much fun to see Jas squirm." I laughed again.

"What's so funny?" Jas asked as soon as she was close enough for us to hear without her yelling. I looked beyond her to Wren and Dave. My brother, Leander, and Boone were halfway across the quad, cutting across the grass to Sir Lancelot's office in the library building, I assumed.

"Nothing much," I said.

Jas scowled at my useless answer.

"Hiya, roomie," Adalia chirped. "Isn't it a splendid day?"

"Yeah, especially since those killer bunnies didn't eat us on the way in. There was a good chance of it."

We all sobered for a moment. Wren and Dave were huddled together like trauma survivors.

I got to my feet as Adalia did. I wrapped Wren and Dave in hugs while Adalia pounced on Jas, squeezing her until Jas batted at the pretty fairy to release her.

"Let's get something clear right now, Adalia," Jas said, smoothing down her tank-top. "I'm not doing your happy shit again this term. If you want to be all happy until you cry, *fine*, but don't try to wrap me up in that crap."

"It's nice to see you too, Jasmine Jolly."

Jas growled, threw her hands in the air, and spun on the heel of her clunky Doc Martens Mary Janes, storming off in the direction of Acquaine Hall. We stared at her retreat.

"I guess we should go with her," Wren said weakly.

"Yeah, we need to check in too," Dave said.

"Maybe in a little bit." Wren shrugged apologetically. "She's been a lot to handle since we met up. I don't know what's up with her."

"She's Jas," I said, and Wren and Dave nodded.

"Well, she's been extra *Jazzy* since we met up with her at the airport in Phoenix," Dave said. "She's got a thorn in her paw, for sure."

"I'd better go make sure she's all right," Adalia said, a little too happily.

"That's nice of you," Wren said. I didn't think she or Dave had realized how much of what Adalia said and did was to rile up the skunk shifter. I stifled a chuckle as Adalia skipped off to catch up to Jas, whose head was down, her shoulders hunched up by her ears, as she stomped toward the admin hall.

"How were your summers?" I asked.

"Good," they answered in unison, then shrugged and smiled. "Nothing special," Wren added. "How about you? How was sharing the summer with the prince?" She waggled her eyebrows suggestively.

"Nothing special."

Wren frowned. "Hmph. That's not what I expected."

Yeah, you and me both. I shrugged nonchalantly, hoping to convince Dave that I didn't care, if not both of them.

"We're still roommates, right?" Wren asked. "We can catch up later."

"For sure." But my heart wasn't in it.

"We should go check in," Dave said. "We're running a little late as it is. Jas had us pull over at rest stops way too often."

"I'll catch up with you guys after. I need to check in with my dad anyway."

But just as I was pulling out my phone, and Dave and Wren were setting off, wind chimes tinkled musically, drawing our attention.

"*Ahem.* All students—except for oners and initiated vampire students—please report to the auditorium in Irele Hall just as soon as you've checked in and received your schedule for the upcoming term. I repeat, head to Irele Hall as soon as you can. Headmaster Sir Lancelot wishes to address you all before the commencement of term. Don't make him wait. He has very important, pressing things to do with his time."

Nessa. I recognized her voice even though a spell delivered the disembodied words to my head. I could picture the tiny fairy puffing out her chest at the importance of Sir Lancelot's message.

The many fae around us got to their feet and began heading toward the auditorium. "I'll grab seats for you guys," I called to Wren and Dave as I hurried to follow the others. Though I'd been in the heart of the fae's lands during summer break, I hadn't exactly been kept in the loop. My brother, Leander, and Boone obviously knew more of what was going on than I did, but they were stingy with the information they shared—in an effort to protect me, I suspected.

I slowed when I reached the granite steps that led toward the large wooden double doors of Irele Hall. A handful of people I'd never seen before bordered the doors, standing beneath the large Corinthian columns that held up the portico.

These men and women were hardened fighters. The edge to their eyes would have suggested it even if their sculpted bodies hadn't. Weapons of every kind peeked out from most available surfaces—swords, daggers, sigils, and quivers. One man even clutched a mace; the way he held it implied he was a master at using it. Who needed to use a mace in these times? Wasn't a gun more efficient? But what did I know of magical warfare? Approximately nothing. Their magic probably interfered with modern weaponry or something.

Every student around me slowed and gave the strangers a wide berth, skirting through the doors as quickly as they could. As I slipped through the doors myself, I felt the attention of every single warrior there like a knife through the back. I might not know who they were, but every one of them knew exactly who I was ... and who was after me.

5

I'D IMAGINED EVERYTHING WOULD BE SIMPLER NOW that I'd survived a complete term at the school. The Academy Spell hadn't kicked me out—score!—I'd survived the shifters' attack; revealed that I indeed possessed magic, even if said magic was peculiar and unstable; and the bizarre environment that was the campus, along with its equally bizarre resident creatures, was somewhat familiar, though I didn't think I'd ever get used to the cantankerous trolls or the way plant life up and moved of its own volition. Compared to my first term, this one should have been easier and more comfortable.

I could already tell I'd been wrong in thinking it.

As the scary-looking warriors who'd lurked on the front steps entered the auditorium and lined up on either side of the raised dais at the front of the room, my stomach churned. The men and women scoured the crowd already assembled. A rustling of unease followed their attention in the form of urgent whispers … until their combined gazes landed on me.

I met their stares as long as I could, well aware that I shouldn't appear weak, not even in front of my fellow students. But after a solid minute of meeting their gazes, during which not a single one of them looked away, I fiddled with my hands in my lap, wishing I had a notebook and a pen—anything—to provide a distraction and disguise my cowardice.

When Jas slid into the seat beside me, I heaved a sigh of relief. Wren, Dave, and Adalia sidled in front of me and took the remaining seats beside me. My breath shuddered.

"Who are *they*?" Wren whispered shakily. "And why do they look like they want to eat you for lunch?"

So it wasn't just me. *Crap*. "They won't stop looking at me," I whined, refusing to look up.

Jas leaned toward me. "Whoever they are, I hope they're on our side."

"Yeah, me too," I whispered. After encountering Damon and Sadie in the parking lot, I suspected the band of hoodlums at the front of the room might be Enforcers as well, though it made no sense, not based on the story we'd been told.

Ky, Leander, and Boone entered the room, and Boone snapped down the kickstand, propping the door open. The three men flicked quick looks from the hoodlums to me. They zeroed in on me right away, I supposed, because all they had to do was follow the stares of the others. Ky scowled, Boone squinted in displeasure, and Leander's face betrayed none of his thoughts. They paused in front of the hoodlums, and tension ratcheted up in the room.

Nessa and Fianna chose that moment to fly through the open doorway, and Nessa, regularly less observant of her surroundings than her cousin, swooped in front of all of them, where she hovered self-importantly at the head of the room. Her diminutive wings flapped so quickly they blurred.

Ahem. "The great headmaster of the Magical Creatures Academy will now address you. Well, not precisely now, but very soon. He's right behind us." The voice of the hummingbird-sized fairy reverberated through my head, enhanced by the Academy Spell. "What he has to say is of utmost importance, so make sure you pay close attention."

The blue fairy glared at all of us students as if we'd already caused trouble. Fianna drew next to her. "With all the recent … events, Sir Lancelot has been busier and more preoccupied than usual. Running an institution of the caliber of the Menagerie is challenging at the best of times." Clearly, these were not the best of times or else a band of thugs wouldn't be lined up behind the fairies.

"Once Sir Lancelot is finished speaking with you," she continued, "don't delay him with questions. If any remains after he leaves, Nessa and I will be available to help you."

"Yeah, because the two of them are nothing but helpful," Jas muttered under her breath. "They cause as many problems as they solve."

Nessa raised both arms in the air. "Without further

ado, your headmaster!" When her announcement wasn't met with thunderous applause, she pouted, and I caught one of the thugs smirking.

When Sir Lancelot flew into the room, landing primly on the desk atop the dais, a hush settled across the assembly. He tucked his wings behind his back and faced us, his brow furrowed so deeply that it shadowed his bright yellow eyes.

"Students," he began in a crisp voice as Nessa and Fianna settled on either side of him. En masse, the assembly leaned forward to catch every one of his words, though they were augmented inside our heads. "I wish I had better news to share with you. But I won't mince words, you deserve the truth, or at least as much of it as is appropriate to share with students. You might have noticed that I requested that oners not attend this meeting. I'll share similar information with them later, but in a way that is more accessible for students new to our world.

"Since all of you here are necessarily survivors, I'll speak more frankly. You overcame the odds and remained students of the academy when the academy dismissed nearly a third of your classmates. They didn't make the cut."

Damn! I'd hoped Sir Lancelot's warnings at the beginning of first term had been exaggerated. But if half the students we'd started out with were expelled, he hadn't exaggerated at all. Because the Academy Spell dismissed the students and whisked them away without notice, none of us was sure how exactly the spell removed them from school. Rumor had it that the students would suddenly find themselves in their homes, their belongings packed for them, every sign that they'd ever attended the academy gone but for their memories. Others said the students would find themselves at the base of Thunder Mountain, the entrance to the school sealed to them forever, appearing as nothing more than ordinary rock. One sixer swore a kid he knew was yanked from his bed in the middle of the night and dragged through the air backwards, hanging from an invisible, spelled hook, until he was pulled clear through the mountain to be unceremoniously deposited at the trailhead. Only one thing was certain: once the academy decided your time here was finished, there was nothing you could do to resist expulsion.

"To be a student of the Menagerie, not only must you be magical and extraordinary in your own way—even if you don't understand your magic or potential yet"—the headmaster's big, serious eyes alighted on me for a moment—"but you must also be fierce and resilient. You must have the kind of courage and fight within you that will allow you to survive in our world, while at school and after, when you join the ranks of the Enforcers.

"Every one of you is required to do a brief stint as an apprentice with the Enforcers, but after the attack at the end of last term, their numbers have dwindled alarmingly. The loss to the supernatural community has been great. I invite each and every one of you to consider a career within the ranks of the Enforcers. Remember, every single Enforcer is a graduate of the

Magical Creatures Academy. They were once exactly like you."

I chortled quietly. I doubted anyone was exactly like me. Not even the millennium-old owl could make sense of me and my odd magic.

"It's an admirable career. There's little more respectable than to selflessly protect others who are too weak or unprepared to defend themselves." He gestured a wing toward the hoodlums gathered in front of him beneath the raised platform. Surely, he wasn't suggesting these misfits were "respectable."

"I realize most of you believed none of the Enforcers survived the attack on them in the night. However, I'm here to share at least some good news with you. Some did survive. Not many, considering they numbered more than seven hundred and now their numbers are in the low double digits. Apparently the Voice didn't anticipate some of the secret patrols the Enforcers undertake, and those who were on duty on these secret missions survived. Some of these survivors stand here among us."

The attention of the crowd shifted to the well-armed goons, who sneered and narrowed their eyes at us, though it wasn't clear whether they were trying to threaten us or if they couldn't help themselves, a habit borne from surviving a dangerous world.

After a few heavy moments passed, Sir Lancelot continued: "I'm sure all of you noticed the commotion in the parking lot this morning. However, I imagine most of you are unaware of its cause. When Leander Verion arrived with Kylan, Boone, Rina, and the rest of the fae that traveled to the Golden Forest, several members of the Shifter Alliance ambushed them."

A communal gasp circled the audience.

"Yes, a grave situation, no doubt. Thankfully, a couple of Enforcers arrived to escort our students to the school and defused the situation."

As if on cue, Damon and Sadie appeared at the open door, each leaning against one side of the threshold, arms crossed over their chests, mess-with-me-if-you-dare attitudes firmly in place. Wren scooted a little closer to me in her seat.

The owl began pacing across the desk. "What the Shifter Alliance's attack at the entrance to our school tells us, very clearly, is that the Voice has not heeded the supernatural community's requests that it back down, that it cease using violence—*murder*—to accomplish its ends." Sir Lancelot pivoted to face us. "The rebel faction will come at us until we crush it."

The hoodlums at the front of the room and at the door nodded, grumbling their agreement.

"They refuse to be civilized, leaving us no option but to defend and secure our position by whatever means necessary. We will always attempt to disarm and talk down before attacking, but if the Voice leaves us no option, we'll do what we must."

Jas turned to me with wide eyes, the thick rim of kohl eyeliner and mascara emphasizing the importance of the gesture. "Shit," she mouthed. "He's talking like we're going to war or something."

I nodded worriedly. Yeah, that's what it sounded like to me too.

The owl dragged the tip of a wing across his face, rubbing at it. "I wish I had better news to share with you. I really do. Perhaps I should have delayed this talk with you until the shock of the ambush this morning had worn off. That the Shifter Alliance should be so open about its actions, attacking students in broad daylight..." He shook his head and sighed heavily, the sound echoing through my head. "It doesn't bode well for their plans for the future.

"Most of you already realize that the leaders of the Shifter Alliance are after two of our own. And though the Shifter Alliance is but a segment of the Voice, it's a powerful one. Kylan and Rina Mont are their targets, and as they're the only clear ones we're aware of, the Enforcers have decided to gather as much of their forces as they can to protect Kylan and Rina. It's the one point where we can be relatively certain they'll attack."

A wave of nausea rumbled through me until it passed as quickly as it arrived. Wren placed a hand on my arm in silent support, and even the moody Jas offered me a sympathetic half-smile.

"Before you ask, the Enforcers haven't abandoned their role in protecting the humans from those paranormal creatures who lack integrity and harm them without care. Nor have they abandoned their role in policing the supernatural community. However, with the vast decrease in their numbers, they've had no choice but to allocate their forces according to priority. Volunteers, mostly those opposed to the despicable tactics of the Voice, have stepped forward to bolster the Enforcers. No, these volunteers aren't trained to be Enforcers, but some are graduates from the Menagerie who've completed their apprenticeships. Most of them are shifters, vampires, and even some mages, who wish to quash the use of violence as a means to solve our problems.

"Anyway, I could talk all day about the finer details of the situation, but that won't serve our purposes here."

No! I wanted to cry out. *Tell us everything!* Maybe understanding more of what was going on would make me feel less helpless...

"The way the magical creatures of the different types and sectors intersect is more complicated and involved than we need to get into here. Suffice it to say, we need to put a stop to the Voice. To that end, the Enforcers you see here"—he nodded toward those in front of him, but also in the direction of Damon and Sadie—"will remain on campus during the entire term. Their role will be to protect the students and staff here, and most especially to defend Kylan and Rina. We cannot afford to allow the leaders of the Shifter Alliance to claim more power, and we most certainly will not allow them to claim it by force, draining the life of two of our pupils in the process."

I sensed the attention of students on all sides of me drifting across me and Ky, who was seated up in the front row of the auditorium where he could shoot to standing without interference.

"For those of you wondering how you can help, the best thing to do is focus on your studies and excel at being you. Master your shifter abilities and magic, learn the skills the professors are so eager to teach you, and consider joining the ranks of the Enforcers after completing your apprenticeships. Also, be on the alert. You all are completely safe within the protection of the campus, but so you should have been last term. Watch your surroundings with vigilance, and if you see anything out of place, notify Fianna or Nessa immediately. If you can't find them, let one of the Enforcers know. They'll be stationed all around campus."

The air in the auditorium grew thick with antic-ipation.

"As I'm sure you've all noticed, after Rasper the Rabbit's death, three of his brothers from the same litter have stepped forward to fill Rasper's role. I assure you, they are equally vicious and equally moti-vated. No one will get by them."

Unless they do... What the owl didn't say hung heavily in the room.

The owl dropped his wings to his sides and huffed. He allowed his exhaustion to bloom across his face; even his feathers appeared to droop. I'd never seen the owl in such an ungentlemanly state before. He opened his beak to continue speaking, then closed it again. He frowned, the feathers around his beak flagging.

"I'm so very sorry to welcome you to a new term when our community is in turmoil. But the world beyond our mountain is even more dangerous. We have the duty to train and prepare to protect it. Though I can't force you to share in this sense of duty with me, I hope that you will want to be a part of the solution. Dear students, do your very best, every single day, and in doing so you'll honor your kind. You'll be part of the force that protects innocents and sets right the many wrongs in the world."

Hmm, yeah, no pressure. Thanks, Sir Lancelot.

A rustling swept his audience, making me think the others were uncomfortable beneath the pressure as well.

"I think that's enough for now," the owl said. "The staff and I have agreed that a mood-booster will be helpful for the student body. So Friday night we will host our very first Paranormal Party of Pleasantries."

Jas smirked beside me. That name ... it was precisely something Sir Lancelot would think made the event seem elegant.

"The soiree will be for all students, chaperoned by staff, of course. So that our initiated vampire students may attend, it will begin promptly after dark, to be held within the dining hall as dusk fades. I'm quite certain this will set the tone for our semester quite wonderfully." The headmaster smiled, but the expression didn't reach his eyes. As his attention trailed off to whatever else preoccupied him, a murmur circled the crowd.

He snapped his gaze back up to us. "That's all for now. You have time to break your fast quickly if you haven't had the chance before arriving at the school. A pleasant staff of trolls awaits you."

The owl clearly defined "pleasant" differently than I did.

59

"You're expected at your first class promptly at nine. Many of you will find an additional class on your schedules. Defensive Creature Magic is now a requirement for all beginning students. It is no longer for the advanced terms only. The staff of the Magical Creatures Academy, and I personally, will do everything in our power to prepare you for what awaits.

"May magic protect us all." With a somber nod to punctuate that somber note, the owl exchanged looks with the Enforcers and Leander, Boone, and Ky, who clearly had already conferred with the owl. Then Sir Lancelot launched himself off the table, caught himself with an efficient flap of his wings, and glided out the open door. Fianna and Nessa flew right behind him, flapping their wings intensely, working to catch up to the owl, who was twice their size.

The assistant fairies must have already forgotten they'd promised to stick around in case any of us had questions. I didn't blame them. From the looks of it, Sir Lancelot's speech had hit us all hard. After last term's half-of-you-won't-make-it speech, I thought this one would be more uplifting. I couldn't have been more wrong.

The weight of the supernatural world settled across my shoulders. I had to find the strength to excel this semester. I didn't have any other choice.

6

WREN, JAS, ADALIA, DAVE, AND I SAT AROUND A TABLE at the dining hall, where I pretended not to be completely overwhelmed. I had the feeling they were doing the same. Sadie sat at the end of our table and didn't bother to disguise her stare—pinned directly on me. Oh sure, it traveled every few seconds, darting across my companions to scan the entirety of the dining hall, especially its apparently foreboding corners, before settling on me—again.

The Enforcer's constant attention made me jumpy, and no matter how much I tried to ignore her, I sensed her gaze across my skin like an itch I couldn't scratch. If this was how the term was going to go, it was going to be a very long one.

"So," Wren said meekly, clutching a steaming cup of jasmine green tea with both hands. She blew the steam, but I suspected it was a delay tactic. My willowy roommate skirted a quick glance at Sadie, whisking across her Smurfette shirt, the same bright

Smurf-blue one she wore this morning when she threatened to kill the hyenas. "You're going to be rooming with Rina and me, huh?"

I admired her effort to appear calm, but her voice came out as a rush of squeaky breath, betraying her true emotions. I didn't blame her. Sadie was terrifying. She was normal-looking enough. In fact, she appeared a little too normal-looking with her medium-length hair, hazel eyes, and average everything else. She was … cute, or she would have been if not for the manic gleam to her otherwise ordinary eyes.

Sadie considered Wren, tilting her head to the side while she studied her. Finally, she gave one curt nod.

"B-but, where will you sleep? There are only two beds in our room," Wren said.

"Don't you worry about me." Sadie's voice was hard enough to slice Wren's ceramic mug in half, making Wren twitch in surprise as she heard the Enforcer's voice for the first time. "I sleep with one eye open."

"Oh." Wren nodded a little too quickly, a little too nervously.

I would've laughed if I hadn't been freaked out about the idea of Sadie watching us while we slept.

"And will the other Enforcer be sleeping in the room with Ky?" Jas asked Sadie, who tilted her head to consider my skunk-shifter friend.

"Yes, and Damon sleeps with *both* eyes open. He won't miss a thing."

"That's good," Jas said, and either she had secret skills as a fantabulous actress, or she genuinely wasn't bothered by the extra dose of weird that had descended upon the school. "We don't want a repeat of last term."

Sadie's eyes grew hard as marbles. "There won't be a repeat of what happened last term, not now, not ever. Not on my watch."

This was dangerous territory. I widened my eyes in an attempt to silently communicate to my friends to back off from this topic. We didn't need to put Sadie through Bad-Memory Ville. Adalia, Dave, and Wren got it right away, though they probably wouldn't have said a word regardless. Jas, however, liked to poke big, angry bears. She'd proven it over and again with the pygmy trolls who worked at the school.

"I can't believe they took out so many of you guys," she said, tucking the lone, shocking white strand of hair behind her ear. "The Enforcers are the best of the best. How'd they manage to get the drop on you like they did?"

I fumed at Jas across the table, but she actually didn't seem like she was trying to upset our crazed Enforcer on purpose. She shook her head, her jet black hair sliding around her chin in shiny waves. "I just … I still can't believe it..."

I waited for Sadie to blow, but what happened was worse. She appeared to cave in on herself; her shoulders hunched ever so slightly, and the hard glint that shone through her eyes softened beneath a wet gleam.

Oh, this was infinitely worse than hardass Sadie. I stretched beneath the table and kicked Jas in the shin.

"Ow," she yelped. "What'd you do that for?"

I quirked an are-you-effing-kidding-me-right-now look while Adalia elbowed her in the side. Jas jerked her head around the table, and when she finally took in Sadie, she had the grace to appear apologetic. It was more than I'd expected from her.

Dave leaned his forearms on the table on the other side of me. "What happened this morning in the parking lot to the trailhead? Were there really shifters from the Voice waiting for you there?"

I grimaced. "Yeah. There definitely were." I relayed the story as succinctly as I could.

"Man, that's really nuts. I'm so glad no one got hurt."

Sadie chortled. "Oh, people got hurt all right. Just not any of us."

Dave and Wren leaned toward me ever so slightly from either side. Crazed maniac Sadie was back.

"Thane's been waiting to get his hands on any of them," she went on, oblivious to our discomfort. "I only wish I could've stuck around to see him punish that bitch Jacinda for killing his wife and the rest of us."

Several beats of intense discomfort circled my friends and me before Sadie's gaze grew wistful for a few moments. "Thane's wife was pregnant, did you know?"

We shook our heads in unison, speechless at the horrors that had befallen the Enforcers—future versions of ourselves. The Voice had even killed those who were apprentices.

"She was my friend." Sadie's voice was too soft,

too vulnerable, and I suddenly wanted the badass protector back.

I pressed through my awkwardness. "Hey, so, they learned their lesson though, right? Never bring a broadsword to a gunfight, am I right?"

Sadie snapped her head up to do a quick sweep of the room before staring at me. I swallowed roughly and blinked too often. When she finally cracked a smile, breath expanded through my chest.

"Yeah, Jacinda should've known better," Sadie said. "Damon won't go anywhere without that gun of his anymore, not after the Attack. He's one of the few lucky supes who can work a gun without it going all wonky with his magic." I waited for Sadie to descend into despair or nostalgia again, but it didn't happen. "Though Damon could kick Jacinda's ass any day of the week, half asleep and blindfolded."

"He certainly looks like he could," I said.

"Jacinda is tough, I won't lie about that, but Damon is tougher. That dude could crack a walnut with his jaw."

I winced, hoping it was simply a colorful exaggeration. "And you guys and Jacinda were really friends at one point?"

"Maybe not friends, but associates. She was an Enforcer in training before turning to the dark side."

Was it a *Star Wars* reference or was there really a dark side of the supernatural world? With magic it was hard to tell, and I sat on my hands to hold myself still. I hadn't had the appetite for so much as a cup of tea after the morning I'd had.

"It happens often enough," she continued. "The rebels, the Voice now, I guess, bribes or blackmails them or whatever it is they do. I've seen some good people end up fighting for them."

"Do they ever come back?" Wren asked, eyes wide and innocent.

"No. None of them ever does."

"Whoa," Jas said. "That's some crazy shit right there."

"Indeed."

"Speaking of crazy shit," I said, "what do you guys think about this Paranormal Party of Pleasantries?"

"I think it's ridiculous," Jas said. When Wren opened her mouth to speak, Jas powered on: "Though if your hot brother will be there, I don't mind attending. There are worse things to do than stare at him all night. Hey, maybe you could hook me up with him and—"

"No," I said. "Not now, not ever. When are you gonna get it through your head?"

"Damn. You didn't have to be that harsh."

"I think you actually offended the unoffendable Jas," Dave said. "I didn't think that was possible."

"I'm not offended," Jas snapped.

"Hey, I'm sorry," I said. "I'm just under a lot of pressure right now."

"I told you, I'm not offended." And to prove her point, Jas proceeded to talk about the upcoming party with the animation of a teeny-bopper dreaming of prom. I tuned her out, mulling over my own concerned thoughts: Were Ky and I really safe on campus? Would we bring danger to everyone else just by being here? Was that fair to the others or should we just run away and hide out somewhere? I still had to check up on Dad and see how he'd fared over the summer without both his children.

A clanking clattered through the large dining hall like a monkey clapping cymbals. Then silence settled around the students in a hush of anticipation. Sadie shot to her feet, hands dropping to the curved blades in sheaths around both thighs.

We all waited for the source of the commotion to reveal itself. The pygmy trolls ran a tight ship, and they'd soon be out from the kitchens and serving areas to scold whoever had disrupted their domain.

But when the pygmy trolls emerged from the kitchens, my heart thudded in a rapid beat; Wren and Dave scooted closer to me, squeezing me in a freaked-out-friend sandwich. Even Jas bit her lip and ran nervous fingertips across her eyebrows.

"What's going on?" Adalia whispered.

"Whatever it is, it can't be good," Wren whispered back.

A dozen-ish pygmy trolls tottered into the eating area of the dining hall, war paint in rough, dark lines across their flesh and below their hardened, black, beady eyes, transforming their disgruntled little old man faces into a formidable sight.

"What the...?" Dave said.

That's right. Dave hadn't seen the trolls in warrior mode. Ky, Leander, Boone, and I were the only students to have seen the trolls rise to the school's defense at the end of last term.

The trolls had discarded their kitchen aprons for loincloths that fully exposed their round little butts, which were thankfully more like babies' tushies than old men's … well, no need to go there. They brandished axes, short swords, and daggers. And when they stalked across the room in an array of gumball colors—two-feet-tall fluorescent fro-hawks peeking above the tabletops—Sadie was the only one to move.

She stepped directly in front of them, blocking their path out of the hall. "What's going on?"

Orangesicle emerged from the group, crossing his arms across his bare, hairless chest. "Intruders are at the gate." He narrowed sharp eyes at Sadie, silently daring her to stand in their way.

"How many?"

"More than the three rabbits can handle."

"They haven't entered the campus though?"

"Not last we heard." Orangesicle tipped his orange fro-hawk at her. "Are you going to let us pass?"

She swept out of the way. "Of course. Kick some slimy shifter ass for me."

"Will do." Then Orangesicle led the rest of the trolls toward the dining hall doors.

"Fight hard!" Sadie called after them. "But live to—"

"Fight another day!" the trolls chimed in.

"That's right," Sadie said more softly. "Live to fight another day," and from the way she said it, I knew she was thinking of all the friends she'd lost.

Orangesicle paused with a knobby hand on one of the doors. "Students, you're to transport every single dish and utensil to the dish depository. Just because we won't be here doesn't mean we won't hold you accountable for any messes you leave behind. We'll know who did what when we get back."

With that, he slammed both stubby hands against the door, which slammed open with a loud slap to the wall behind it, and led the small army of waist-high trolls, including hair, outside. When the last of the round butts faded from sight and the door closed behind them, Jas whispered, "They don't actually have a way of knowing who does what while they're gone, right?"

In unison, Adalia, Wren, Dave, and I faced her. "Do you really want to test that?" Wren asked.

From the mischievous twinkle in Jas' ice-blue eyes, yes, yes she did.

"We're in a school of *magic*, Jasmine," Wren pressed, while Jas' eyelid twitched at the use of her full name. "It's a school of magic for shifters, but it's still a school of magic. If you want to be reckless and stupid, that's fine by me. Just don't drag any of us into your mess."

Dave gave Wren an appreciative look, and I had to admit I was also appreciating Wren's shift in attitude. But Adalia sobered us all right the eff up. "Jasmine Jolly, are you serious right now?" she said. "We're apparently under attack and all you can think about is causing trouble and other trivial … stuff."

Wren's eyes widened. The upbeat fairy had been about to say "shit."

"Grow up already," Adalia said, and Wren's jaw dropped open. "This is life and death we're talking about. Just because you were safe all summer at your parents' estate doesn't mean the rest of the paranormal world was. We're basically at war and you want to do pranks on the trolls who are stepping it up to defend us? Really?"

"Whoa," Dave muttered under his breath. It was exactly what I'd been thinking.

Adalia sat back from the table, crossed her arms across her ample chest, and glared at Jas. I'd never seen the fairy like this before.

Sadie was stalking back toward us when a trilling erupted throughout the dining hall.

"All students except for initiated vampires," Fianna's voice rang out, "you're to report to the dining hall immediately. Like right now. Stop whatever you're doing and run to the dining hall. Stay there until we tell you to leave. Do *not* go to your 9 AM class until we tell you to. All staff except for general student protection, head to the gates."

Fianna's voice vanished abruptly. A deep, encompassing silence spread across the students in the dining hall before they erupted into a chaos of simultaneous comments.

"Enough!" Sadie roared, spreading her arms wide. The hush was instantaneous. "We don't have time for your squabbling and freaking. You need to get it together right this second." She swept her gaze across the tables; not a single student was willing to object. "Good. We have plenty of shit to do."

She pointed at a table across from us. "You guys. There are a couple of back doors to the kitchens. Find them and barricade them. Shove whatever you can in front of them. Actually, you guys"—she pointed to another table—"go help them. Get it done."

The two tables of students rocketed to their feet. "You think they're going to get into the school?" a burly shifter asked.

"I think," Sadie said, "we want to be prepared if they do. Now go."

While the students streaked across the dining hall, breaking one of the trolls' many rules, she pointed at a couple of other tables. "You, drag the tables closest to the main doors next to them. We'll wait until all the students are inside, then we'll barricade the doors."

She whirled, taking in the rest of the room. "The rest of you, stay quiet until I tell you to do something. I need to focus."

"On what? What are you going to be doing?" I asked.

"Way to follow my rules, Rina." But she answered me anyway: "I'm going to be sealing the large windows that leave us vulnerable to attack."

"But how?"

"No one ever said I was a shifter."

"But I thought mages weren't part of the Enforcers. I thought mages only worked to police their own kind."

"Yeah, well, I've never been one to follow rules myself."

"You seem like a shifter," Dave said.

"Exactly. I'm with my own kind, just in my own way," Sadie said. "Now silence. I need to get to work. If the trolls, rabbits, and other staff can't hold the shifters, they'll be looking for you."

"And Ky," I gasped.

"And Ky." Sadie slapped a hand to my shoulder. "Ky's in good hands. Damon won't let anybody touch him, I promise."

I'd seen enough movies to know that when people said they promised, shit went to hell fast. But there was apparently nothing I could do to help my brother or anyone else. I did as Sadie said and waited in silence, watching her flash waves of orange at the large panes of glass lining the walls until they shimmered with the light of her magic.

7

MORE THAN AN HOUR PASSED IN AGONIZING SLOW motion. All students who were going to report to the dining hall were barricaded inside the large hall with us. Most of the heavy, solid wood bench tables were being used to block the entrances to the hall, and the students huddled along the sides of the bare room, leaning against the walls.

Though the students conversed in a non-stop buzz of subdued, nervous whispers, the hush within the room vibrated against my mind until I couldn't stand it anymore. I shot to my feet.

"What is it, Rina?" Wren asked. She and Dave rocketed to their feet too. They leaned toward me, concern etched across their kind faces.

"Nothing, it's nothing. I just can't wait anymore without knowing what's going on. Ky's out there somewhere."

"But Ky is fine, he must be," Dave said. "He's a tough shifter in his own right. Besides, he's sure to be with Boone and Leo, and both of them can hold their own too."

"Don't forget about that Enforcer with the dreads," Wren said. "There's no way he's a pushover."

My shoulders relaxed a fraction of an inch, but it wasn't enough. "Thanks for trying to help, guys." I linked my hands behind my back, arched my chest, and popped my back. "I'm just super stressed. I need to walk off some of this energy."

Wren offered me big, sympathetic eyes. "Want us to come with you?"

"Thanks, really, but I just need some time alone with my thoughts." My freaked-out, frantic thoughts. I remembered everything that had happened at the end of last term in vivid detail. Rage's hard, determined face as he promised to steal my power and Ky's. He'd kill us without flinching. Fury's distorted mountain lion, too weak to fight. Leander's firm body and soft touch as he pulled me against him...

I walked away from my friends, wishing there was a place to go within the hall where all these eyes wouldn't follow. There had to be at least a hundred students inside this one space, all waiting for news. Were we at war within the school? Was there nowhere safe to go anymore? Would Ky and I be hunted until our inevitable deaths? Would we get those we cared about killed in the process of protecting us?

Shit!

I meandered through the serving areas and into the kitchens, usually off limits when manned by the trolls. How had this become my life? Not that long ago, my greatest concern had been that the paranormal world would pass me by. Now I was smack-dab in the middle of it all, putting my friends and the entire Menagerie in danger. And Dad ... what would happen to him if he didn't have Ky or me anymore?

Wood and metal creaked then snapped, pulling me out of my fruitless reverie. I gasped and shuffled backward a couple of feet, and though the smart thing might've been to run back where the others were to find Sadie, my feet were rooted to the spot, waiting to see what would emerge through the back door to the kitchens.

Another straining groan and the doors tore from their hinges, only to push against a large stainless steel cabinet and a massive stove the students had wedged against the doors.

Whoever was on the other side of that door was strong; when they pushed again, the cabinet and stove skidded across the tile floor with a grating screech. The contents of the cabinet rattled, a din of metal and ceramic crashing around inside it.

My breath hitched, and my brain returned online with a flood of realizations: I was stupid for standing there, gawking at the double doors. Whoever was coming through that doorway was probably hunting me. I needed to get Sadie. I needed to get her fast.

I pivoted on my heel and moved in the direction of the common area, but a ferocious force slammed against the doors, sending the stove stumbling and bouncing across the tile, cracking a few of them. The cabinet slid across the floor until one of its legs hitched on the depressed grout between tiles and the entire thing tipped. It balanced precariously for a second, and then crashed to the floor.

I jumped as the cacophony of rattling metal and breaking porcelain assaulted my eardrums. Well, Sadie had certainly heard that. No need to call her now.

I reminded myself that not only was I a mountain lion shifter, but I was also a mage—probably, maybe; it was a working theory. I also struggled to forget that my shifts remained wholly unpredictable and that there was no guarantee I'd manage to shift before whatever monster was coming through those doors walked through them. I was better off forgetting as well that my glowy-goopy mage powers hadn't made a repeat appearance and that I couldn't count on them to help me in the least.

Then a cowgirl boot appeared between the double doors and all thoughts of what I was supposed to be forgetting and what I was supposed to be remembering vanished. Like the proverbial deer in the headlights, I waited, staring at the doorway. Shouts rang out in the common area—probably Sadie—but I couldn't make out what she was saying.

Then an ordinary woman walked through the doors...

With her highlighted, caramel-tinted hair swept into a high ponytail, and bangs riding low around soft brown eyes, and a round, unassuming face, this woman couldn't have crashed open the locked and barricaded doors … could she? In tight jeans and a coral-colored sleeveless polo t-shirt, she strolled into the kitchens. Immediately, her attention landed on me. "Hello there."

"Hi...? Uh, why'd you break in here?"

"Oh. I was just checking in to make sure everyone is all right. I especially want to make sure the girl Rina is okay."

"She's fine. Who are you?"

She beamed a winning smile and brushed the bangs from her face, oblivious to the destruction her entrance caused. "I'm Wendi, with an 'I.' I'm an Enforcer."

"Well, Wendi with an 'I,' you could have just knocked on the front door and Sadie would've let you in."

"Oh, Sadie's here?"

I wasn't buying the nonchalance. She wasn't happy Sadie was here, no matter what she said.

With impeccable timing, Sadie ran through the open archways that connected the kitchens to the rest of the dining area. She held a curved blade in each hand, but slid to a stop when she spotted Wendi.

"What are you doing here?" she accused.

"Checking that everyone's okay."

"You could've asked to enter through the front doors."

"That's what I said," I interjected.

"Yes, well, we're under attack," Wendi said. "I arrived at the back entrance first. I took action to get inside as quickly as I could." She shrugged, but Sadie only narrowed her eyes at her.

"And beyond checking that everyone's okay, what other reasons do you have for coming inside?"

"What do you mean? What other reasons would I have? You know what we Enforcers do. We protect. That's what I'm trying to do."

"Hmph. I didn't realize you were being assigned to the school."

"I was, just this morning. After Thane interrogated Jacinda and discovered that more attacks are planned."

"More attacks?" Sadie asked sharply. "Tell me."

Wendi gave me an askance look. "Later."

Sadie moved to my side. "If there are more attacks coming, she needs to know. This is Rina Mont."

Surprise flitted across Wendi's soft brown eyes, hardening for a few moments before they returned to normal. "You're Rina?" she said to me like we were about to become fast friends.

"I am," I said tightly.

"Well, if only I'd known before…"

"What would that have changed?"

Wendi smiled winningly. "I would've offered you my protection right away." She waltzed over to Sadie and me, invading my bubble of personal space, and placed a soft hand on my forearm. I looked down at it, wondering how her fingernails were so perfectly manicured in a coral tone that exactly matched her shirt and lipstick when she could ram doors open.

"I'm looking forward to getting to know you. I've heard so much about you."

I raised my arm to flip the loose strands of my hair

over my shoulder—and to dislodge her hand from my arm. I took a step back. "Well, I don't know anything about you. Do you have news of what's going on out there?"

"Oh, that? Yeah, everything's fine now."

"What happened?" Sadie asked.

"A bunch of shifters tried to force their way through the rabbits and the gate, but I showed up at just the right time. I took most of them out, and the rabbits helped take out the others. By the time Sir Lancelot showed up with the staff, I had everything under control."

"How many shifters were there exactly?" Sadie crossed her arms, arched her eyebrows, and looked Wendi up and down.

Wendi shrugged and glanced at her manicure. "About eight of them."

"You took out eight shifters on your own."

"That's what I said. You know I'm more than capable of it."

But Sadie didn't reply. Someone pounded on the front doors to the hall, loudly enough that the sound thumped through my chest all the way in the kitchens.

"You're sure it's fully safe out there now?" Sadie asked of Wendi.

"A hundred percent."

Sadie hesitated, but when the pounding continued, she grabbed me by the arm and led me toward the common area.

"Wait," Wendi said. "You should leave her here with me, just to be safe."

"I thought you just said it was safe," Sadie said.

"It is, it is. But it never hurts to be extra careful."

"That's precisely my thought. You stay here and get those doors barricaded again, just in case. Surely your super strength is up for the challenge. Or are you worn out from taking out eight shifters all on your own?"

Wendi scowled at Sadie. "Of course I can do it."

"Good. Then do it." Sadie smiled, but her eyes remained cold.

She pulled me through the kitchens and into the dining area, where half the students had gathered in front of the rattling doors.

"Make way! Coming through," Sadie yelled, and students dispersed immediately. "Who is it?" she called through the three-inch-thick wood of the doors.

"Damon. The threat has been neutralized."

"How much wood would a woodchuck chuck if a woodchuck could chuck wood?"

Okay. So Sadie had lost her mind. It was bound to happen. She hadn't seemed that stable to begin with.

I searched for my friends, looking to get away from the kooky lady. I found Wren, Dave, Adalia, and Jas right away; they were already staring at me. But when I moved to step away from Sadie, she didn't release her hold on my arm.

"A woodchuck would chuck wood at you just to punish you for your stupid joke," Damon's voice rumbled through the wood.

Sadie sighed in relief. "Help me get this barricade cleared."

I nodded, and along with several other students I heaved and pulled, and in minutes Sadie yanked the doors to the dining hall wide open.

Damon stood immediately beyond them, his semi-automatic hanging from one hand, Ky at his other side. I breathed in my relief, my chest expanding fully for what felt like the first time since Fianna's panicked announcement. When I spotted Leander a few steps behind Ky, I had to lean on the threshold as my knees buckled from relief. Boone was next to Leander.

The guys stood among what appeared to be the entire staff, including a dozen-ish ornery trolls, who seemed disappointed they hadn't gotten to kill anyone. Even the gnome Professor Quickfoot's battle ax was blood free, when it had been coated after the Attack. At least he didn't seem annoyed he hadn't gotten to shed blood this time.

Sir Lancelot swooped above the heads of everyone and flew into the dining hall. Fianna and Nessa zoomed in behind him, flapping their wings so fast to keep up that they were barely visible. He landed on one of the tables to the side of the entrance, the fairies alighting immediately behind him. The headmaster cleared his throat tiredly, and for the first time I noticed hints of the bird's long life. Ordinarily prim and proper, he sagged, as if the burden of our current conflict weighed on him as much as it did on me.

"Everyone, settle down," he called. If not for the magical augmentation of his voice, I doubted his words would have carried across those of us assembled. He appeared beaten though we'd just scored a victory—if there was such a thing as a true win during war, when all parties lost to some degree or another.

"The threat has been dealt with. Not a single shifter managed to enter the school's campus. The rabbits and Enforcers halted their progress. We're all safe." A relieved hush settled across the crowd. "We'll continue to be safe. The Enforcers have sent everyone they can afford to the campus, and the trolls will bolster their numbers so continuous patrols and watches can take place across the entirety of our large institution. Do not be alarmed if you notice the Enforcers or trolls in unusual places. The Voice, whether through its subgroups the Shifter Alliance or the Undead League or other supernaturals, will not have the chance to harm any of us again."

Those amassed outside the doors trickled inside as the owl sucked in a big breath and squared his petite, feathered shoulders, scanning the crowd with his large, serious eyes. "I realize that current events are unsettling. Even I feel shaken to my core. But please know that you're in the midst of the finest institution for magical creatures in the entire world. And though you certainly are already aware, our sister institutions are also the strongest in their fields. The Magical Arts Academy and its several subsidiaries will not abandon us in our time of need. If it becomes necessary, I will call on the mages and dragons to help us."

No. Way. Dragons would come help us? On campus? I sensed the disbelief circling through our ranks. Sure, two dragons had descended upon the school last term so their riders could warn Sir

Lancelot with some secret news. But they'd departed quickly, and the beasts that'd been relegated to legend up until then had mostly remained elusive—a vision one barely dared believe.

The owl rubbed a wingtip across his tired face. "Nothing has changed, other than I hope this morning's attempt will serve to encourage you to press forward in your studies harder than ever before. Do not feel helpless. Rather, channel that energy into training to become the most powerful shifters you can be. I fear the world will need every single one of us before this war is over. Give everything you have to excelling. Not only will you benefit, but so will the entirety of your community, and there is no greater honor than serving others."

Ky, Leander, and Boone wove through the students and appeared at my side. I pushed away an irrational urge to bury myself in Leander's arms and pretend we had no greater concern than his father's dislike of me. The elfin prince met my eyes. Something flashed across the silver of his own that made me wonder if he could possibly be thinking the same thing—unlikely. Regardless, I took half a step toward him, thinking no one would notice. When I sensed Ky's stare on me, I stopped moving and trained my attention on the owl, but Leander took half a step toward me as well so that the sides of our bodies pressed together. His fingertips brushed mine.

"No misguided shifter, vampire, or other magical creature will tarnish our way of life," the headmaster was saying. "I won't allow it. *We* won't allow it."

"Hear, hear," Damon called out, as Sadie whooped.

"They won't disrupt our lives or our purpose," Sir Lancelot continued, standing as tall as he could at six inches, his own declaration appearing to bolster his resolve. "Proceed to your first class immediately. We'll learn, we'll train, and we'll excel. We'll beat them at their own game, because we'll play it better if for no other reason than that our motives are true. We don't aim to hurt, we aim to protect. We don't wish to crush anyone, only to elevate all the races. We seek to defend the humans and animals as they inhabit this Earth with us. We will prevail for our hearts are earnest, and there's nothing more powerful than that in this world. Only those true of heart can perform the strongest magic."

The owl brought both wingtips to what might have been his waist if he'd been a very tiny man. "I believe in every single one of you. So does the school. You wouldn't be here otherwise. Now all that's left is for you to believe in yourselves." He allowed his message to sink in, then barked, "Now, off to class you go. Those shifters made us waste enough time. You have ten minutes to arrive at your first class for a late start. Dismissed!"

Students stirred to action as if returning from a stupor and began filing outside. I noticed Sir Lancelot's attention settle on something in the distance and turned to find Wendi at the back of the hall. The owl gave her a short nod, from which I read thanks and respect. Wendi nodded back.

So she actually had been a big part of saving the day? Maybe Wendi with an "I" wouldn't be so bad after all.

"Come on, Rina," Sadie said from behind me. "I'm going to be stuck to you like white on rice."

Leander brushed my hand again as we turned to face her, and I couldn't help but smile at the determined look on her face. Sadie was all grit and business in her Smurf-blue Smurfette shirt. "You heard the owl. Time to get to class and learn to kick ass. You don't get to be this awesome without a ton of hard work. Am I right, Damon?"

"Hell yeah. You're in good hands, Rina. You can trust Sadie with your life." Damon moved to Ky's side, preparing to escort him to his own first class, no doubt.

"Let's just hope she won't have to." Sadie grimaced and ushered me through the throngs of people, elbowing students out of the way as she went. I offered Ky and Leander wary smiles, then allowed myself to be swept up in Sadie's momentum, leaving a trail of protesting students in her wake. Wren, Dave, Adalia, and Jas hurried to catch up with me.

The first day of school had barely started, and already nothing was as I'd expected it to be.

Just peachy.

❦ 8 ❦

Wren, Dave, Jas, Adalia, and I huddled past the main auditorium in Irele Hall and continued down a wide hallway toward a smaller version of the room. Sadie was at our backs, making us all nervous by constantly glancing in every direction, like we were in some B-grade cop movie and bad guys might pop out at us at every turn. Her fingertips twitched around the hilts of the curved blades that hung from her belt, though I wasn't sure she even realized she was doing it. I sensed her behind me like a big sack of Smurf-colored stress. I hunched and released my shoulders, trying to rid myself of the tension, but there was no way to accomplish it while my high-strung protector was shadowing my every move.

When we arrived at the appointed room, Wren and Dave stopped at the open doorway, peered inside, then stepped to the side to consult their schedules.

"What? What is it?" Jas asked, tilting her head to see around them.

"There are advanced students in there." Wren peered at her schedule. "But it's the right room. The Illumination Room in Irele Hall for Defensive Creature Magic 101."

"Yeah," Dave said. "We're at the right place."

"Ky's in there," Jas said excitedly, and Ky whipped his head around to look at her, and then me. Did Jas really not realize that my brother had super hearing thanks to his shifter powers? Or worse, did she not care?

I rolled my eyes at her back until I realized that if Ky was in the room, there was a decent chance that his best friends would be as well. I tried to be subtle about peering around my friends' heads, but when I did, I discovered Leander's searing eyes already on me.

Shit. I whipped my gaze away and turned to find Sadie staring at me with a smirk. "The prince of the elves? Really?" She waggled her eyebrows at me.

"Shut up. It's nothing." Was I allowed to speak to an Enforcer that way? I had no idea, but she needed to butt out of my business—my very nonexistent business. There was nothing official between Leander and me, or at least there wasn't supposed to be.

When I snapped my gaze from Sadie, I found Adalia also looking at me. Her eyes were gentle … almost as if she pitied me for falling for someone I couldn't have. Well, there might be plenty of reasons to pity me—first and foremost the fact that I was one of the two most hunted shifters on the planet right now—but rejection wouldn't be one of them. I'd be damned if I'd allow it.

I shrugged off thoughts of the prince I couldn't have and straightened my back, smoothing my shirt and pleated skirt. I was here to learn. I should be the most motivated of all the students to study. Not only was I still very nearly a novice, there was every chance I'd be forced to defend myself, no matter that I'd been assigned my very own high-strung protection detail.

"Well, what the hell are you guys waiting for?" Jas asked. "The advanced students won't bite, you know."

But at this school they actually might.

Wren and Dave folded their schedules back up as they prepared to lead us into the room, then Wendi appeared around the corner behind us. "What are you doing here?" Sadie asked, her voice as hard as the blades at her side.

Wendi smiled winningly as her ponytail swung behind her head. "Sir Lancelot asked me if I'd help you watch over Rina."

Sadie growled, a rumbling low in her chest. It was difficult to remember that she wasn't a shifter but a witch. With the way she behaved, I expected fur to erupt across her arms at any moment. She was wound tighter than a corkscrew.

Adalia stepped closer to me as if to protect me from my growling protector.

"If you don't like the headmaster's order, take it up with him," Wendi said. "I'm just trying to do my job."

"I'm already doing the job. I don't need you," Sadie grumbled, low and menacing.

Wendi's smile broadened until it couldn't possibly be genuine. "Clearly, Sir Lancelot didn't think you had it covered." She shrugged bare shoulders. "Don't blame me for your shortcomings." Wendi's voice dripped with saccharine, and Adalia took my arm.

Sadie narrowed her eyes and flared her nostrils. "I don't have shortcomings. What I do have is a pest trying to cramp my style."

Wendi flipped her ponytail. "Girl, do you seriously think a Smurfette shirt is the pinnacle of style?"

"Them are fightin' words." Sadie grinned like taking down Wendi would be the best thing to happen to her all day. She put up her fists and bounced on her feet. "Come on. Bring it. I've been waiting to take you down forever. You've had it coming, with your stupid hair and your stupid outfits and your stupid nails."

Wendi studied her manicure again. "You're just jealous because I took down those rogue shifters all on my own. I saved the day." She flicked innocent-looking eyes up at Sadie, but she was laying it on too thick. "Maybe someday you'll get to save the day. Or someone. Anything, really."

Sadie snarled and charged at Wendi, whose eyes widened as if she hadn't actually believed the wild Enforcer would follow through. That was stupid. I'm pretty sure every single one of us there could tell that Sadie was about to give Wendi a beatdown.

Sadie tackled Wendi. The two of them went flying onto the marble floor, hitting it with a loud smack and a groan—Wendi's. I was starting to think Sadie was too tough to complain about pain.

"*Ahem.*"

We all turned to look at the entrance to the small auditorium classroom, including Sadie, straddling Wendi with her fist pulled back, ready to let it fly.

"While I enjoy a good smackdown as much as the next person, this isn't the place for it. I have students to prepare to direct their own smackdowns on the assholes threatening our school."

Marcy June. The petite professor of advanced students who was fiercer than a man ten times her size. And I hadn't even seen her in her animal form yet.

The tiny woman placed both hands on her hips. I slid my gaze down her tank-top, well-worn jeans, and kickass boots, then swung it back up to take in the well-defined muscles of her arms. She was ripped. Not bodybuilder ripped—thankfully—but she made the most of her slight frame. She was all muscle, no fat, and plenty of gristle from the looks of her.

"Well? Are you waiting for a formal invitation or something? Because all you're going to get is a good ass-whooping if you don't listen."

I couldn't tell whom exactly Marcy June was talking to, but Sadie stood, allowing Wendi to get up, and my friends and I slipped into the room, receiving a friendly-ish glare from the petite professor as we slid past her. Dave and Wren halted as soon as we were in the room and twenty or so faces turned our way, including Leander's and my brother's protector, Damon.

Jas huffed from behind me. "You guys are ridiculous. Take a seat already." But as she moved to the front of our group, the buxom redhead, who'd been draped all over Leander every chance she got last term, swooped past us to lead her crew of groupies to the open seats in the front rows next to Leander, Ky, and Boone. Damon sat a few seats over from them, his semi-automatic weapon absent, though the Enforcer continued to appear lethal despite his chill demeanor.

"What the fuck?" Jas whispered, though I was sure most everyone in the room heard her, including my brother. Subtle, Jas was not.

She stomped past the front rows and deposited herself in the open row immediately behind them. She sat behind Ky, crossed her arms over her chest defiantly, and crossed her legs, highlighting stretches of creamy skin beneath her skirt that was shorter than school regulations permitted. She narrowed heavily made-up eyes at the ginger, but the curvy redhead didn't respond, training her own narrowed eyes at me instead.

I sighed audibly. I thought I'd left the cutthroat catfights behind at Berry Bramble High. With attention thick enough to make me want to squirm with every step I took, I moved across the front of the room, up the center aisle, and claimed a seat next to Jas, which happened to be directly behind Leander. Wren, Dave, and Adalia sat next to me.

Ginger and two of her equally bosomy clones in different shades swiveled in their seats to offer me the full-on glare treatment. I rolled my eyes so hard that my eyeballs actually ached, and when I returned them to front and center, Leander was looking straight at me, which made Ginger and crew fume. He winked at me, and I laughed—softly. I didn't have a death wish, and Ginger and crew looked ready to pummel me to the ground à la Sadie.

Sadie tromped into the room with Wendi on her heels. Sadie shooed the student from the seat immediately behind me and sank into it with enough noise to guarantee she disturbed the class. When Wendi tried to sit next to her, Sadie growled until the enforcer took a seat behind her.

"Well," Marcy June said from the front of the room, drawing my attention. "I think we've had enough distraction for one day. We have important shit to do."

I started at the teacher's language, but Jas grinned. Marcy June seemed just her style.

"You'll have noticed that this is a mixed level class, unlike your other classes. This is because this is the first time the school is offering Defensive Creature Magic 101. It's a new required class, and yes, you'll be all mine every single day, Monday through Friday, so get used to me. And get used to your classmates. You don't have to like each other to learn to kick ass."

Jas nodded enthusiastically, setting the gemstone hanging from her hoop nose ring to swinging and sparkling.

"Your schedule lists me as Professor Marsh, but for those of you who don't know me, call me Marcy June. I don't stand by formalities. Also, while this is the official classroom for our class, we'll meet at the shifter practice room in Bundry Hall often, so make sure you pay attention at the end of each class to find out where to show up for the next one. You should also pay close attention because I don't repeat myself. I'm here to teach, not coddle. If your mommies didn't do enough hand holding before you showed up here, well, you're flat out of luck."

I snapped my gaze to Ky and noticed him go rigid just as I did. Though I was certain Marcy June didn't realize Ky and I didn't have a mother to do anything for us, she also didn't seem like the type to worry about diplomacy and tender feelings.

"No one's going to hold your hand here, especially not me. Any questions? None? Good. Let's get started. Every one of you here is at least a twoer, which means you all should have some basic shifter skills by now, unless McGinty is going soft in his basic shifting classes, but I've known the man long enough to know he's a hardass. So don't bother using the excuse that you haven't learned something about your shifter animal on me. I won't buy it. Sure, you learn more as you go, obviously, but being a shifter, and eventually being an Enforcer, is all about learning on the fly. Flexibility is your friend. If you allow yourself to form rigid beliefs about what you can and can't do—or what your opponent can or can't do—you're setting yourself up for a world of hurt.

"You need to teach yourself to think outside the box. Keep your mind sharp and access it even while you're in your animal form. And before you ask, yes, every one of you in here is a shifter. The other supes and vamps will train a different way. I'm a shifter, so you got me."

What kind of shifter? I was desperate to know what kind of animal belonged to this instructor's steely attitude.

"We won't be working on your shift or how to develop your shifter powers. I'm leaving that to McGinty. That's obviously an important part of defending yourself, but in this class we'll work on using your skills to throw your opponent off balance, to allow you to dominate even when your animal might be the weakest in a fight. Size is important, it's true, boys"—she flashed a quick grin—"but in shifter fights, like in real life, it's not always the biggest and strongest that will win. How you use your skills is more important than size, and I'm going to teach you why and how. And if you're lucky enough to be the strongest and fastest in the room, there's always more to learn, trust me on that. Arrogance will get you killed quicker than anything else. Never underestimate a shifter. If you do, it might very well be the last thing you do."

Marcy June stopped her pacing across the front of the room to scan her audience to confirm that we all hung on her every word. "I'm also going to train you to fight in your human forms. We can't always rely on our animals, especially when the magic of our opponents is varied and unpredictable. Some of the stronger mages can block a shift. There are also some magical objects that can interfere. Or maybe you might be too injured in your human form to conjure the strength of your magic to shift. Since we can't anticipate the exact circumstances of your fight, we need to train for as many bizarre situations as we can think of. It's the only way to truly prepare.

"I'll pair you up so that you start by fighting other students that evenly match you. As the term progresses, I'll make the odds tougher. By the end of the term, every single one of you will have to fight someone who outpowers you, or you might fight me. And trust me, I won't hold back. It won't serve you if I don't show you what you might be up against. When you're a shifter, it pays to be tough as nails. Right, Sadie?"

"Hell yeah," she said from behind me. "The tougher, the better."

Marcy June scanned her audience again, dark eyes intense. "Girls, you'll want to wear shorts under your skirts. There's no room for delicate flowers in this class. Be ready to be thrown … unless you can throw your opponent first." She grinned as if she'd made a joke. Sadie was the only one to chuckle.

The professor proceeded, undoubtedly saying more things to freak me out about the rest of the term, but I didn't hear a thing for several solid minutes as a realization hit me—hard.

Marcy June had said this class was for shifters several times. Further, since Ky and Boone were such great friends with Leander, they spent a lot of time together. And in this school, creatures were clustered according to type—by necessity; we had different skills and couldn't all be grouped together. If Leander was in this class, that meant the elfin prince was a shifter.

Why on earth hadn't I considered that before?

Then I knew why. I'd seen his wings and assumed he was a creature who constantly maintained his form. But ... holy shit. He wasn't sporting wings right now. His back, sans wings, rested completely against the back of his seat, directly in front of me. And I hadn't even noticed.

Dumbfounded that I could be so stupid, I stared at the back of his light blue shirt. His back appeared smooth beneath it. *WTF?* What kind of shifter was he that he could retract his wings? Was there such a thing as a partial shift? Even though I wasn't as ignorant as I'd been last term, I still had no idea.

Leander was a shifter. He had to be. I was crushing on a guy and I had no idea what he might turn into...

As if he sensed my attention on his back, he turned in his seat. When his eyes met mine, he raised his eyebrows in question. Slowly, those around him turned to face me too. Ky was first, then Boone, but their groupies soon followed. Ginger tried to sear me with the force of her stare. Jas leaned forward in her seat to try to sear Ginger with her own stare. It was getting ridiculous, and in two seconds we'd have Marcy June on our asses for interrupting class.

I swallowed my shock—both that Leander was a shifter and that I'd been stupid enough not to notice—and blinked my link to him away. I smiled blandly and pinned my attention on Marcy June up front. It took a while, but eventually everyone did the same.

But even though I stared at the tiny professor with

the dark hair and the dark eyes, I didn't absorb a single word she was saying.

Leander was a shifter.

Like me.

Maybe that meant we were similar enough that we could be together. Even if for a term or two on campus...

9

I NEVER THOUGHT I'D BE RELIEVED TO BE IN BASIC Shifting 201 after how much I'd flubbed my shifts in McGinty's class last term, but after the tension of Defensive Creature Magic, I was ready to be free of Ginger and her equally catty friends. If I had to leave her to rub her paws all over Leander to get away from her, so be it. Besides, Marcy June was *intense*, too intense for the first day of classes, especially with the way the day had started.

My relief, however, was short-lived. Though Basic Shifting was also held in the Illumination Room, McGinty directed us to the shifter practice room in Bundry Hall before most students' butts hit their seats. And he assigned me as a partner to the best shifter in the class: Jas. She grinned at me from the other side of the padded mat, bouncing on the balls of her feet as if we were about to spar.

"You do realize you're not supposed to hit me or

anything, right?" I said. "Because you're looking a little unhinged."

"According to you, I always look unhinged."

"True enough, but you look particularly so."

"It's nothing. I'm just picturing all the ways I'm gonna take down Tracy." She jabbed the air between us, her white-striped black hair and dangling nose ring swinging with each punch. "Take that, bitch," she hissed to her imaginary opponent.

"Who the hell is Tracy?"

"The bitch who couldn't take her eyes off Ky. She's encroaching on my territory, and I'm gonna put her in her place." She jabbed again. "Teach her a lesson."

I breathed in some patience; with Jas, I could always count on needing a whole lot of it. "First of all, my *brother* is *not* your *territory*. And secondly, is Tracy one of the redhead's friends?"

"If you mean the redhead with the huge boobs who can't keep her grubby hands off your man, then yeah." She punched a quick one-two combo. "You know, if you roll your eyes like that they might get stuck facing the back of your head."

I scoffed. "No they won't." But just in case, I kept my eyeballs where they belonged. "And Leander isn't my 'man,' you know that."

She shrugged. "Whatever. You can let Stacy take Leo if you want, but I'm staking my claim on Ky."

"Wait. Stacy and Tracy? Are you for real?"

"Yep." She grinned and brought her fists down to

her sides. "Their little grabby, buxomy trio is Stacy, Tracy, and Swan. You can't make that shit up."

I chuckled. "I'm pretty sure it'd be impossible to make up half the shit that goes down at this school."

"Eh-hem."

I turned my head to find Professor Conan McGinty behind me, towering over me with his full, bushy beard and full, bushy head of auburn hair.

"What do you think, lasses? Are ya actually going to do any coursework today?" His voice was a slight brogue. Now that I knew what shifter magic felt like, I sensed it on any shifter powerful enough to put off shifty vibes when they were in human form. I was sensing lots of power rolling off of him. "You're supposed to be practicing your shifts, not gossiping like old maids."

Jas pouted and opened her mouth, probably to complain about being called an "old maid," so I rushed to keep her from sticking her proverbial foot in her mouth. I tried not to alienate my teachers, even if she apparently didn't care. I blurted out the first thing that popped into my head: "I practiced a lot over the summer."

"I'd hoped you would. The better you get, the safer you'll be."

"Yeah, my brother and Boone coached me quite a lot since we didn't have much to do in the fae's Golden Forest over the break."

"Glad to hear it. Leander didn't help?"

I schooled my features into indifference. "No, his

father kept him pretty busy. I didn't see him all that much."

"Hm. That surprises me."

"Why?"

"Well, Leander's shown quite an interest in you is all."

"Hm-hmm," Jas said from behind me in a singsongy I-told-you-so tune, though she'd never told me any such thing.

Don't ask, don't ask—"How so?"

McGinty's eyes twinkled as he looked down at me. I thought he was actually going to answer my question for a few moments, before his expression grew serious and he tucked his arms behind his back. I suspected he'd just realized he was beginning to gossip like an "old maid."

"Show me your shift," he said. "Let's see where you're at now, lass."

I pushed the many questions and doubts I had to the back of my mind for later analysis—or even better, where I'd hopefully forget them—and stepped into the center of the mat, encouraging Jas off it. I closed my eyes and pictured my essence embodied in a strong, powerful, muscular mountain lion. During last term, McGinty had specifically instructed me not to do it this way. But it worked for me, so whatever. I was pretty sure the instructor would encourage me to embrace however I could get to the desired end result. I'd seen him encourage Dave Bailey to shift a dozen different ways, so long as he stopped ending up part bobcat, part boy. After my many struggles in shifting last term, I was just grateful I'd found a way that got it done more or less predictably; I still only managed to shift maybe seventy percent of the time.

I envisioned my thick fur, the golden color of a sandy desert, glistening in the sunlight. I pictured my eyes, golden, copper-toned, so much like my human eyes. I envisioned the way my muscles glided under my flesh in the pinnacle of grace and efficiency. This was easy as I'd watched Ky as a mountain lion over the summer until I'd had my fill, and our lions were much the same, though mine was slightly smaller.

I breathed in deeply, gathering my energy in the center of my abdomen, deep in my core. My magic pulsed there like a beacon for my power … and then I pushed it out, sending it toward that image of myself as a mountain lion, a majestic creature perfectly in tune with nature and all creation. I directed my magic toward the image I held in my mind and … *poof*.

I shook myself and opened my eyes, knowing I'd managed it. And in record time. I was nowhere near as fast at it as Ky or Boone, or even Jas, but compared to my performance of last semester, I was a superstar.

"Damn, girl, that was awesome," Jas said, and I noticed Wren and Dave grinning at me from a few mats over.

I looked up at McGinty. His face was far too serious. "Well, you didn't blur, vibrate, or flicker. But neither did you shift the cracking-breaking way." Finally, he grinned as wide as my friends. "I suppose I always figured you were unique. You came up with your own way, and it suits you just fine. You're a mighty beautiful lion, that's for sure."

I smiled, though I had no idea what that might look like in my animal form. He reached down and patted me awkwardly on the shoulder. "This is a vast improvement from last term, no doubt about it. But there's always room for more improvement. You've seen what your brother can do, right?"

I nodded.

"Keep practicing until you achieve his fluidity. Or until you surpass it." He smiled again, the enthusiasm twinkling in his eyes. "I bet Ky would like that, huh, his squirt of a sister shifting better than him?"

Wait, was McGinty pitting me against my brother? And how many people knew Ky called me "squirt?" I still had to get back at him for that...

"Shifters are competitive by nature," McGinty continued. "But the only one you should compete with is yourself. Keep it up until you've managed *your best*. You'll know when that is." He squatted down to examine my face. "It's really quite remarkable. So few of you in the world..."

He studied me for long enough that I would have definitely been fidgeting in human form. He stood again. "Now, let's see you shift back. I want to hear all about how you shift without the three usual steps."

But when I went to shift, reaching for the image of my human self in the reverse of what I'd done, I couldn't quite hold on to the image long enough to return to my usual self. My lion seemed to be asserting her dominance, her power.

It took me the rest of the hour-and-forty-five-minute long class to finally grab hold of myself, my long blond hair, copper eyes, bare arms and legs, school uniform, before things began to happen in the right direction. I channeled all the strength and ferocity of my lion into holding onto the image of myself as a young woman. My lion resisted; I pushed onward.

The bell rang just as I finally returned to myself as a girl. Panting and exhausted, I sprawled on the mat that reeked even to my human nose of stinky feet and old sweat. I wished the staff mages would do some kind of spell to keep them sparkling clean.

"Class dismissed!" McGinty yelled out to the rest of the class of mostly exhausted shifters before focusing back on me. "I'm glad to see you made it back, lass. You had me worried there for a bit. We'll have to talk about how things went tomorrow."

Joy. A conversation to look forward to—not.

I heaved myself up from the mat and joined my waiting friends in heading to the dining hall. Dave appeared as exhausted as I was; he must still be struggling with his shift. Sadie and Wendi settled behind our group, constant shadows. I caught Sadie elbowing Wendi before I turned back around.

I was famished. Shifting, or struggling to shift as it were, really took it out of me.

DESPITE THE MANY PERSONALITY QUIRKS OF THE pygmy trolls, there wasn't a thing I could say against their cooking. The selection of food in the dining hall was varied and smelled delicious, as usual. And as usual, Wren and I chose our food not based on what was most appetizing, but on which station was manned by the least frightening-looking troll. It varied from day to day, the trolls' moods as fickle as Jas suffering from PMS.

I settled at the bench table with two slices of veggie pizza and a salad drenched in ranch dressing, which kind of negated the fact that I was eating a salad, but whatever. I'd probably burned about five thousand calories trying to shift for so long.

Sadie and Jas were already there. Sadie had two trays of food, piled high with a salami sub with all the fixings, two slices of pepperoni and mushroom pizza, three tacos smothered in hot sauce, and a bowl of chili topped with raw onions and Mexican cheese. I really hoped she was going to brush her teeth before sleeping with "one eye open" in our room tonight.

Jas sat in front of her spicy Szechuan stir-fry and stared at Sadie, plucked eyebrows raised. "Where are you gonna fit all that?"

"In my belly," Sadie said around a bite, smiling as we got a view of sub sandwich. "Man, I missed the dining hall. It was one of my highlights while studying here."

"I'll bet," I said.

"Mmm. The food is as good as I remember. A bonus of watching your ass all term."

I choked on a bite of salad. "You're going to be here with me the entire term?"

"Yup. What, don't you want me watching your back?"

Actually, yes, yes I did. I nodded. "For sure. You look like you could kick anyone's ass."

Wendi took a seat on the opposite end of the table from Sadie. Her tray contained a salad and nothing else, and it wasn't coated in ranch.

"Too bad she has to be here too." Sadie's shoulders slumped glumly as she shoveled another bite of salami into her mouth.

Wendi pretended not to hear—shifters have superb hearing—and took a dainty bite of cucumber and tomato and washed it down with sparkling water.

Sadie watched her. "Puke," she said under her breath. I wasn't sure whether to groan or chuckle.

"Okay, what is it with you two?" Jas asked, never afraid of conflict, while Wren and Dave sat next to me, and Adalia claimed her usual seat next to the prickly skunk shifter.

"Why, whatever do you mean?" Wendi said like a Southern belle.

Sadie growled, "I just don't like people who put on airs. There's enough hot air around that chick to inflate a hot air balloon. When you're the best at what you do, there's no need for pretense."

"You just don't like that *I'm* the one who took out the shifters attacking the place this morning. You can't handle that someone else might get the limelight for once. You always want it to be all about Sadie, Sadie,

Sadie. She's one of the best Enforcers, don't you know? She kicks butt. Yada, yada, yada. I'm sick of it. You're just going to have to deal with me getting more attention than you for once."

"It's not that, you idiot. You're——"

"Hey there, ladies," Damon interrupted.

Thank God. I was pretty sure Sadie and Wendi were ten seconds from grappling on the floor of the dining hall, and then we would've had to deal with the trolls' wrath in addition to their fighting.

"What's goin' on?" he asked, and it was hard not to picture him with a joint hanging from his lips; he was that chill—until I remembered him with his semi-automatic, then the chill picture in my head vanished like smoke.

"Just Wendi being 'Wendi with an I,'" Sadie said sulkily.

Damon nodded knowingly as Ky, Boone, and Leander sidled up beside our table—along with Stacy, Tracy, and Swan shadowing each of the boys. The ginger Stacy actually had her hand on Leander's shoulder from behind, though his eyes were pinned on me.

"Hi, Rina," he said, and the entire table hushed.

"Hi, Leander," I replied, mostly because I wanted to see Stacy fume. I could tell she was pissed, even though her face was mostly hidden behind the prince's tall, strong frame. I made out an irritated flip of long, gorgeous red hair from behind his shoulder.

Tracy and Swan—so similar to Stacy except the first was a blonde and the other a brunette—placed possessive hands on Ky and Boone's shoulders. Stacy's head popped up from around Leander. She forced a tight smile. "Well, we must be going. We need time to eat before our next class."

"True enough," Boone said, but I think it was mostly because the large shifter wanted food.

Leander inclined his head toward me. "I hope to catch ya later, Rina."

I smiled. "Yeah, see ya."

"Bye, *squirt*," Ky said, and I renewed my vow to kill him later.

"Bye, *Kylan*," I said, since he preferred his nickname to his full name. His copper eyes tightened, but he tilted his head at me in a stalemate gesture I'd seen from him before. Or maybe it was a warning to stay away from his friend, though I hadn't done anything.

"Are you ladies going to be okay if I sit with them?" Damon asked, his penetrating gaze pinned on the grumpy Sadie.

"We'll be fine," she said, and under her breath, "And if not, I'll kick her ass."

"I like her," Jas said cheerily, trying to catch Ky's eye, but my brother was already leading the way to another table, his friends and their groupies following.

Damon shared a meaningful look with Sadie that held volumes I didn't understand, then gave what appeared to be a warning look at Wendi, before moving his protective self over to Ky.

"I think I'm going to invite him to the dance," Jas said, and none of us had to ask whom she was talking about.

"You can't do that right now," Wren whispered frantically. "Don't you see the girl draped all over him?"

"Seeing and caring are two different things." Jas pushed up from the table, and Wren, Dave, Adalia, and I watched her move toward Ky with enough apprehension to make up for her lack of concern.

"I thought we didn't need dates for this dance party thing?" Dave said.

"I assumed the same," I said. Though maybe it was more like I'd hoped that was the case.

"It'd better be," Wren said. "I think we have enough pressure on us right now without worrying about dates."

"For sure." I'd better not need a date...

We watched Jas as one watched a train wreck, our food forgotten, waiting for the inevitable. But when Jas tapped Ky on the shoulder and managed to separate him from the tentacle-fingered blonde, he gave her his full attention. And when she'd said whatever she said, he shot an alarmed look at me.

So she'd asked him to the dance...

Damn, that girl had a pair.

I was in the process of mentally cataloging all the comforting things I could say to the abrasive shifter once she returned to our table when she turned and started back toward us... and her smile took up most of her face.

I snapped an accusing glare at Ky, but he shrugged like he hadn't known what else to do. And then he had bigger problems to deal with. Tracy tapped him on the shoulder, he swiveled to face her, and I directed my attention pointedly at my food.

Jas was so not going to date my brother. It wasn't going to happen. No way. That was as uncomfortable as it could get. What if they had ... sex? Ew. No. Un-unh. It wasn't going to work.

Was this yucky feeling that slithered down me like slime the reason Ky didn't like Leander paying attention to me? Okay. I guess it made sense. Because if he was picturing Leander and me in half the compromising situations I was picturing Ky and Jas, he had a valid point. Maybe I wouldn't think of the elf anymore. That would make me a good sister and—

My thoughts cut off abruptly as Wren and Dave swiveled on their seats to stare behind me, and Adalia gawked from across the table.

"What are you guys looking at?" I turned and looked straight up into the expectant—and gorgeous —face of the second prince of the elves.

"Rina, may I have a word please?"

My legs shot me to standing before my brain managed to catch up and suggest restraint. When Jas started *ooohing* loudly enough to tint my entire face pink, I stalked as far away from the table as I could. I stopped in the corner nearest the double doors, but farthest from the messenger flowers. I didn't need any witnesses to this embarrassing conversation, even if they were of the flora kind.

When I about-faced and stared up into his silver eyes that rolled like liquid mercury, my heart started thumping, my mouth went bone dry, and I couldn't think of a single thing to say.

"Would you like to go to the party with me on Friday?" he asked, and I found myself following the movements of his full lips as they formed each word. "…Rina?"

Oops, apparently I was still staring at his lips when I was supposed to be replying. I snapped my attention to the rest of his face. "Uh … yeah, sure. But do we need dates for the party? I didn't realize we did."

He smiled at my evident nervousness. "I don't think we *need* them, but I'd like to go with you."

"Really? You would?" *Gah, stop talking, Rina.*

"Yes, I would. I would have liked to spend more time with you over the summer too, but my father kept me too busy for that." His silver eyes became stormy in an instant.

"I'd hoped to get to know you better then too," I said in a soft, timid voice.

"So you'll go to the dance with me as my date?"

I fiddled with the pleats of my skirt. "What about Stacy?"

He raised both eyebrows. "What about her?"

"Well, won't she be upset if you take me as your date?"

He didn't even flinch. "Maybe. But that's her problem, not ours. I've never done anything to encourage her affections."

You also don't appear to discourage them, I thought.

"I've always been clear with her. She's a friend, nothing more," he continued, making me grateful I hadn't spoken my thought aloud. "What others think of me isn't my business. I only have to be the kind of man I can feel good about."

Wow, how very mature of him. I wasn't nearly that mature. I nodded my agreement, however.

"So we'll chat more Friday?"

"Yeah, definitely. Yep. For sure."

He smiled broadly, as if he realized I'd had to force myself to stop rambling, and took a few backward steps toward the tables. "I'll be looking forward to it."

I nodded like my head was on a spring. "Me too. Lots." I clamped my lips shut as heat rushed up my neck and across my cheeks. Why did I always have to say embarrassing stuff?

He chuckled, his eyes alight with delicious, wicked mischief, and turned, striding back toward Boone, Ky, and their groupies with sure steps like he owned the world. His wings were nowhere in sight.

I waited a minute to give my heart a chance to stop pounding, then attempted to walk with equal grace and confidence. The tip of my Converse snagged on a depression in the tile floor and I tripped, but managed to catch myself quickly. It was possible that no one would have noticed.

But I sensed someone's attention on me like a laser beam. I really didn't want to, because I had a good idea whose attention it was, but I looked over to Leander's table anyway. Yep, Stacy was glaring at me like I'd killed her pet kitten. And she'd definitely seen me trip; her sneer was as malicious as it was prominent.

I purposely avoided her and Ky, who was bound to be looking at me too, and made my way toward my table of friends with my head held high. Like Leander, I didn't care what others thought of me—and maybe if I said it enough, I'd actually believe it.

I took my seat and slid my plate toward me, though my stomach was too filled with butterflies to eat. Finally, I looked up. Everyone at the table was staring and waiting, even Sadie and Wendi.

"Well?" Wren prompted.

"Well what?" I said.

"Don't be coy with us," Jas snapped. "It doesn't suit you. Did he ask you to the dance or not?"

I tried to play it cool, but failed with flying colors. A grin stretched my face. "He did."

Wren squealed a little too loudly, but I was too happy to care.

10

"IT'S NOT EVEN SUPPOSED TO BE A 'DANCE' WITH dates," I was complaining once the nerves really got to me. Leander was supposed to meet me in fifteen minutes. "Sir Lancelot called it the Paranormal Party of Pleasantries. That implies no dates."

"Are you seriously griping that you're going to the party with Leo as your date?" Wren asked from where she was casually draped across her bed. She wore a simple yet pretty dress in a dusky rose that suited her willowy body and complexion perfectly.

I was fretting over my own dress in front of the standing mirror, though since the dresses had magically appeared in our closets before Wren and I arrived at our rooms after our final class of the day— Beginning Creature History 201 with Professor Whittle, the most boring werewolf teacher ever—I understood that my dress suited me as well as Wren's suited her. Still, it was a date with an elfin prince—a very off-limits elfin prince.

"Come on," Wren said. "You look beautiful in that dress, and I love that you're still wearing your sneaks. Leo is going to love the look."

"Yeah, well, he isn't going to have a choice, now is he? I don't even get to choose between outfits."

"Thank goodness," Sadie groaned from the other room. "If not I'd have to hear you whine even more. It's a dress. Who cares?"

"That's easy for you to say," I grumbled. "You get to wear jeans and a t-shirt. I wish I could."

"You can if you want to."

"Hmph." I abruptly realized I was being a stereotypical whiny teen and sank onto Wren's bed. "I'm sorry. I'm just really nervous. You get to go with Dave. That sounds so … comfortable."

She smiled. "It is. I'm actually looking forward to the evening. It'll be a nice change from all the classes and hard work, not to mention all the stress of the … situation."

It was an unspoken agreement. Neither one of us talked much about the Voice, the Shifter Alliance, or any of the other supernatural groups out to get us in general, and me in particular. Any discussion of the dangers we had so little control over left us both unsettled and depressed.

"Aren't you looking forward to spending the evening with Leo?" she asked.

"I would be. That elf is hot." Wendi's voice drifted through the open door from the common room, where it was a miracle that Sadie hadn't killed her yet as she lounged on the couch, regularly offering her opinions. I was actually glad the two of them would be at the party too; I didn't think it wise to leave them alone and unsupervised.

Wren and I ignored Wendi. We'd had plenty of practice at it during the couple of hours we'd been hanging out in our dorm room, which the staff witch Nancy had magically expanded to include two additional rooms, with locking doors and a single bed within each. Apparently she was familiar with the temperaments of my two bodyguards. Our room looked no different from the outside than it had before —magic was seriously awesome.

I leaned closer to Wren in hopes of having a private conversation. "Of course I'm looking forward to it. You know I like him, it's just … he's so intimidating. He's super sure of himself, and I told you what happened over the summer. We're not even allowed to be together. His father would probably flip if he found out Leander had asked me to the dance. Not to mention Ky. He's been trying to corner me to talk all week."

"I don't think Ky can say much about you going with Leander. He's going with Jas."

"Ugh. Don't remind me." I flopped back on the bed and draped a forearm over my face.

Wren chuckled. "You're so dramatic sometimes."

I laughed. "I know, and I hate it." I sat up and patted her on the leg. "You know just what to say to snap me out of myself. Thanks, girl."

"You got it." She grinned and stood from the bed, admiring herself in the mirror.

"You look beautiful," I said.

"Thank you. So do you."

I smiled my thanks. "Ready?"

She nodded, and we exited the room we shared into the common room.

Wendi rocketed to standing from the couch right away. "Hold up. *This* is how you're going?"

"Uh, yeah..." I said.

"Neither one of you is wearing a speck of makeup. And your hair! It's so … normal. You both have this gorgeous, long hair. You could do all sorts of fun things with it. You could twist it or braid it up—"

Wren and I evaded her outstretched hands as she reached for our heads.

"Thanks," Wren said, "but we like ourselves just as we are."

I blinked at her. I hadn't told her what Leander said.

Sadie moved toward us when Wren and I reached the door. "I'll do my best not to crowd you," she said to me. "But my job is to never let you out of my sight."

"Thanks, Sadie," I said. But while I was thankful for her commitment to protect me—and maybe Wendi's as well; I hadn't decided yet—I really wasn't grateful for the fresh reminder that I wasn't safe. Even inside the heart of Thunder Mountain, probably concealed within a million advanced spells, surrounded by magical creatures of all sorts, I was still vulnerable.

If the shifters Rage and Fury wanted to get to me, it seemed like it might only be a matter of time before they found their opportunity. They'd managed it last term, when the Menagerie had already been supposedly impregnable.

"I've seen that look before," Sadie said. "I know how you feel. But don't let worries about the future, about things that might never come to pass, ruin your present. There's no place safer in the entire world right now. Remember, it isn't just me watching your back."

"Obviously, because I'm here too," Wendi said.

Sadie, in a bright pink *Powerpuff Girls* t-shirt, gripped my shoulders. "There are Enforcers, trolls, and all sorts of creatures patrolling the grounds too. Just because you can't see them doesn't mean they aren't there, and the school has more magical defenses than I can count."

"That's because you can barely count to a hundred," Wendi snapped.

Sadie's eyelid twitched but she steadfastly ignored the other Enforcer. "Have fun and don't worry about anything else. Don't let Rage and Fury ruin things for you even when they're not an immediate threat."

I nodded, wanting her to convince me, even though I was pretty sure the mountain lion shifter brothers were an immediate threat so long as they were alive.

Sadie slapped me on the back hard enough to

rattle my insides. "Now, off you go. Remember, have fun … but not too much fun, if you know what I mean. That elf might be sexy, but that doesn't mean you have to have sex with him on the first date."

I groaned. "Come on, Sadie, really? Do you have to go there?"

"No more than you do."

I flung my hands in the air. "I'm not going to have sex with him. I'm not even supposed to be going on a date with him. His dad would probably kill us if he found out. Leander and I are too different, the wrong species and all that."

"You're not as different as you think. That's probably why the king was so worried. I see the look in Leo's eyes when he takes you in. The king doesn't miss much; I'm sure he saw it too."

Wren was looking between Sadie and me with intrigue, but I was finished with this conversation. I was so over how complicated my life had gotten.

I slunk through the door, wishing the night over already.

I'M NOT SURE WHAT KY SAID TO LEANDER TO GET HIM to agree, but Ky, Jas, Leander, and I were going on a double date. Quadruple date really if you added in that Wren and Dave, and Adalia and Boone, were tagging along too. When you added in Ky's and my bodyguards, we were a party all on our own.

I arched my brows in question at Adalia, but she

only shrugged. I wasn't sure who'd asked whom to the dance, but I liked the match. Adalia and Boone were agreeable and pleasant, and a logical pairing to complete our group. Maybe that's all it was between them, two friends hanging out.

Jas, however, was surlier than usual. She wasn't happy to have a gaggle of creatures tagging along as a buffer between her and Ky. I, on the other hand, didn't mind giving up my privacy with Leander if it foiled any come-ons she might have planned to direct at my brother. Seeing the two of them standing in close proximity was enough to weird me out. When Jas snaked her arm through his, I had to look away.

But the moment we stepped into the dining hall, I forgot all about the company I kept and the shifters plotting to attack my brother and me. The dining hall had transformed into an extraordinary space—magical to the extreme.

Absent were the rows of utilitarian tables and buffet islands. Thousands of tiny twinkling lights illuminated the open dance floor, and a mystical-feeling fog drifted across the room, converting the large space into something cozy while affording some privacy to the students assembled, but not enough to hide indiscretions.

Silver vines culminating in pink, coral, violet, and buttercream flowers hung from the ceiling, stopping several feet above the tallest head; stars sparkled overhead, as if we were standing outside. A shooting star raced across the high, vaulted ceiling, and I couldn't help but gasp. I wasn't the only one.

"This is incredible," I whispered as Leander leaned in to catch my soft words.

He grinned and took my arm. "It's going to be an incredible night since I get to share it with you," he said against my ear, and I didn't manage to conceal the shivers that ran through me.

"Are you cold?" he asked.

"No. Happy."

He nodded as if he understood and led me farther into the hall. Soft Classical music wafted toward us from the far left corner of the ballroom. I gasped again. "Are the … trolls playing?"

"Pygmy trolls are superb musicians, when they put their minds to it, that is."

"Wow." I couldn't help my awe. The music from their odd instruments was as fine as that of a modern symphony. "What are they even playing? Those aren't regular instruments, are they?"

"They definitely aren't. The trolls do everything their own way."

"I can't believe they can sound that amazing with homemade instruments."

"Remember that trolls have magic. The pygmy trolls that work at the school have more than most. Their instruments might remind you of your average violin or cello, but they're bound to hide as many secrets as the trolls."

"Can we get closer? I want to see."

He chuckled. "I didn't imagine you'd be asking to get closer to the trolls. You always seem a bit afraid of them."

"That's because they're terrifying. At least they're wearing cute little suits now." Wait. "You watch me?" I directed my gaze from the orchestra to him.

"Of course I do. I'm interested in you, Rina. Or can't you tell? You fascinate me."

Despite the fact that our friends stood only a few feet away from us, the music cocooned us in a semblance of privacy. We were surrounded by people, and yet I felt as if it were just Leander and me.

I leaned into his arm. "After this summer, I wasn't sure how you felt about me."

He opened his mouth to respond, but someone bumped into me from behind. I lost my balance, but Leander's strong arms shot out to wrap around me, pulling me close.

I spun on whoever had pushed me. "What the hell?" But whatever else I'd been about to say froze on my lips as I stared into unblinking, predatory eyes.

The vampire's face crept upward slowly until his mouth revealed pointy fangs. "Hi, princess. Long time no see."

It was the same guy who'd pushed me in the auditorium on the first day of classes as a oner, before the vampires were fully initiated and could no longer tolerate direct sunlight—at least not for another century or two. His three buddies stood at his back, just as they had the last time I'd seen the unpleasant bunch.

But last time Leander hadn't been witness to their bullying—nor had my brother.

Apparently Ky was watching us despite the foggy

haze and the drifting musical cocooning. A few long, hard strides placed him between me and Vamp Bully. Leander drew next to my brother, keeping me in sight, but just behind them.

"What do you think you're doing?" Ky said in that tone of voice that made lesser creatures cower.

"Oh, nothing. Just saying hi to the princess."

"Well, you shove my sister again, Anton, you and I are going to have big problems, you get me?"

Anton didn't seem as intimidated as I would've expected him to be when facing two large, fearsome men, and Boone was already moving in the direction of his friends while Damon and Sadie glared at the vamps from nearby.

"You and your sister are the problem," Anton said. "You're the reason we have all this ridiculous security and can't come and go as we please. Rage and Fury just want you, no one else."

Boone arrived and growled right away. Leander leaned forward, getting right in Anton's space. The vamp's buddies didn't intervene, though they didn't back up either.

I wasn't usually one for letting the boys handle my problems, but they were so outraged on my behalf, it was kind of sweet.

"Ky and Rina aren't going anywhere," Boone said, his voice low and gravelly. "They belong here as much as you do. More so even."

"Why's that, wolfy?"

"Because they don't go out of their way to be pricks."

Anton put his hands up. "Hey, I call it like I see it. If they'd go, all our problems would just … disappear."

"Is that a threat?" Ky said.

"Not at all. When I threaten you, you'll know it, trust me." Fully extended, Anton's fangs protruded over his bottom lip. With his dark brown hair, pale skin, and eyes a degree too large for his face, there was no disguising what he was.

In unison, Ky, Leander, and Boone advanced on him, and Anton's cronies stepped forward, joining him on either side. The shifters growled, the vampires hissed, and I spotted Damon and Sadie walking toward the scuffle. Jas, Adalia, Wren, and Dave moved next to me, anticipating a fight.

But then Fianna and Nessa dive-bombed the vamps and my brother and his friends with the zooming sound of mosquitoes. Fianna landed on Anton's face while Nessa zipped around the two bands of men in a non-stop buzzing circle.

"You'd better back off, buddy boy," Fianna said, staring into one of Anton's eyeballs. "This here is a party. You're not supposed to fight at parties. If you do fight, Nessa and I'll be forced to deal with you as we see fit, and trust me, you don't want that. Nessa and I've been forced to behave more than we'd like lately, and there's nothing I'd like more than to beat your mean, scrawny butt into submission."

"Fianna," Nessa hissed, shifting to hover behind her cousin. "Remember that you're not supposed to talk to the students like that. You're supposed to be nice. No beating anyone."

Fianna scowled. "You're lucky Nessa's coming to your defense, or you'd have some real problems on your hands. Vamp or not, I'd take you down."

Anton didn't seem to know what to say when the person threatening him was a few inches tall. Hell, he probably couldn't even focus on her as she was right next to his eye.

His crew held their positions but didn't advance. Neither did my brother and his friends.

Fianna looked between all involved parties, scowling. "I don't want to see any more fighting, got it?"

Anton nodded, but Boone said, "Then this jerk had better keep his pointy mouth shut."

"Granted," Fianna said, and I had to swallow a laugh.

The crimson fairy flew from the vamp's face to float in the middle of everyone. She looked back and forth between them all once more, then pointed a diminutive finger at them in turn. "I'll have my eye on you." Her eye was probably the size of a grape seed. "Don't you forget it."

The men didn't say a word.

"Well? What are you doing standing around?" She shooed them with her hands. "Disperse. Cavort. Socialize in a friendly and appropriate manner." When no one moved, she roared, "Now!"

Anton and friends turned and merged with the crowd, and Fianna and Nessa turned to face the rest of us. "Nessa and I'll keep an eye on them. I don't trust them," Fianna said, though I was pretty sure she shouldn't have. Though tiny, she was still a member of the staff. I couldn't imagine Sir Lancelot speaking like that, and they were his messenger assistants.

"I don't trust them either," Boone said, and though the big shifter didn't seem like the type to hold a grudge, I had the feeling he was about to make an exception. He crossed his arms across his wide, muscular chest, which strained the seams of his fine suit, and scowled in the direction the vamps had disappeared.

"Hey!" Fianna yelled. She'd spotted some other commotion across the hall, and she and Nessa zoomed out of sight.

The band struck up a particularly jovial tune—an odd jaunt that mixed elements of bluegrass and alternative rock and did so with surprising success—and Leander reached for me again. He leaned toward my ear. "Now, where were we?"

I barely remembered, and I had no idea how he could behave so casually after that, but I let him lead me onto the dance floor. At least there no one would threaten me—I hoped—and I'd escape my brother's scrutiny.

Leander brought a hand to my waist, pinned me in his rolling silver gaze, and the rest of the world faded away. The hazy fog enveloped us as I gave myself over to the moment beneath a pristine starlit sky. I didn't give a damn that it wasn't real. I'd take it.

Anton and the other vamps had served to remind me that, if certain sectors of the supernatural community had their way, I wouldn't be at the academy. Hell, I wouldn't be alive.

I stepped closer to Leander despite the upbeat tempo of the music.

Carpe diem—seize the day. I willed the rest of the world beyond the two of us away.

❦ 11 ❦

I LOST TRACK OF WHERE THE OTHERS WERE AS Leander whisked me across the dance floor with practiced ease. After the summer I'd spent in the fae's Golden Forest, I understood that a royal like him was expected to possess every social grace. Besides, the fae in general were festive, embracing any excuse they could as a reason to celebrate. Surely Leander had had plenty of occasions to dance in his life, whereas I'd had close to none. Dances at Berry Bramble High didn't count, trust me on that one, where twerking and grinding were real travesties.

I barely registered the music beyond noting that it changed constantly between genres. The trolls were as fickle with their music as they were with their moods. Regardless, Leander knew exactly how to move to each song, even the ones I was certain the trolls must have invented.

He wore a charcoal suit, a light cobalt blue shirt, which happened to match the tones of my dress, with the top two buttons undone. He'd pulled his wavy silver hair back into a ponytail at the base of his neck and tucked his wings away—however it was that he managed that. And though he looked a bit like a god the way he filled out his suit, I struggled to focus beyond his eyes. The silver orbs were like twin full moons, beckoning me further into their depths.

"You look beautiful tonight," he said, pulling me against him to be heard over the music.

"So do you." I briefly wondered if I shouldn't have spoken so bluntly, but then dismissed my concern. I was too happy to worry about sharing my heart.

He smiled. "When Ky mentioned he had a sister, I never imagined you'd be how you are. He made you sound so … plain and uninteresting."

I laughed despite myself. "I'll bet he did." I hesitated, but only for a moment. "Has he talked to you about staying away from me?"

Leander paused to twirl me to the rhythm of the current ballad before continuing. "He has."

"But you're ignoring him?"

"It would appear so." He looked away, in the direction of Ky, I presumed, and when he looked back at me his eyes were extra intense. "I'm drawn to you, Rina. You feel different from everyone else. I see you watching the world around you, and it's like you view things in a new way. Your magic is magnetic. All of you is. I tried to stay away last term, but I finally gave up."

"Are you saying I'm irresistible?" I joked.

"Yes."

My heart jumped in my chest. I stared into his eyes and wondered if I'd ever be able to stop. This wasn't normal, was it? I'd never dated in any real sense before, but this seemed like too much, too fast. How could he feel this while barely knowing me?

As if he'd read my mind, he said, "I know this might surprise you, but I've always been sure of myself … and what I want."

I gulped. "And you want me?" My pulse thumped in my head loudly, overcoming the tempo of the music.

Leander grinned like the Cheshire Cat and gave a single nod that set my heart to racing anew.

Holy shmoly, this man was amazing. And though I tried my best to remind myself that he was extremely off limits, my heart didn't give a damn about rules and shoulds and shouldn'ts.

I lost track of time as the space grew more idyllic. The perfume of fresh flowers overpowered the scent of so many creatures gathered in the large hall, and the fog that enveloped the room caressed my skin, leaving it tingling, blotting out those I didn't want to think about. Or maybe that was Leander, it was hard to tell with the way I was consumed by him.

Eventually, he led me to a slender row of tables pushed to the side of the room, covered in all sorts of delicacies. There were cakes, chocolates, bonbons, and mini sandwiches with unrecognizable ingredients minced into tiny pieces. There was punch and flavored sparkling waters. The glasses and small plates appeared to be real, etched crystal.

"Wow, Sir Lancelot really went all out with this," I said.

"It's been my experience that the owl doesn't do things halfway. He's probably been looking forward to having an elegant event for ages. He loves that stuff."

As if we'd called him with our attention, Sir Lancelot swooped past us, alighting on the branch of a miniature tree that moved in rhythm with the music, its delicate silver leaves shaking and ringing like a whispering maraca. "Good evening, Lady Rina and Prince Leander Verion. I do hope you're enjoying yourselves."

I blinked at the owl, taking in his black smoking jacket, with the sleeves omitted to allow room for his wings, and the black bowtie wrapped beneath his feathered head.

"We're having a fine time, thank you very much, Sir Lancelot," Leander said.

"You look quite dashing, Sir Lancelot," I added, and got to enjoy the way the bird flustered under my praise.

"You're too kind, Lady Rina, too kind indeed." He puffed his chest out more than before. "Well, may your night continue to be most pleasurable. I must continue my rounds, you do understand. In a party of this sort, one can never remain in the company of one guest for too long."

"Of course." Leander tilted his head graciously while I thought the owl crazy for wanting to leave the prince's side.

"Hey," Jas said, poking my bare shoulder to get my

attention. I turned to find her, Wren, and Adalia standing in a huddle.

"We're going to the ladies' room," Wren said. "Want to come?"

"Uh, thanks, but not really. I'm—"

"Coming with us." Jas swooped in, took my arm, and called to Leander over her shoulder. "We'll bring her back soon. A girl needs to refresh, ya know?"

"Jas," I hissed. "What are you doing? I don't need to pee."

"I know, I know. All you need is your smoking hot prince. But you can't leave us hanging like this. You two have been mooning over each other for ages, and here we are just waiting to find out how it's going."

"You could've waited until the party was over..."

"No, we most definitely could not have. Friends don't make friends wait that long."

"Since when?"

"Since she hasn't been able to get Ky alone," Wren interjected.

"Though she's been trying," Adalia said loud enough to be heard over the music, an odd blend of soul and Elvis-style early rock and roll.

"Hey," Jas said, "it's not my fault Boone won't leave his side."

I smiled to myself. Ky had probably asked Boone to be his wingman—in the reverse. I didn't want Jas to be bummed, but I didn't want her to get it on with my brother more. She'd get over her disappointment, and I wouldn't have to be forever scarred with images of the two of them together. There were plenty of other handsome shifters she could crush on.

When we reached the door to the restroom, I had to stop to admire it. The paneling was adorned with multi-colored flowers that swayed in tempo with the trolls' music, and they appeared to be growing out of the wood of the door itself. Twinkling, magical lights floated like stars among the blossoms, peeking in and out of view as the flowers danced. Reaching for the stars, I pulled my hand back before tracing them, not sure the magical illusion would hold up to my touch.

Jas drew next to me and huffed. "Come on. What's the hold up?"

Then Sadie caught up to us, Wendi a few paces behind her. Jas spun on Sadie, the short skirt of her black dress flaring as she turned. "She doesn't need you to follow her into the bathroom. No one can kidnap her from a stall."

Sadie frowned. "It's my job to shadow her."

"We'll watch her back." And before Sadie could complain, Jas reached through the sparkling stars, dispersing them as if they were tiny puffs of clouds, while the flowers dove out of the way of her hand, and pushed the door open. Once Wren, Adalia, and I were through it, Jas pushed it closed and leaned against it. "So? Spill the beans."

"What beans?" I said. "There are no beans to spill. We're in the middle of the entire school."

"Whatever. You guys are acting like the rest of us don't exist."

"It's so romantic," Wren sighed. "Ouch!"

Someone was pushing the door inward, shoving us out of the way.

"Wow, Sadie doesn't give it a rest," Jas growled and whipped around to glare at the Enforcer.

Only it wasn't the Enforcer. Four vampires slunk into the room, pointing cold, feral grins at us.

"What are you doing here?" Jas crossed her arms over her chest and straightened to her full five-foot-two height.

"This is a public restroom, isn't it?" said the girl with hair the color of blood in perfect ringlets down the middle of her back. Her dress was the same color, making the pallor of her face more noticeable under the room's incandescent lighting.

"Well, it's taken right now. You'll have to come back later." Jas tilted her head up, and Wren and Adalia moved behind her.

"Why? Because the princess is in here? And she's so special that we can't risk any of us bothering her?"

"Hey," I snapped. I hadn't intended on saying a word; I'd had enough of this stupid conflict before it even started. But I'd be damned if I'd let vamps call me "princess" and get away with it. "Knock it off. I'm not a princess, and I'm sure as hell not your princess. So leave me the hell alone."

The three vamps shifted closer to the one with the gorgeous red hair, preparing for a cat fight, but Sadie shoved the door open hard enough to dislodge all of us. "Come on, vampies. You're leaving with me."

"Why?" Blood Red said. "We have as much right to be here as anyone else. You can't—"

"I can, and I will, so save us all some time and stuff it." Sadie wrapped fingers around her pale, spindly arm and yanked.

"Hey! You can't manhandle me like this. You can't—" But the rest of her protest was drowned out by the start of a new song as Sadie dragged her through the door. Blood Red's friends scurried behind them. The second the door slammed shut again, I sighed heavily. "What the hell is up with the vamps? I didn't do anything to them. None of this mess is my fault."

"Agreed," Adalia said. "But vamps aren't known for their level-headedness."

"Well, they'd better watch themselves, or they're going to lose their heads," Jas growled.

"You can't mean that," Wren said. "They're students. You can't—"

"They're stupid students. It's a freaking good thing we don't need to see them during the daytime or else I legit would've strangled one of them by now."

The door pushed open again, and the four of us swiveled as one to see who would enter this time.

Stacy, Tracy, and Swan entered with noses and boobs held high, entitled pissed-off airs clinging to them like cloying perfume. Their gazes sought out Jas, Wren, and me right away. Even though Adalia was theoretically on a date with Boone, they left her alone.

Before Stacy opened her mouth, I threw my hands in the air with a loud huff. "Hell no. I'm so not doing this." I whipped right past the lot of them, yanked the door open, and waltzed back into the large room that held Leander somewhere.

I stomped around the dance floor until my jets cooled and I sighted my elfin prince. He was with Ky, Boone, Dave, and Damon, but when he spotted me he walked over to me.

He studied me as he placed a hand on either of my upper arms. "What is it? What happened?"

"More vamps hating me, along with your groupies. Nothing worth wasting my breath on." I blew away a few strands of hair that had landed across my face. "The chicks at this school are nuts."

Leander stared at me for a few seconds before throwing his head back with a bark of laughter. "You sure do have a way with words."

I felt my cheeks heating. "Well, it's true."

"You can say that again." He chuckled some more. "What do you say? Wanna get out of here?"

I sharpened my gaze on his. "Are we allowed to?"

He smiled broadly. "I'm of the mindset that it's better to ask for forgiveness than permission."

I nodded. "I like your way of thinking."

"As much as I'd like to lose your bodyguards, it's probably not a good idea. But maybe we'll get lucky and they'll give us some space."

"And Ky?"

"Like I said, forgiveness over permission. I learned that the hard way, or else I wouldn't have been able to have any kind of life in my father's court. I'll deal with Ky later. He knows that I'd never do anything with you that wasn't appropriate. He trusts me."

I gave a darting look across the dark, hazy space and took Leander's hand. There were so many people here, so many eyes on us. "Let's do it. Sadie said she'd try not to crowd me."

Leander squeezed my hand and led me outside, where we slunk into the night like spies. My friends would give me hell for leaving without saying goodbye later, but I wasn't worrying about laters now. They'd understand—eventually—and accept my apology. All I had was my moment with my prince, and I was seizing it.

❦

Leander and I meandered without aim, keeping to the main quad of the campus, and Sadie—and probably Wendi, though I hadn't spotted her—kept far enough behind us that I could almost believe we were alone beneath the starry night—a striking illusion of the Academy Spell.

His hand was warm in mine, and the temperature was pleasant despite the fact that the night would already have a chill to it beyond our mountain. In Sedona, fall was coming. Here, we'd never experience the season.

"We should have left the party at the start," I said. "It's so peaceful out here."

"Definitely."

Several minutes passed in companionable silence before I remembered there was something I wanted to ask. "So … I've been wondering. How come you can do partial shifts? If that's what they are. I mean, sometimes you have wings, sometimes you don't. But you're a shifter. Right...?" It was far from my most elegant effort, but I didn't really understand what he did or how he did it. "I haven't seen any other shifters have part of their creatures showing. And I'm pretty sure what Dave does doesn't count."

"Not every shifter can do what I do. Partial shifts are only possible if the shifter has high level magic." He shrugged it off as if it were no big deal. "I leave my wings out almost all of the time when I'm home, but here I try to pull them in as often as I can stand it. I don't like to draw more attention to myself than I need to."

The look I gave him must have revealed my many questions because he continued: "It's uncomfortable to keep my wings in for too long. A bit like an itch I can't scratch. It feels like I'm trapping them under my skin."

"But only with your wings?"

"A bit with all of it, I guess, but my wings are what gets to me the most."

"And why don't you like to draw attention to yourself?"

He sighed, and I could tell there was a lot more to his story than he would share tonight. "When you're a prince of the elves, everybody expects something from you. Whether it's a favor or whether they expect you to do incredible things. It's hard to find friends who like you for who you are and not for what you can do for them, now or eventually. When you're a prince, even the second one in line to inherit, people tend to forget that you're a lot like them. I just happened to have been born to a title, to a position, but that doesn't mean I don't experience the same things they do. It doesn't mean I was born with every answer.

"I've always imagined it would be nice to be anonymous. To not have everyone stare at you no matter where you go or what you do. My wings only make that more pronounced. Everyone's curious about the shifter who walks around in a partial change."

Everyone except me, apparently. Dope.

"I'd keep my wings in all the time if the sensation didn't drive me up the wall."

He hadn't offered the information, but surely it couldn't be a secret at a school for paranormal creatures, where shifting was a class requirement. "And what do you shift into?"

He looked away, gazing absently into the night. "A silver eagle."

My breath hitched. An eagle? From the size of his wings, his eagle must be huge. I followed the direction of his gaze, but there was nothing there but dark, clear night. "What's it like to fly?" I whispered, as if the night had suddenly become sacred.

He smiled wistfully. "Magical. Like nothing can touch you. Like you're truly free."

"That sounds really amazing."

"It is." My prince sounded like he was somewhere else, so I leaned into his chest and rested my head there, allowing him whatever time he needed.

His heart beat evenly beneath my ear until he gently pressed me back and slid a finger beneath my chin to tilt my face toward his. In an instant, his eyes called to me, drawing me to stare into their depths as if they were truly magnetic.

"Rina, may I kiss you?" His words sounded far away, as if I were in a dream.

"Of course." My heart rate sped up to unreasonable levels as he slowly lowered his lips to mine, and when they touched, I closed my eyes without meaning to, breaking the connection to his gaze, but opening to so much more.

His lips were soft and gentle as they told me all the things his words hadn't. Time fell away, leaving him and me alone in the quiet night. He pulled me closer to him in stages until my body pressed fully against his, his hands wrapped around my waist. At some point, I wove my hands around his neck, the silky strands of his long hair brushing against them.

He kissed me until I decided we had to find the way to be together beyond this one night. My heart, mind, and body responded to him like he was the only one in the world for me—a terrifying thought. When our kiss grew more urgent, more passionate, and I opened my lips to him, inviting his tongue to dance with mine, I became certain of one thing—I needed more of him. Lots more.

His hands traced my shoulders, my back, my hips. His fingers wove through the long strands of my hair, his breathing heavy. Then he abruptly pulled away. "We have to stop."

I blinked at him, working to jumpstart my brain back to rational thought. "Why?"

"I don't know anymore, Rina, I really don't." Anguish coated his words.

I brought my hands to his chest. "You don't think we can be together?"

He pulled a hand from my back and I instantly missed the touch. He ran the hand through his hair, discovered it tied back, tore the tie from his hair, and flung it to the ground. He breathed audibly while I waited. Finally, he moved away from me to retrieve the tie and stuffed it roughly in his pocket. I shivered in the sudden absence of his warmth as if it were a cold winter night.

"We're too different," he finally said. "My father warned me against it. Again and again."

"I see," I said, though I really didn't. "I thought we were just two shifters. How different could we be? We both have shifter magic. We're both supernatural creatures."

"But you aren't fae. You aren't an elf." Torment dripped from his words. He sighed loudly, running both hands through his hair before flinging it across his shoulder. "What the hell was I thinking? I should never have..." He growled. "Rina, I'm so sorry. I should have resisted my pull to you. It was irresponsible to involve you in my life when my father will never allow our relationship to go anywhere of consequence. Please forgive me."

I crossed my arms in front of my chest "Forgive you for what? For kissing me or for telling me it was a mistake?"

He swallowed, his throat bobbing visibly. "For both. I should never have asked you out tonight."

It was difficult to reconcile the confident prince who'd invited me on a date and courted me all night with this man. I'd never imagined him flustered. It was so unlike him.

"Well, I'm glad you asked me out, and I'm glad you kissed me. I don't regret a second of it."

Well, maybe I was starting to regret this part.

He looked at me and I could hardly bear to look into those silver eyes that swirled with his torment—or was it regret I saw there? "You really wish we'd never shared this night?" I asked.

The night filled the silence.

"Fine. Whatever."

"No, Rina, no. Of course I don't wish we hadn't shared this. I'm just … I've never been in this position before. I don't know what to do."

I breathed in a few times to calm myself, then took a tentative step toward him. "What happened to ask for forgiveness, not permission?" My hands itched to reach out for him, but I didn't.

"I'm not sure my father would forgive me this, not when he knows it means something to me."

"Why? Why is it so bad to go on a stupid date with me?" Though it had been far from insignificant, and he had to know it.

"Because we can never be together, not in any true sense. I'll be promised to another. My life hasn't been mine since my birth."

"We're not talking about getting serious here,

we're talking about connecting and having a little fun." But my heart recognized the lie for what it was. That kiss had felt too right, too meaningful. There was a connection between the prince and me, no matter what either of us said.

"I don't think I can spend time with you and not want more than a 'little fun.' I'm just not made that way."

I bit my lip. "Yeah, neither am I."

There was so much more to say, and yet nothing that would make a real difference. We stood there, a foot between us, like strangers in the night, before I couldn't take it anymore. My heart was a mess of confused emotions, and if the look on his face was anything to go by, his was in turmoil too.

When I finally moved right up to him, he exhaled as if he'd been waiting for me to do just that. His shoulders relaxed, and he wrapped strong arms around me and held me fiercely against him, as if the force of his will was enough to override his fate and bind us together.

12

THE DAYS PASSED IN A BLUR. BETWEEN MY THREE DAILY classes, each an hour and forty-five minutes long, and extra practice time with Ky after dinner, I collapsed into bed most days in a heap of physical and mental exhaustion. I could've done without the physical exhaustion bit, but at least an exhausted brain didn't bother overly much with thoughts of Leander and what might have been.

From the frequent looks he gave me when he assumed I wouldn't notice, I knew Leander was thinking about us. But if he wasn't willing or able to move past his father's judgments, then I had to let it go. He was an elfin prince; I was neither an elf nor royalty. I had no dowry to impress a king of the elves. End of story. At least, that's what I kept telling my heart, which was devilishly persistent despite my rational arguments.

"Where'd you go just now?" Wren asked, prodding me with her elbow.

My own elbow slid out from under me atop the dining table and my fork clattered loudly onto my plate. I cringed until I was certain the cutlery hadn't broken the plate. I had no desire to start my day endangering my life by telling one of the pygmy trolls I'd broken one of their plates. They took any offense to the dining hall personally, and if I'd learned anything since arriving at the Menagerie, it was that you never wanted to offend the trolls. Like ever.

"She was mooning over Leo," Jas said, though I'd asked her not to keep saying shit like that. As usual, Jas did what she wanted and didn't seem to care much about how her words were received by others.

I sighed and pushed my plate away. I'd tried for fresh fruit and a bagel piled high with cream cheese this morning, but, as of late, my appetite just wasn't what it normally was.

"I wasn't *mooning* over Leander." I hoped I hadn't been. I'd been working hard not to. "I've just been tired lately."

"You have been pushing pretty hard." Wren's concerned eyes traveled the length of me. "Couldn't you ask Ky to give you a break from the extra practice for a bit?"

"Trust me, I've tried. He says the dangers are too great and that I can't rely on anyone else to protect me. Sorry, Sadie," I added with a flash of apologetic eyes to the perpetually hungry shifter in her usual seat at the end of our table.

"No worries," she said as she shoveled a small mountain of scrambled eggs drenched in hot sauce into her mouth. "He's right. Even I can't anticipate every single attack, and I can't be there to watch your back every second of every day—though I try."

"Are you finally admitting to some limitations?" Wendi asked from the opposite end of the table, where as a rule Wren, Dave, Jas, Adalia, and I did our best to ignore her. As feisty as Sadie was, at least we could always count on her to be real. Wendi … well, real wasn't her style.

Sadie didn't even bother looking at the other Enforcer, who sat prim and straight in her lemon-yellow button-down sleeveless blouse. Sadie pretended to scratch her cheek with her middle finger while shoving more food into her mouth.

Wendi growled low in her chest, but Sadie looked at me. "The more you know about your shifter powers, the better. We're obviously hoping you won't have any more encounters with any of the Voice, but they're persistent fuckers. It's always better to be prepared."

"Hopefully more practice helps you more than it helps me," Dave said to me, his shoulders droopier than usual.

As was our habit, he sat on one side of me, and Wren on the other. I placed a hand on his shoulder and squeezed. "Hey, you've been improving lots lately. Think how far you've come since last term."

He chortled darkly. "I guess when you start out by monumentally sucking, just regular ol' sucking is an improvement."

"There you go," Sadie said, as if that would encourage him.

He slid pieces of half-eaten omelet around his plate. "I don't think McGinty knows what to do with me anymore."

"He does seem to have Melinda on call," Jas said.

Wren and I glared at her.

"What? What'd I do wrong this time?"

Adalia shook her head from beside her, but we didn't bother to answer. Jas would apparently be Jas, no matter how many times we explained her many offenses. With a pointed look at her, Wren leaned across me to look at Dave. "You haven't gotten stuck in a partial shift all term. That's a huge improvement."

"That's right," Adalia said. "You've barely needed the Magical Moving Mousse at all lately."

"Thank goodness, because that shit reeks," Jas said.

Adalia rolled her eyes, and I chuckled, because Jas still hadn't figured out that the happy-go-lucky fairy was messing with her pretty much all of the time.

"Adalia's right," Wren powered on. "You haven't even had to carry the mousse around with you lately."

"But I'm probably the only student on campus that Melinda gave his own personal jar to," Dave said.

"Probably," I said. "But that doesn't mean you haven't improved a lot lately. And remember that we're all different. We have different strengths and weaknesses."

Jas opened her mouth, and Adalia elbowed her in

the ribs sharply. While Jas glared at the fairy, she smiled at Dave. "You wouldn't be at the school if you weren't amazing in your own way."

"She's right," Wren said, smiling broadly at our gentle fairy friend.

"Thanks for the pep talk, guys," he said. "I've just gotten tired of constantly worrying the school will kick me out, of being the odd one out all the time, you know what I mean?"

"Do I ever..." I said.

"Are you going to eat that?" Sadie asked, and I thought she was talking to Dave, but she was talking to both of us. As had become our habit, we slid our plates of uneaten food toward the average-sized witch.

"I swear, I'll never figure out where you stuff it all," Jas said. For once, I agreed with her sentiment.

"What can I say?" Sadie mumbled over a mouthful. "I have a fast metabolism."

"It's gotta be more than that." Jas eyed her up and down. "You eat like a grizzly bear shifter—like three grizzlies."

Sadie shrugged and bit into my bagel. "At least I don't waste. The trolls hate waste."

"Do they ever," Wren said. "I think they might hate everything."

"They don't," Adalia said. "They just have really strong beliefs … and equally strong personalities."

"Well, strong personality isn't an excuse for their non-stop grumpiness," Jas said. "I've never seen one of them even smile."

All of us, even Sadie, blinked at Jas a few times,

who was obviously oblivious to the finer details of her sparkling personality. Then Jas' attention shot to the door behind us. "There they are."

I didn't need to turn around to figure out who she was talking about. I wished I could leave and head to class early, but if I did, Sadie would have to go with me, and she still had most of an omelet and half a bagel to go.

"Hi, Ky," Jas called across the dining hall, forcing my brother and his crew—with Damon trailing them —over to our table. I debated the effect of giving Jas a sharp kick to the shin before deciding not to bother. What would be the point? Jas was … Jas.

"Hi, Jas," Ky said, but his eyes were on me. "How you feeling today?"

"I'm fine." I pinned my gaze on him and only him. As soon as Stacy saw me, she did her best to imitate an octopus with a thing for silver-haired princes. Her fingertips, capped in fire-engine red nail polish, swept across Leander's shoulder to rest on his chest. I refused to look at either of them head-on.

"Good," Ky was saying. "I was a little worried. You took quite a beating last night, squirt."

"You would know. You were the one beating me."

"I can't take it easy on you. Rage won't."

"I know, I know."

Boone stepped out from under the brunette groupie. "Maybe I could help. You've been sparring with her for a while. Maybe it'd be good to have someone different."

Swan pouted over his shoulder, and I wondered, not for the first time, why the guys let these girls hang all over them. None of the boys seemed particularly into any of them. Maybe it was simply easier than dealing with their scorn.

While my brother and Boone debated the torturous routines they'd put me through later that evening, Sadie finally finished her breakfast. Feeling Leander's eyes on me the whole time, I stood. "I'm heading to class early."

Wren looked up at me. "Want me to come with you?" Dave prepared to stand too.

"No, thanks. I could use some quiet time alone. I haven't had enough of it lately." And by that I meant hardly any at all. Of course, time to myself was relative. I wouldn't be going anywhere without Sadie behind me, and Wendi somewhere behind her.

But at least Sadie would give me space, and I'd be free from Leander's stare, the one I could hardly bear anymore. No matter how much I tried, I couldn't forget the way his lips had felt on mine or the way his hands held my hips possessively. I couldn't avoid the memory of how his eyes had seared into mine. So much intensity … for a whole lot of nothing.

I picked up my teacup and silverware and headed for the dish depository. I sensed someone a few paces behind me; I figured it was Sadie with her pile of plates. Even the hardened Enforcer followed the trolls' directions.

But when a hand wrapped around my upper arm,

I knew exactly who it was. I went rigid and flung my fork and butter knife into the appointed tub with a loud clang. When I turned, I tried not to meet Leander's eyes, but my traitorous heart had me looking right up into them.

"Can we talk, Rina? Please?"

I hesitated, wanting to say no, but discovered myself unable to resist the intense emotion rolling through his mercurial eyes. "About what?"

"You know about what."

"Okay. Maybe I do. But what would be the point? Nothing's changed, has it?"

He merely stared at me, and I had my confirmation. "Exactly. You already told me you don't want me as part of your life."

"That's not true at all, and I hope you know it." He wrapped both hands around my upper arms.

We were drawing unwanted attention. Every student who filed toward the dish depository flicked underhanded glances at us; some openly stared. Leander was slightly famous. I was slightly notorious. I didn't blame the students; they couldn't help themselves.

Leander captured my gaze as if we weren't inside a packed dining hall. "I very much want to be with you."

My heart thudded, and I just wanted to run away. Running from my problems wasn't a long-term solution, but it was better than the squirming mess of desire and disappointment roiling through my insides.

"My father is extremely powerful. His influence is

far reaching, and not just with the fae. He'd make things *very* hard for you if I chose to be with you. It wouldn't be fair to do that to you. I can't."

"No, because you won't even give us a chance." Heat was building behind my eyes, and I hated that this mess had me wanting to cry. I would not cry in front of Leander, or any man—save my brother, of course; he didn't count as a man.

"Rina..." His eyes implored me to understand, and while I suppose I did, this still sucked, big-time. "Let's talk somewhere private. I can't stand to have you angry at me."

"I'm not mad at you. I'm just … disappointed, I guess, but I'll get over it." Eventually. I hoped.

"We can still be friends, can't we?"

I chuckled without mirth, my heart chipping at his unintended blow. "No, Leander, I don't think I can be friends with you. Not right now. Maybe not ever. I need some time to forget about you."

Orangesicle and Rainbow squinted beady troll eyes at the two of us from the dish-washing area. We were probably breaking several of their rules, including congesting student traffic. But the trolls held back more than usual when the elfin prince was involved. They returned to their duties, flashing round troll butts in our general direction.

Leander stared at me for several long beats, during which the sensation of his hands on my arms heated the entirety of my body. "I don't want you to forget about me."

"Well, you can't have it both ways. That's not fair to me."

"I know."

"You don't want to be with me——" He opened his mouth to protest again, but I powered on. Despite his father's rules, he still had a choice. There was always a choice—maybe not an easy choice or even a good one, but a choice nonetheless. "You choose not to be with me, fine. But you can't both have me and not. I owe myself better than that."

"I can't stop thinking about you." His eyes widened as if he hadn't meant to blurt that out.

I offered him a faint smile. "I think about you too, but thinking isn't enough for me. I either want to be with you, or I want to be free of you." I wasn't sure that was a fair expression of how I felt, but I didn't care. I had enough on my plate with Rage and company; I didn't need my heart spazzing out on me to boot.

"Look, I need to go. Besides, Stacy's waiting for you." I worked to deaden my eyes. I was *not* jealous. "She doesn't know what to do with her gropey paws now that you're not there."

"I told you, it's not like that between us. She's just a classmate, a friend. We've been in classes together since first term."

"Whatever. You do you, I'm gonna do me." I plastered a winning smile on my face, one that was sure to fall short of convincing him of my nonchalance, but it was the best I could do. "Have a great day."

"We have the next class together, Rina."

As if I could forget... "Well then I guess I'll see ya there." I slipped from his hold and stalked past him, blinking rapidly to clear the wet heat behind my eyes, sensing every one of my friends and his trailing me. I didn't meet a single one of their curious gazes. I strode straight to the double doors, pushed them open, and escaped outside.

I walked with purpose down the path that circumnavigated the grassy quad, though it was far too early to head to Defensive Creature Magic. When I heard the faint sound of the doors opening and closing behind me, I knew Sadie was tailing me. But Sadie, unlike Leander, would give me the space I needed. Damn the prince and his thoughtful heart. Damn those eyes that claimed he wanted to be with me as much as I wanted to be with him. And screw the king of the elves and his racist requirements for his son and kingdom.

My feet took off in a run as if they understood what I needed better than I did. I ran until I reached the end of the quad, slipped between the buildings that housed the girls' dormitory and the library, and stilled long enough to call on my mountain lion.

The connection between her and me had grown stronger over the weeks of McGinty's class and the practice sessions with my brother. I experienced her urge to run free as if it were my own—hell, maybe it was my own. The more I connected with her, the more difficult it became to distinguish where my lion ended and I started.

Picturing my lion's thick fur, her golden-copper

eyes, and the strength of her muscles, I *felt* what it was like to be her. I wrapped the sensation of her perfect design around my human body. I pictured my lion apart from me as well as one with me. Then I pulsed the energy—my shifter magic, I now knew—which had collected without thought within my core, outward toward the image of my lion. My magic flooded my senses and my body, tingling along my limbs.

I landed on four massive paws and took off running without checking behind me. I needed to run free more than I needed Sadie shadowing every one of my steps. I ran through the forest that surrounded the campus until my spirit lost some of its restlessness and my breathing came heavy but steady. I ran until the first bell announced I had fifteen minutes to get to my first class, then pivoted and sprinted in the direction of Bundry Hall, where Defensive Creature Magic was meeting this morning.

I had a lot of ground to cover and I had to be on time. Marcy June liked to make examples of those who were late to class, or otherwise acted up, by making them demonstrate her defensive exercises. Like Marcy June, who didn't waste time on gentle maneuvers, her demonstrations were brutal and to the point.

I tore across the thick forest, trees and bushes and flowers whipping past me so fast they merged into a sea of color. I released a burst of speed and pulled in a true breath of freedom. Now that I knew what it was like to be in the body of my lion, I didn't think I could do without her. She was powerful and free from the mess of emotions that burdened my mind and heart. Within her, the only thing that mattered was magic and power—two things I apparently had in spades.

Now all I had to do was master them...

❧ 13 ❧

I MANAGED TO SHIFT BACK TO HUMAN FORM AFTER only a few failed attempts, which was definitely significant progress. By the time I eased into the shifter practice room in Bundry Hall, the large high-ceilinged space was packed. Students and staff alike lined the walls to watch whatever was about to go down in the middle of the room on the padded mats.

My stomach churned. What did Marcy June have in mind? The professor wasn't one to hold back, not even in her classes. I wondered which poor sod she was going to use to demonstrate, hoping it wouldn't be me or any of my friends. Selfish, I know, but I couldn't help it.

I slid next to Wren and the rest of my friends just as the bell announcing the start of classes rang out. Phew. I'd made it in time. Today was definitely not the day to give Marcy June reason to pay extra attention to you.

"What's going on?" I whispered to Wren, while

Sadie slipped through the door behind me. Her sharp eyes scanned the crowd in a continuous sweep until they alighted upon me, then they relaxed. Sadie took her job seriously, which was more than I could say for Wendi, whom I saw less often than I probably should —though I definitely wasn't complaining. The prim enforcer hadn't done much to endear herself to me, though she was careful to go through the motions of what she thought would win me over—and that was the main reason she hadn't.

Dave answered for Wren, leaning across her. "Marcy June is going to spar with Sadie." His eyebrows danced across his brow. "This is going to be so effing cool."

"Marcy June told those of us who were here early," Wren said, "and a few of the students ran out, to spread the news I guess. I have no idea how everyone got here so quickly. They must've dropped what they were doing and booked it here."

The news had obviously spread far and wide. Orangesicle and Rainbow were here, along with the newly nicknamed Berry Crush with the fuchsia fro-hawk, and a handful of other pygmy trolls I hadn't made up names for yet. Professors McGinty and Quickfoot stood off to the side, conferring with their heads together, and even Professor Damante had deigned to come. He stood apart from everyone, leaning against the wall as if he didn't have a care in the world, drawing the eye of many of the girls there.

Even the Gropey Gaggle, consisting of Stacy,

Tracy, and Swan, flicked the occasional glance at the vampire professor, whose smug understated smile indicated he knew precisely the effect he was garnering. He wore his arrogance with the same ease as he sported his pale gray suit that accentuated the perfect lines of his body, the defined angles of his face, and the intensity of his eyes. His lips were nearly cherry red, and I had to remind myself that this man was a predator—most likely a highly dangerous one, professor or not.

Standing with my brother and Boone, and their ever-present devotees, Leander caught my eye—of course he did—and I hurried to look away, but not before he brushed Stacy's hand away from where it encroached on his shoulder. She trained a glare on me as if I'd been the one to reject her instead of him, and I turned away. I'd had enough drama for one morning.

Whispers circled the room, and students gawked as Damon entered with … a centaur. No, the creature wasn't a centaur—he had wings, and he walked alongside the tall Enforcer.

"Who is that?" I whispered, succumbing to the tangible awe that imbued the room.

"That's Egan," Adalia said. "He's a professor here, though I'm pretty sure he only teaches the really advanced material. He's a legend."

"Why? Why's he a legend?" Dave asked in a reverent whisper.

"All I know is he's supposed to be amazing. And he's one of the last of his kind. Creatures like him were hunted nearly to extinction. They're supposed to contain more power than three supes their size."

"Wow," Dave said. "He's huge."

He was. The size of a giant stallion; there was no way you'd miss him in a crowd.

"Hey, everybody," Marcy June called out, drawing everyone's attention to the center of the room and hushing the excited whispers. "I see word got around about what I have planned for today's class. So y'all came to enjoy a good fight, huh?" Affirmative murmurs whisked across the space. "Well, you're creatures after my own heart. There's nothing better than a good, solid fight."

Actually, I could think of about a thousand things I'd rather do than spar: watch a good movie with a tub of pralines and cream ice cream, hang out with my friends, sleep … kiss Leander. *Shit.*

Marcy June was working her audience, arms spread wide like she was the ringleader of a circus, egging everyone on. "You're about to see one heck of a fight!"

A few people hollered, and I was pretty sure two of them were the shifter Professor McGinty and the gnome Professor Quickfoot. Memories of Quickfoot with his bloody ax after the Attack last term invaded my mind, and I forcefully pushed them away.

"Sadie, come out here." Marcy June waved my protector out into the middle of the floor. Sadie stalked into the center in a Wonder Woman t-shirt, ripped jeans, shit-kicker boots, and enough confidence imbuing her stride that I couldn't decide who would win this match. Sadie started unfastening the sheaths that hung from either side of her waist, placing the curved blades off to the side.

"Sadie and I've known each other since our time as students at the Menagerie," Marcy June said. "We were friends and fierce competitors. I owe a few broken bones to this lady right here." She looked at Sadie wistfully, like broken bones were a cool thing, further cementing the notion that the petite professor and I had markedly different priorities.

"As y'all know, we've been under constant threat for a while now, hence the creation of this Defensive Creature Magic class. And while the greatest threat we're currently under comes from shifters and vamps, in the supernatural world nothing is predictable, nothing at all, and that's a guarantee. So while mages usually keep to their own in this fight, it's far better to prepare for the unexpected than to be taken by surprise. Surprise in the wrong circumstances gets you as dead as you get."

Wren leaned into me. I knew enough of the willowy girl now to realize she was trying to offer me comfort in case Marcy June's words were freaking me out, and yeah, they kind of were. She wasn't known for being tactful, that was for damn sure.

Marcy June spun to take in everyone gathered. "Now, some of you might not realize that Sadie is a special case. She comes off as a feisty-as-fuck shifter, but she isn't a shifter. She's a witch. Still, even the Academy Spell recognized that she wouldn't have fit in with tight-assed magicians, so she studied here.

Always, magic is fluid. You've gotta remember that. Even a hundred-year-old spell gets that, and the sooner you do, the sooner you'll be prepared to take on whatever's coming.

"Sadie fights like a shifter, but she uses magic instead of animal powers. She's fierce and unpredictable, which means you won't see her coming unless you stay sharp."

Sadie, sans blades, walked out onto the grouping of four large padded mats. She swung her arms behind her a few times and cracked her neck, back, and knuckles.

"Shit," I said. "This makes me nervous."

"I'm trying to decide who will win, and I can't," Jas said, sounding as excited as Dave, who was so jittery he could barely stand still.

"I know. They seem so evenly matched," he said, "though Sadie is a bit taller than Marcy June."

"Everyone's taller than Marcy June," Wren said, flashing a grimace at Jas. "Sorry, I forgot about you."

Jas was about as tall as Marcy June, and equally petite. But size did nothing to determine ferocity in either case. Jas growled and narrowed her eyes at Wren, but she was too excited to really be mad. Her eyes danced as she pinned them on the two women.

Marcy June inched closer to Sadie, her attention on her now and no longer her audience. "I'm not going to bother with rules and warnings," she called out, starting to circle Sadie on the mat. "Sadie and I've done this many times, though it's been a long while, hasn't it?"

Sadie growled a response, sounding exactly like a feisty shifter. If I hadn't seen her orange magic myself, I would have struggled to believe she wasn't about to turn into some kind of animal.

"Egan?" Marcy June called out, but her gaze was already latched onto Sadie's. "Will you call the match, for old times' sake?"

In unison, the crowd shifted to take in the centaur with wings—a pegataur? I had no idea what they might be called. I didn't even realize they existed. I had to get a move-on reading through Dad's *Compendium*.

I thought Egan might have bristled under all the attention, but he didn't do or say anything to make me sure of it. His hooves clopped across hardwood planks as he edged the mats that all but covered the floor. His upper body was that of a man, his lower body that of a horse with wings. His chestnut hair matched his coat, though his tail was shiny, ebony black that swished with each step he took.

When Egan reached the two women, he waved a hand toward them and they approached. Whatever he said, I couldn't make it out, and in two minutes Marcy June and Sadie were back on the mats and the giant pegataur was backing up to give them room.

"Who do you think will win?" Dave asked. "I'm betting on Sadie. She's a badass."

"Hmm," Jas said. "Marcy June is pretty freaking intense herself. I mean, just look at her."

Marcy June's teeth were bared and her fingers were arched like claws, though she remained in human form. She hunched over like a beast, circling Sadie, whose eyes darted all across her.

Marcy June lunged at Sadie, and Wren and I shrieked. We weren't the only ones, but I still flushed with embarrassment. "Shit. I thought Egan was going to announce the start of the match..." I trailed off. No one was paying attention to what I was saying, not even me.

Halfway through her attack, Marcy June transformed into an average-sized coyote, which was to say she possessed the size and demeanor of a wily, underfed street dog. If she blurred, vibrated, and flickered, it'd been too quick for me to notice.

But Sadie was ready for her. When Marcy June dove at her leg, sharp teeth bared to bite, Sadie flung a wall of orange light straight at her, slamming into the coyote and throwing her back. The coyote tumbled and rocketed back to her paws while Sadie was busy gathering more orange magic between her open palms.

The coyote lunged at her calves again, impossibly fast. Sadie jumped as she twisted out of the way, and blasted a ray of orange straight at the coyote's butt. The coyote jumped like her tail was on fire, but instead of whimpering and cowering, the animal pivoted on quick paws and lunged again. This time the coyote's jaws latched onto Sadie's leg, tearing through her jeans.

Sadie cried out and kicked the coyote free. The coyote sailed through the air in a squealing snarl. Marcy June landed on her side with a dull thump.

Sadie was already stalking toward her, ignoring the red that was soaking through the bottom of her pant leg.

Melinda, the healer, and Nancy, the main staff witch, entered through the doors at a run, Fianna and Nessa zooming over their heads. The badger and witch brought their hands to their thighs as they bent over catching their breath, their attention going straight to the fighters I imagined they were there to assist.

The coyote was back on her feet, teeth bared in a low growl, when Sadie flung an orange beam at her. The coyote jumped out of the way and sprinted toward Sadie, who got off another orange ray, aimed straight at the animal's chest. Marcy June flattened herself to the ground, the beam whizzed across her fur, singeing it, and flew past her.

Startled students dove out of the way as orange light slammed into the brick wall behind them with a thunderous *boom*. Brick cracked and crumbled, shooting shards in every direction.

Sadie brought her hands to her chest, flattened them there, and when she flipped them back around to face Marcy June, they glowed like the sun. But the coyote flung herself at Sadie's injured calf before the witch could release her magic.

I gasped, and Wren huddled closer. Adalia, always thoughtful, moved to my other side and pressed into me, allowing us to suffer through this together.

It wasn't like Sadie and Marcy June were my favorite people, but it wasn't like I didn't like them either; I liked them just fine. I might've even admired them and their don't-give-a-shit-what-anyone-thinks attitudes. They were ferocious in a world that had made them that way; they'd found the way to survive in a cutthroat supernatural community that rewarded strength. Both were average to small women, and yet they fought with a fierceness often reserved for men, or those far larger than them. I didn't want either of them to get hurt.

The coyote shook Sadie's calf in her mouth. Sadie reached down with both hands and wrenched the animal's jaws wide open. Sadie's hands bled freely when she threw Marcy June across the room.

The audience held its breath. If everyone else was like me, I couldn't breathe.

The coyote landed with a heavy thud on the edge of the mat and didn't pop right back up. When she did rise, she limped her way back over to Sadie, who held what looked like a fireball between both hands. The Enforcer's eyes were narrowed, her mouth a thin, grim line.

The coyote ran at her in a jagged line. Sadie fired and missed, burning a smoking hole in one of the mats. She aimed and fired again. This time, the animal's coat caught on fire.

Marcy June stopped, dropped, and rolled, and then kept coming at Sadie, full speed. She launched and slammed into Sadie squarely in the chest. The witch stumbled, swung her arms wide as if enclosing the coyote in her magic, and then pressed her palms against the snarling creature's body. When Sadie moved her hands forward, the coyote moved with them, suspended in the middle of a bubble of orange, fiery magic.

The coyote snarled and bit at the orange glow, trying to tear through it, without success. Sweat dripped down Sadie's temple as she fought to maintain her magic against the force of the coyote's resistance. Her hands began to tremble slightly while the coyote thrashed to break free.

I sucked in a ragged breath, trying to calm myself, reminding myself to breathe, that I wasn't the one in the fight—the two stupid chicks with a death wish were.

Sadie's orange glow began to flicker. She launched the coyote across the room again, but this time the animal landed on her feet. One of her legs caved under her, but she ran straight back at the witch, even with her gimpy gait.

My protector amassed the same orange magic between her palms again, but it sputtered a few times, not nearly as bright, nor as strong. When the coyote charged at her injured calf once more, ripping through the shredded material and tearing a chunk of flesh from her leg, Sadie roared and threw every bit of orange in her hands at the shifter.

Sadie's magic flashed as it made contact; the coyote started to shake so hard that she dropped the chunk of bloodied flesh from her mouth, convulsing.

"All right!" Egan yelled out. "I'm calling it. Disengage."

"Oh thank God," Wren said, huddling into me, speaking my thoughts aloud. Even the less shakable

Adalia seemed unsettled, and the sparks of enthusiasm had long faded from Dave's eyes. Only Jas continued to appear alive with excitement and adrenaline.

Sadie's magic fizzled out to nothing as the witch plopped unceremoniously on the mat where she stood. The coyote flopped onto the mat next to her, sides heaving.

The audience seemed to hold its breath.

"I call a tie," Egan called out, his voice ringing across the crowd easily. Murmurs began to build into a frenzy as Melinda and Nancy, with Fianna and Nessa flying overhead, ran over to the fighters. Melinda clutched her apron, covered in delicate flowers, her badger face settled into determined lines. She knelt by Sadie and Marcy June and dug in the deep pockets of her apron for her magical healing ointments. Nancy hovered behind her, apparently waiting for instructions.

"Holy shit that was intense," Wren said, drawing my attention back to my friends. "What the hell was Sadie thinking? What the hell was Marcy June thinking? They're both fucking nuts!"

I couldn't remember if I'd ever heard the big-hearted flower-child let the F-bomb fly before, but if ever there was an occasion for it, this was it. My heart was beating far too fast considering all I'd done was observe.

"Students, head to your next class," Fianna's voice rang through my head. "No need to dilly-dally. Everything's under control here. Show's over, now move it."

"The crimson fairy reminds me of you," I said to Jas, who smiled broadly.

"Yeah, she's got some attitude, huh?"

I hadn't really meant it as a good thing, but Jas skewed everything the way she wanted it.

"Come on, let's go," Adalia said, and I allowed her to lead me through the mass of students with a few final glances at Sadie. Was I supposed to wait for her? She didn't look ready to do any protecting at the moment.

But as my friends and I moved along with the exodus, I convinced myself that I was surely safe enough at the academy surrounded by shifters as fierce as Marcy June and Sadie, who was shifter fierce despite her witchy magic. Everyone here wanted the same thing: balance and peace in the supernatural world, and between it and the humans. We were all on the same page, right?

Regardless, unease prickled against my senses while I walked. I just didn't know why.

❧ 14 ❧

Weeks later, Sadie leaned against the wall next to Damon on the floor of the shifter practice room, legs out in front of her. She was wide-eyed and alert despite the long day and the fact that it was past eight at night. Maybe it was because of the nap she'd taken during Beginning Creature History 201.

"Someone could make a fortune bottling up Wendell Whittle and selling him as a sleep aid," she was saying to Damon. "The man could put sprites to sleep, and you know how they are—they won't stay still for a second."

Damon laughed, a low and soothing rumble I'd come to enjoy from the man who didn't say much.

"Why would anyone choose him as a professor? Surely there were better options than the most boring werewolf in all history. Probably the only boring werewolf to have ever existed. Werewolves aren't supposed to be boring. They're supposed to be feisty, fiery, and ferocious." She punctuated each adjective with a flick of an enthused hand.

"Has he caught you sleeping yet?" Damon asked in that deep, smoky voice of his.

Sadie beamed a grin wide enough to crinkle her eyes. "Nope. Not a single time."

"He's probably not paying attention to you," I said while I stretched my arms and legs. "You're not a student. He shouldn't care whether you sleep through his class or not."

"Oh, he cares, trust me. He's been trying to catch me sleeping since I was a oner."

"You were a student of his when you were here?"

Sadie nodded, her ponytail flopping behind her. "He's been teaching here since the start of the school. A few of the teachers have, though not all. The vamps had some major turnover during the last few years. Though not Vladimir Vabu. He's been here from the very start. He was involved in the original Magical Arts Academy, but not that Lorenzo Damante. He's new, and I don't trust him."

"He hasn't done anything to make you distrust him though, has he?" Damon asked.

"No, not yet, but he's too … good looking. He bugs me."

Damon threw his head back and laughed, his heavy dreads brushing the floor. "You can't seriously be suggesting you don't trust him because he's too fine."

No … she couldn't be. Lots of supernaturals were

imbued with above average looks thanks to the way their magic worked to achieve balance and harmony.

"He always looks like he's ready for a walk-off," Sadie scoffed. "He's a vampire, for fuck's sake, not a Ken doll. A man shouldn't look that perfect." When Ky, Boone, and Leander joined Damon and me in staring at her, she added, "But no, I'm not saying that's why I don't trust him—not entirely. He just feels off to me, and I'm not sure why."

Damon nodded thoughtfully, and from the way his deep brown eyes became pensive, I could tell these Enforcers were used to paying attention to their intuition, even when it didn't entirely make sense.

Ky sidled next to me. "As entertaining as it is to watch Sadie lose it over Professor Damante, we have work to do."

I struggled to internalize the groan that bubbled up at the thought of what was coming. "I'm starting to think we should name our little practice sessions "Beat Up Rina Time" or something. I'm still sore from last night, and I'm a shifter with super healing."

Ky opened his mouth. I put up a hand to stop him. "Don't bother. I know what you're going to say already, and yes I realize that Rage and Fury and whatever other numbnuts decide to come after me won't take it easy."

I moved to the center of the padded mats, where a few weeks ago Sadie had sparred Marcy June and become the talk of the school for days. "Who's going to beat me up first? You or Boone?"

We'd gotten into a rhythm. For the first few weeks of the term, Ky had trained me alone. Several weeks ago, Boone had joined us. And while the addition of the large wolf shifter meant double the fun and double the bruises, I couldn't deny that I'd improved noticeably since they'd been helping me.

Leander hadn't come before tonight. I didn't know what he did while his best friends were sparring with me, and in case it had something to do with Stacy, I didn't ask. I purposefully didn't look his way, yet I could still sense his attention on me like a warm, sunny breeze.

I wouldn't allow the presence of the prince to distract me. I had to be fully present for whatever Ky and Boone had planned. They'd been whispering together earlier, and with the way Ky kept grinning at me, I'd bet it meant they were about to unleash a particularly nasty attack—to test my reactions, of course.

I was in workout clothes—leggings, a crop tank-top, and my ever-present Converse—and I was as ready as I'd get. The sooner we started, the sooner I'd get to veg with Wren for a while and get some sleep.

"Let's get this party started," I said, and before I'd finished the last word, Ky charged me.

Though he remained in human form, he was still half a foot taller than me and who knew how many pounds of muscle heavier. He wrapped strong arms around my waist and took me down with him.

My back hit the mat with a loud smack; the air rushed painfully from my lungs. It was like taking a belly-flop from a ten-story building. I groaned before I could stop myself; Ky seemed to count my groans as points for them or some such boyish nonsense.

When I looked up into his smiling face, I bucked my hips and legs until I threw him off me. We both rolled and popped up to our feet. He wasn't going to take me by surprise again.

I flicked my gaze between Ky and Boone, who was too close, circling me around the mat on the other side. Just in case, I glanced at Sadie, Damon, and Leander. The Enforcers remained where they'd been, though their conversation had ceased, all attention on the match in front of them.

I shouldn't have looked at Leander. The moment my eyes skimmed the lines of his body, wings on full, glorious display, I hesitated, drawn by the pull he had over me—the same magnetism I hadn't been able to shrug off no matter how hard I tried. His eyes blazed as they skimmed across my body. Then they widened, and I knew I'd made a huge mistake.

I snapped my head around to find Ky more or less where he'd been, though he'd stepped inside the zone of my personal space. I didn't spot Boone before I was airborne. He rammed into me with his head and shoulders down and sent me sprawling several feet off the floor.

A month before, I would've landed flatter than a lumpy pancake. But these little training sessions had helped hone my reflexes, and even though I was in the body of a girl, my lion was never far away anymore.

I twisted in the air and managed to get my feet

under me before dropping lightly to the mat. I stumbled but caught myself, and the next second I had my fists raised, protecting my face, and my forearms shielding my upper body. I stepped to the back of the mats so I could view both Ky and Boone ... and Leander.

"Don't let the eye candy distract you," Sadie called out.

Sadie had about as much tact as Jas, which was to say none at all. I grimaced at my protector. At least no one would notice me blushing when I was already working up a sweat.

Ky and Boone shared a look that spoke of nefarious intentions. Hell no. While they were flicking looks at each other, I ran toward them. I dipped my shoulder low and rammed into Ky—and it was like hitting a brick wall. I swallowed my groan of pain as the impact ricocheted down my entire side or I'd never hear the end of it.

I brought both hands to his ribcage and pushed with all my strength like I was some defensive back, and managed to push him backwards a couple of inches. I grunted and pushed some more. "How the hell am I supposed to accomplish anything against two dudes who're twice my size? I can't even budge you, Ky!"

"Your size is a disadvantage in this fight," Damon said, standing to move closer to us. "Which means you have to find your advantage and use that. Don't fight them the way they want you to, fight them the way that benefits you the most."

Thanks for nothing, Yoda. What the hell did that mean? I had no advantages against the two massive shifters.

Sadie walked over to stand at Damon's side, barely coming up to his shoulder. "What he means is that you have to find a way to make it work for you, no matter what comes up against you. If you can't beat them in size and brute strength, then find some way you can beat them. In other words, fight like an alley cat."

If this was all the advice they were coming over to dispense, then they could march right back over to the wall. But while everyone was distracted...

I dove at Ky and Boone like I was diving into a damn swimming pool, hands outstretched above my head, and linked an arm around each of their calves. As I slid across the mat along my stomach, the momentum brought them down to the floor with me. Ky smashed to the floor, but was already gathering his legs beneath him to stand back up. I plopped the entirety of my weight on Boone, sitting on his chest, pinning his arms beneath my knees. When he bent his feet beneath him and prepared to buck and roll me off him, I slid farther down his chest so that I sat on his hips, and leaned forward, pressing my hands against his shoulders to hold him down, my knees still digging into his arms.

I flicked a frantic glance behind me, trying to pinpoint Ky's location lest he attack me from behind, when I noticed Leander, his eyes wide and blazing. What...?

I looked down at Boone. His hazel eyes were

bright and alert, zeroed in on me. His face was flush with an intensity I'd never seen on him before.

Oh.

I was straddling his hips, and Boone was a very sexy, very hot-blooded wolf man.

Shit. No wonder Leander was looking at me like that.

Before the moment could devolve any further, I slid off him and got to my feet, backing up from Ky, making sure no one was behind me. Nothing like straddling your brother's best friend in front of him and the guy you're sweet on to get the blood pumping.

The door opened and closed behind me, and I spun toward it. Wendi slipped in, and for once I was grateful for the distraction she offered. She smiled, and I returned the gesture, though as usual it felt fake.

"I think that's enough grappling for now," Ky said, an extra edge to his voice. "Time to shift. You'll fight one of us at a time, squirt, starting with me."

I knew better than to wait. When the edges of Ky's body began to blur, I'd already closed my eyes and was picturing my lion. Was it ideal to close my eyes when an attack was imminent? Of course not. But I hadn't figured out how to send my shifter magic to my animal without picturing her first. I couldn't do it with my eyes open, taking in other images. It was a significant disadvantage, which meant I had to hurry. Ky's shift would be complete in seconds.

I envisioned my mountain lion, strong and power-ful. I imagined her lean, muscled body and stared into those bright amber-copper eyes. I stared into her gaze so intensely … that I suddenly felt myself within her, a part of her.

I hadn't intended to merge with her yet, but I was already one with my lion. I pulsed the energy I'd managed to build in my core toward me as the lion just in case, and opened my eyes.

The outlines of Ky's human body flickered a few times … and then he stood in full magnificence, a majestic mountain lion.

I stared into those eyes so much like my own as they glowed faintly. He growled, and I returned the favor. Boone, Leander, Damon, and Sadie backed off the mats, giving us a wide berth.

When Ky lowered his head into his shoulders and went completely still, I took off at full speed, straight for him. We met in the middle, reared onto our hind legs, and clashed heavy paws. We batted at each other, neither coming on top, a chorus of snaps and snarls marking time.

Though we were relatively evenly matched, Ky was slightly larger than me. He was also a bit stronger. Eventually, he'd gain ground on me, and I wasn't having it. He'd beaten me too many times, and as he liked to remind me, Rage wouldn't hold back, and his lion was as potent as my brother's.

I put all my strength into shoving Ky, and the momentum rocked him back a few inches. He scooted the distance on his hind legs as I opened my mouth and roared, letting loose all my pent-up frustration, and trust me, it was a crap-ton.

He landed on all four feet, only to bounce back onto his hind legs. He was about to lunge at me.

I let him, rearing up to meet him. But this time, when he connected with my paws, I rolled backward onto my back. As he dropped at the unexpected lack of resistance, I slid slightly down the mat so his paws would land on either side of my head, and just as he was bringing down his wide, open jaws—probably to wrap around my throat in victory—I lashed out with my hind legs, catching him in the fleshy part of the abdomen between his hips. I pushed out, flinging him over my head.

He hadn't seen it coming, the shock evident in his wide lion eyes and enraged snarl.

My brother landed on his side, slamming into his shoulder—hard. But before he could retaliate, I claimed my feet, sides heaving from the exertion.

Damon started clapping just as Sadie hooted and ran toward the center of the room. "Damn, girl!" She leapt a couple of feet into the air. "Now that's what I'm talking about. Smarts are more important than size—well, most of the time anyway." She winked.

I glanced from Ky to Boone, and when neither appeared ready to attack me, I settled onto the floor, head leaning on my front paws, eyes wide open. When Ky's lion started blurring, vibrating, and then flickering, I released a sigh of relief. The session was over for tonight.

Now if only I could shift back to human form as easily as Ky had...

I closed my eyes again and pictured myself as if I were looking into the full-length mirror in the bedroom I shared with Wren. I stared into my eyes, and just as had happened when I shifted into my lion, the distance between my awareness and my eyes shortened to nothing. Before I realized what had happened, I found myself inside my human body, every part in the right place. As I'd done before, I pulsed my magic into the image of myself as a girl, settled into her, then opened my eyes.

I was face-down on the mat, returned to my long limbs and long hair. I nudged my chin more comfortably into the tops of my hands, figuring I might as well stay there for a while. I was beat.

"That was good, squirt," Ky said. "You're learning to think outside the box."

"And your shifts are getting faster too," Boone added. I tilted my head up to take in the werewolf towering over me. His expression was as relaxed and congenial as ever. Good. No weird feelings there.

When Ky and Leander moved to either side of Boone, and Sadie and Damon hovered above me, Wendi in the background, I dragged myself to my feet. Even though I trusted every one of them, the part of me that continually remained a lion now didn't appreciate being in such a vulnerable position.

I felt dead on my feet, but I refused to let it show. Half the battle was in appearances, or so Ky had told me. Shifters respected strength, so I had to appear strong whenever possible.

"Are you hurt?" Ky asked.

"No, just beat. How 'bout you? Boone?"

"We're good," Boone said.

"Great. Can I go to bed now?" I rubbed at the tension in one of my shoulders.

Ky smiled. "I think today you've earned it. We'll meet after dinner again tomorrow."

"How long do we have to keep meeting for practice like this?" I managed not to whine, but just barely.

"As long as it takes to get you strong enough to fight Rage, Fury, and whomever they might show up with. Remember—"

"I remember. They're hunting me—us—I know. How could I possibly forget?" I trailed my gaze from Sadie to Wendi, across Damon and back. The reminders of the dangers were everywhere.

The group of us started toward the doors, but when we reached them, Leander held me back. "Can I talk with you for a sec?"

Ky, Boone, and Sadie stopped walking to look back at us. "Go on ahead," Leander said. "We'll only be a moment."

Ky hesitated longer than the rest of them, but eventually he followed Boone out of earshot, where he stopped, turned in our direction, crossed his arms over his chest, and waited.

I met the prince's eyes and immediately was lost to the torrent of emotion swirling within them. He flicked a nervous glance at my brother, then took my hands anyway.

"Rina, I need to talk with you."

"We are talking." But immediately I felt like a jerk and wished I could take back my snarky response. Something was clearly on the elf's mind—or maybe it was his heart that had him so evidently twisted in knots.

"In private, where Ky isn't trying to read my lips."

I chuckled. My brother did kind of look like that was what he was trying to do.

I wanted to say no. There didn't seem much more to say between us that would make any difference. But Leander seemed so earnest that the words were out of my mouth before I could take them back. "Okay. We can meet. But how about tomorrow? I'm really tired, and I'd rather be alert when we talk." Not to mention not sweaty.

He smiled, and the way his entire face lit up at my acceptance had my heart speeding up. *Down, traitorous heart, down.*

"Tomorrow, then," he said. "After your history class and before dinner, that should give us enough time."

Time for what, I wondered while trying not to get hopeful. I'd worked hard to quash my expectations where he was concerned, and I didn't plan to undo my efforts.

"I'll meet you outside your classroom," he said. "I'll be looking forward to it."

I nodded, not sure what to say. "I'll see you tomorrow then."

"Perfect." And Leander seemed happier than I'd seen him in several weeks, since our last talk, in fact.

But as we moved to join the rest of our crew, I should have known better—never leave till tomorrow what you can do today. Wasn't that the saying? Well, I was about to learn that there was some serious merit to the phrase.

❧ 15 ❧

I STARTLED AWAKE, MY HEART POUNDING, AND LISTENED in the darkness to discern what had woken me. But beyond the soft, rhythmic breathing of Wren, in her bed on the other side of our shared bedroom, the night was quiet. I turned my head atop my pillow, trying to make out the outlines of the space, but the shutters were closed tightly; not even a flicker of moonlight filtered into the room. It felt late, like it was the middle of the night, but the alarm clock rested next to Wren, too far away for me to reach it to confirm the hour—she said I snoozed too many times in the morning.

The night was still, yet a tangible unease told me something was wrong. But what?

I turned my head in the other direction and discovered a thin trail of warm drool on the side of my face. Gross. I wiped at my face with the back of my hand ... and a stifled laugh whispered through the silence, grating against my nerves like fingernails along a chalkboard.

I froze, my hand still against my face, my pulse beating frantically.

There was definitely someone in the room with us. And though the laughter had been quickly smothered, I had a feeling I knew whom it belonged to, and if I was right, it was bad news. Everything about the vampires seemed like bad news lately. They went out of their way to run into me after dark just to glare and hiss at me.

I slowly moved my hand from my face and slid upward in my bed gradually until I was leaning against the headboard behind me. A chance still remained that the person who'd invaded our room—Blood Red if I was right, whose name was actually Paige—hadn't realized I'd made her. The chance was perhaps infinitesimally small, but I'd take whatever chance I could get. I was at a disadvantage tucked within the blankets of my bed, and Wren was wholly vulnerable no more than a few feet away from me.

Vampires were apex predators of the night, when their vision was superior to all but shifters in animal form. All of their senses were heightened in the night-time, and I couldn't shake the feeling that Paige was staring straight at me. The sensation of being watched crawled across my skin.

I sat and waited, scrambling to come up with a plan that would get me out of this mess and not drag Wren any deeper into it. I didn't know exactly what Paige wanted with me by sneaking into our room like this, but I could guess. At a minimum, she intended to inflict discomfort or pain. But I couldn't shake the feeling that her intentions were far more nefarious. I imagined the consequences for sneaking into another student's room in the night to cause them some sort of harm would be punished severely. Sir Lancelot would certainly be outraged. For Paige to risk the severity of punishment, she had to be here for an important reason. There was no way that reason boded well for me.

The seconds sped past, but I didn't come up with any coherent plan beyond hopping out of bed and racing past the intruder toward the common room. That would get Paige away from Wren, and hopefully I could rouse Sadie and possibly Wendi, both of whom slept with the doors to their individual rooms open. While I called out for my Enforcer protectors, I'd shift into my mountain lion—hopefully. I'd gotten better at shifting, but it still didn't work a hundred percent of the time, more like eighty-five percent. My odds weren't great, but nothing good was going to come from me waiting for Paige to make the first move.

I started peeling the comforter from my legs, one slow inch at a time, when I heard another rustle from the opposite side of the room from where I'd thought Paige was. Shit. Either my own senses were distorting information or Paige had brought friends. I had to move, and I had to move now.

I tore the blanket the rest of the way from my body, flinging it to the bottom of the bed, and jumped to the floor. My bare feet hit the hardwood floor running and I slid into the common room, mouth already open to call for Sadie.

But Sadie's door, which was always open when we were sleeping, was firmly shut, and Wendi's door was closed too. Definitely not a good sign. "Sadie!" I yelled, and a moment later a hand slapped against my face harder than necessary, an arm snaking around my neck and latching onto my shoulder, tugging me backward, pressing against my windpipe and cutting off my ability to scream.

"Don't bother," Paige whispered harshly against my ear in that nasally voice that was uniquely hers. "She won't hear you. We made sure of it."

My heart skipped a beat. "You killed her?"

The two seconds it took Paige to answer felt like a thousand. Sadie and her crazy ways had grown on me. Finally, the vamp laughed again, sending shivers across my mostly bare skin. I slept in nothing more than panties and a thin camisole that bared my waist.

"No, we didn't kill her, she's only sleeping," she said, "though I wish we had. Watching you die will have to be enough reward."

I tried to figure out how many of them "we" might be while pondering why she would hate me so much. I couldn't think of a single vamp I liked, especially among the students, but I didn't want any of them to die. Well, maybe now I did. Paige had raced to the very top of my shit list. I wouldn't mind if she was wiped from the face of the earth.

A rustle and a shuffle on opposing sides of the

common room told me there were at least three intruders here. Since they were probably part of Paige's crew, and she didn't go anywhere without the three submissive vamps that trailed her every move, there might be a total of four intruders. If Sadie couldn't help me, and I couldn't call out for Wendi, who was probably out of commission for the same reason Sadie was, it was all on me.

Paige tightened her hold around my throat, gagging me. "No one's coming to save you, princess. Come with us without a fight, and maybe the shifters will take it easier on you." She chuckled happily. "No, there's probably no chance of that. Rage wants you too badly." The others chortled with her, but I still couldn't decide whether there were two or three more of them.

The best way out of this was to shift. At least as a lion I could rip through them and cause some serious damage. I closed my eyes to the overpowering darkness and envisioned myself as my lion. She was staring back at me, hurrying me along, ready to pounce and deliver some punishment already.

But just as I was closing the gap between us, reaching the magic that pooled in my center toward her, Paige's hold vanished from around my throat— and a metallic collar snapped around my neck in its place.

The vision of my lion disappeared as if it had been no more than a figment of my imagination.

I whipped my hands up to the collar and pulled and tugged, but I already knew there was no budging it, not with brute force. It was a magical object, it had to be, which meant there was no escaping it through ordinary means.

While Paige laughed behind me like some cartoon villain, I stomped on her toes. When her head whipped down to look at her foot, I grabbed onto that thick, beautiful curly hair of hers and pulled down, slamming her face into my knee hard enough to break her nose. I felt the bone and cartilage crunch; warm blood gushed onto my leg.

"You fucking bitch," she hissed as she straightened, her words slightly slurred.

I took that as an invitation to slam my fist into her face. I couldn't see to make sure to hit her straight in the nose again, but my fist made contact with her cheek before deflecting off, and this time she howled in pain.

I couldn't make out the others, but now I could call for help—once I made it out of the dorm. I wouldn't call for other students to help, that'd only put them in harm's way. I sprinted toward the door that led out to the hallway and had it halfway open when my legs gave out beneath me.

I slumped to the floor, my hand slipping from the doorknob and dragging along the door. My body weight slouched against the door, slamming it shut. "What's … happening?" My words were slurred, and I was struggling to keep my eyes open.

Paige was at my side, her voice traveling from very far away to reach me. "You're going to take a long nap, just like your friends. And when you wake up …

well, if we're lucky, you'll never wake up again. Time to die, princess."

She punctuated her statement with a kick to the ribs, and unlike me, Paige wore boots. I thought I should curl into the fetal position and protect my head with my arms, but no movement followed the intention. My eyelids fluttered heavily until they failed to win their fight. As my eyes closed, consciousness vanished. I slid to the floor, dead weight.

I WOKE WITH A START BUT DIDN'T OPEN MY EYES RIGHT away as the memories of Paige and her band of bloodthirsty bitches flooded in. My hands and feet were tightly bound; the cold weight of the metallic collar remained around my neck. A dull throb pulsing through both sides of my ribcage suggested that Paige had gotten in another kick or two after I'd lost consciousness.

I moved my fingertips and brushed across carpet. Where the hell was I?

I peeked open my eyes, caught sight of Ky slumped in an unconscious heap across from me, and had to work to keep my panic under control. I focused on keeping my breathing and heart rate steady, two factors vampires were particularly attuned to. There was no way I wanted to alert any vamps that I was awake.

The room we occupied was dark, but a sliver of light shone beneath the closed door, revealing a sparsely furnished, windowless room. There were two cushy gaming chairs and a couple of couches arranged around a monstrous flat-screen TV. Free-weights, a mini-fridge, and a card table pushed to one corner rounded out the room. There were only two doors, the one with the light under it, which I presumed was the only way out of here, and another one, partially open to reveal bathroom tiling.

Ky's arms were bound behind his back and tied to a narrow column. His body slumped awkwardly to one side. He was going to have some serious neck kinks to work out once he roused—after he freaked out about our confinement and tried to kill whoever held us captive, of course.

Like me, Ky sported a shiny silver collar that was undoubtedly disconnecting him from his lion, just as mine was. A faint blue glow surrounded the metal, casting his normally tanned flesh in an eerie glow. He was seriously going to lose his shit when he woke up and found us here. He might be a jerk of a big brother sometimes, but not when it really counted.

I strained my ears, listening for any sign that someone was coming to check on us. When I was certain no one was heading our way, I yanked my hands against the column behind them, but only succeeded in chafing my wrists. I checked out the binds around my feet. Zip ties, dammit. There was no way I was breaking free without magic.

"Ky," I whispered a few times, but he didn't react. "Ky," I whisper-screamed again, searching for anything within reach to throw at him. Nothing, of course. I wasn't even wearing a shoe I could scoot his way.

"Are you sure they're still asleep?" The words slithered through the crack under the door and I froze. Though the words were far away, I recognized that prim voice.

Wendi. Motherfreaking Wendi!

"I checked on them five minutes ago," said a deep male voice I hadn't heard before. "They're both out cold."

"Okay, good. I need to get back before anyone wakes up and discovers them gone. I can't be linked to this. Those rabbits will kill me if they find out I'm the one who knocked them out."

"Rage said that was part of the deal."

"And does Rage keep his deals?"

The man didn't respond.

Wendi growled. "He'd better keep his bargain with me or he'll regret it. I want my mom back home by the end of the night. I've done my part, now you tell him that if he ever calls on me again for anything else, I'll kill him on sight. And if he *ever* lays another finger on my family, he'll beg for death before I'm finished with him. And once he's dead, I'll turn him over to Thane."

The artificial, saccharine chirp was absent from Wendi's voice. I had no doubt she meant every word she said. And though Wendi didn't owe Ky or me any loyalty beyond that required of her role as an Enforcer, I couldn't prevent the stab of betrayal that wound its way through my guts. I'd trusted her. All of us had trusted her. She'd slept in the next room over.

If I hadn't happened to wake up at precisely the right moment, I might have never learned of her involvement. She might have gotten away with handing us over to Rage. She'd probably drugged Sadie and Wren, or whatever the magical equivalent of slipping someone a roofie was, to make sure the vamps could slip in while she was away, likely securing her alibi.

Oh, Sadie was going to rip Wendi's head off with her bare hands and dropkick it across campus. But in order to inform Sadie of Wendi's betrayal, I had to get out of here first.

I imagined that Ky had arrived to share this man cave basement with me after a similar string of events. Damon, Boone, and Leander had probably been forced into a deep sleep while the male vamps had taken Ky. It had probably been Anton and his lackeys, since the Academy Spell ensured only males were allowed in the boys' dormitories after dark and only females in the girls'—to prevent any after-hours hanky-panky.

I'd work out the exact details of our kidnapping later. For now, I had to get us out of here before Rage or Fury arrived to claim their prizes. With our shifter animals out of reach thanks to our new jewelry, it was time to think outside the box. How on earth were Ky and I going to get ourselves out of this one? No ready answers had arrived by the time footfalls padded toward the closed door.

I snapped my eyes shut and slumped back down the column, ignoring the painful pull on my arms and ribcage as I settled my face into relaxed inexpressiveness. My insides boiled with a desperate determination as the door clicked open.

❧ 16 ❧

"THEY HAVEN'T STIRRED AT ALL SINCE THEY GOT here," said the same deep, unfamiliar male voice from before. "I've been checking on them every five minutes. They've been out cold."

"You weren't supposed to leave their side," said another voice I'd probably never forget, and I struggled to maintain my ruse of sleep as an icy chill settled deep in my veins. *Rage.* I'd spent every day since I'd last seen him trying to block out our last encounter.

"I told you to stay with them at all times," he said, his voice vibrating with power.

"But they have the shift blocking collars on, and their hands and feet are tied. They can't do anything."

"If I wanted you to think for yourself, I'd tell you to. You're lucky nothing happened or I'd be dealing with you right now. Since they're still here, then I'll give some thought to how I'll deal with your disobedience later."

"I didn't mean to disobey," said the male voice, not

so deep anymore as he scrambled to appease Rage. "I just figured there was no way they could go anywhere."

"Well, you figured wrong. They're mountain lions."

"With shift blocking collars on."

Rage growled, and I heard scuffling footsteps as I imagined they backpedaled from the furious leader of the Shifter Alliance.

"I'll deal with you later," Rage said, ire simmering in every short word. "Now go get the sorcerer. The sooner we get this over with, the sooner my brother can go back to being himself."

"Yes, Rage," the male said in a submissive chirp, and the creaking of the door opening and closing soon followed.

Ky and I were completely vulnerable, and in the room alone with Rage. There was no one to protect us here. No one to keep him from killing us right now.

Never before had it been so difficult to remain still, and never before had it been so important.

Shifters' senses weren't like those of vampires; they were sharper than those of most humans, but they weren't overly heightened unless we were in our animal forms. But someone as powerful as Rage, strong enough to dominate every other shifter in North America, might scent my fear anyway. I had so much of it pumping through my body that I had no doubt it was permeating through my pores. Still, I couldn't control it. I couldn't keep my heart from straining to leap from my chest in a burst of panic. My instincts were to jump up, grab Ky, and run so fast and so far that Rage would never find us.

And yet Rage had managed what was supposed to be impossible. He'd stolen Ky and me from the Menagerie right out from under more protectors than ever before. Beyond our personal guards, there were other Enforcers across the campus. Vicious trolls and killer rabbits protected the secret mountain oasis, and Sir Lancelot had the entire staff on high alert. Half of the students were advanced enough in their studies to put up a worthy fight.

But none of the academy's heightened defenses had managed to halt Rage. What were the odds that I, bound and limited, could do what the others hadn't? Slim to none, surely. Still, it didn't matter. Just as Rage had found the way to beat the odds, I'd have to do the same. Because there was no way in hell I was going to allow Rage to take my brother from me ... from Dad. If something happened to Ky, Dad would break, I just knew it. And I'd been a crummy daughter lately. I hadn't spoken to Dad more than a couple of times since the term started. I had to find the way to make things right.

Sharp inhales punctuated the silence, and I thought my heart might seize up then and there and put an end to all this suffering. Dying from fear was a real risk as I sensed the shifter's body heat against my mostly bare skin. He was right next to me, hovering over me, sniffing me.

Oh God. I wasn't a good enough actress to maintain the illusion of sleep. I was two seconds away from crawling out of my skin, and it'd probably be less than that before Rage discovered I was awake, negating my one and only advantage.

When the door creaked open, I very nearly gave myself away. My breath hiccupped in my chest. But Rage didn't say anything before another voice spoke over the loud whooshing of my pulse.

"There you are, brother. I've been looking for you."

Fury. It had to be.

"It won't be long now," Rage said. "Before the night is over, you'll be restored to your full power. I'll have finally made things right."

A few moments passed before Fury spoke again. "Are you sure this is the way to make things right? I sacrificed my power for your life with full under-standing of what I was giving up. Saving your life was worth it. I made a choice after weighing the costs. You didn't steal my power, I gave it to you. But we'll be stealing their power, and their lives, if we do this."

"Not if, brother, when. I'm not turning back now. I can't live with what I've done to you. I have to fix it."

"But you can live with taking their lives, or at the very least their power?"

"Damn right I can. You're my brother. They're strangers. It's an easy choice."

So basically Ky and I were at the mercy of a megalomaniac without a conscience. The brother with a semblance of a moral compass was too weak to do more than protest. Just dandy.

"Excuse me, Fury," a new voice said. "I'd like to

get a look at my subjects." Two sets of muted footfalls made their way over to me. "The resemblance between the siblings is certainly strong. You're certain they're both mountain lions?"

"A hundred percent," Rage said. "Fury and I saw both of them a few months ago. They're both fine specimens."

"Hmm, how remarkable. Such an oddity for the same shifter magic to manifest among siblings, and yet there are two sets of you in the room with me."

"Save your marveling for later, sorcerer. We're in a hurry. The Enforcers are sure to start looking for them soon. We're on borrowed time."

"Very well. Our deal remains?"

"Yes. Once the spell is complete and you've succeeded in transferring one of their powers to my brother, restoring his shifter magic to its original state, then I'll give you the second sibling to do with as you wish."

"What will you do with the second one, Jevan?" Fury asked.

"Experiment with him … or her. There is still so much we don't understand about shifter magic. Since the Magical Council banned experimentation on living creatures, the expansion of our knowledge has been stunted." The crazy-ass sorcerer tsked. "I look forward to learning how the identical shifter magic manifested in mother and her two children. It's most unusual. Pity the mother is dead. I would have liked to study them all."

Jevan's voice was clinical, cold and detached. What the hell was wrong with these fruitcakes?

"I already got everything you asked for the spell. Your list was long and many of the items were difficult to procure, but I managed it," Rage said. "I'll have one of my men fetch them for you."

"Very good, very good indeed." The sorcerer's voice was greedy, and I imagined him licking reptilian lips. "I'm impressed you managed to find the dwarf bone marrow. Dwarves are notoriously hard to kill."

"Like I said, I managed. Now on with it, Jevan."

"First I'll need you to transport them outside. My magic is increased when I'm outdoors, connected to the elements."

"Fine." Rage's voice was tight. "We can move to the back yard."

"No, not the backyard. Thunder Mountain."

"Have you lost your damn mind?" Rage snarled. "Didn't I just say the Enforcers will be looking for them? And the ones who survived our attack are the hardened ones who don't go down as easily as the others. They'll put up a fight."

"It's either Thunder Mountain or we risk the success of the transference spell. It's a super complex spell. Surely you know that or you wouldn't have asked me to be involved. I need access to the strongest magic in the area. With the academy inside the mountain, its magic will have soaked into the earth around it. Tons of spells are needed to maintain the school. I already told you there's no guarantee the transference spell will work. It's incredibly dark, uncommon magic. To increase our chances, we need to be next to the school."

"Motherfucker!" Rage roared, and I jumped, then immediately tensed in preparation for whatever would come of their discovery that I'd been listening to their conversation all along. But they didn't notice my jerk, and my heart stuttered when I realized why.

Ky groaned as if he were in pain, and the three men in the room with us focused on him. I peeked through half-shuttered eyelids. The two shifters were large and bulky, taller even than Ky and as broad in the shoulders as Boone. Fury might have been stunted in his mountain lion form, but he wasn't in his human form. He was as muscled and solid as his brother.

The sorcerer, however, was as petite as Jas and Marcy June, but with none of their evident aggression and ferocity. In skinny jeans and a cable knit sweater, he appeared totally insignificant. In the faint lighting, I pegged him at a scrawny mid-thirties, though with dark sorcerers without scruples, and access to myriad spells that could probably affect the rate of their aging, I suspected it was hard to tell.

The three men hovered over Ky, allowing me a limited view between their backs. I opened my eyes all the way, struggling to make out the features of his face in the dim light. At least Fury had left the door open, allowing more light from the hallway into the room, but I still couldn't be sure how badly Ky was injured. I didn't see blood anywhere, but that didn't mean much in a world where a blast of magic could end your life in a flash that wouldn't leave a single mark on your body.

Ky came to with a start. It took a full three seconds before he registered that Rage, Fury, and Jevan leaned over him. When he did, he kicked out at them with his bound legs while simultaneously tugging on the bindings around his wrists.

Rage and Fury swiftly evaded his kicks, but Jevan wasn't quick enough, and the sorcerer stumbled backward, tripping on his own feet, and fell flat on his ass. He sat up gingerly, hissing at my brother. "I hope he's mine."

Ky growled, perhaps too furious for words, and kicked out again. But Rage and Fury were out of reach. He heaved and jerked his arms until the column behind him groaned—but it wasn't going anywhere.

"Where am I? What have you done to me? Why can't I shift?"

Jevan claimed his feet and strutted back toward Ky, though this time he kept his distance. "That would be me. You're wearing one of my inventions. I like to call it the *You're Fucked Collar*."

"How very quaint." Ky snarled ... until his gaze landed on me across from him. "Rina?" he whispered, and my stomach sank. I hadn't sensed any panic or fear from my brother ... until now. Until he discovered me in the *You're Screwed Scenario* right along with him.

He stared at me for a few, tense beats, and then he struggled against his bindings with renewed fury. He yanked on his fastenings so hard that the column shook and a fine dust of plaster rained down from above him. "Let. Her. Go," he panted, nostrils flared as if he were embodying his lion without the shift of form.

Rage stared at him, and then turned to look at me. I didn't close my eyes in time, though I didn't suppose there was much point to my ruse anymore anyway. He crouched in front of Ky, his thigh muscles bulging against the fabric of his jeans. "No. I'm not letting either one of you go until you've given me what I want. So there's no point fighting. You won't escape, and I'll do as I please. With both of you."

"I won't let you touch her. You'll have to kill me first."

Fury grimaced, obviously uncomfortable with the situation, but Rage smiled with a lethal determination that had me wishing Ky would stop antagonizing him. "Have you not figured it out yet, boy? You have no control here. Not over your fate, or your sister's. The best you can hope for is to make it painless for both of you. Do as we ask and I'll make your death swift. Fight me, and I'll make you beg for death before I'm through with you."

I expected Ky to bite back with another snarky comment, but instead he studied the three men in the room. He scanned the man cave that enclosed us and finally examined my own bindings, identical to his. When he trained his attention back on Rage, his tone was calm—too calm. "If your plan is to take our powers, you don't need to kill us. We could live on without our shifter powers."

"You're right. I don't need to. Play your cards right and maybe I won't."

Ky's nostrils flared again as he stared at the muscled shifter. He didn't say anything, I imagined because he didn't believe him, and the two stared at each other until Fury shifted on his feet next to them.

Jevan cleared his throat. "If you want to get this done before the Enforcers find them, then we'd better get a move on. The sun will rise in a few hours, and then we won't have the vamps' help anymore."

Fury placed a hand on Rage's shoulder. "Come on, brother. If you're set on doing this, then let's do it."

Rage growled at his prisoner in a show of dominance, but Ky growled back loudly enough to send chills racing across my bare skin, pebbling it with goosebumps. Ky hadn't said it in words, but he'd just threatened to tear Rage apart. I dearly hoped Ky would have the chance.

Rage stood and faced Fury. "Go tell the men we're moving out. Make sure they grab Jevan's ingredients. You can carry the girl, I'll deal with this one."

Fury glanced at me before nodding at his brother and disappearing through the doorway.

"You go with him too," Rage told Jevan.

The sorcerer turned so that his profile faced me. Fully in shadow, its lines were sinister, capped by a slightly upturned nose that was a bit too small for his face. "Don't think for a second that you command me. I'm not one of your men. You called me here because you need my skills. We aren't friends, and I'm not your minion. Be sure to mind the respect you owe me."

Rage stalked toward the short sorcerer until he towered over him. "I'll be sure to keep that in mind," he said with a thick mocking tone that indicated he didn't respect the sorcerer an ounce.

"You're lucky to have me, since the other sorcerer you used to work with … conveniently left town."

I wasn't sure if that meant the other sorcerer had fled to avoid working with Rage, or if Rage had done something to make the other sorcerer disappear. Either proposition was ominous. I didn't imagine dark sorcerers were known for their high standards in working partners.

"I do feel lucky," Rage added while I wondered if the leader of the Shifter Alliance might have a screw loose. He looked down at the sorcerer and smiled tightly at him. "Are you ready to move now, respected sorcerer?"

Jevan bunched his fists at his sides, hesitated, but finally turned on his heel and stalked from the room, slamming the door behind him.

"The bloody man has an ego the size of this house," Rage said as if forgetting that his only audience was his prisoners. "It's lucky indeed that I need him, if not I'd have strangled that scrawny little neck of his twice over by now."

He stalked over to me and Ky yelled, "Don't you hurt her!"

Hot tears stung my eyes that my big brother should care so much about me, then I told my eyes to stop being so wimpy and woman up. Thankfully, they obeyed, and by the time Rage settled into a menacing crouch above me, I had a death glare firmly in place. If my eyes could kill, the man would be a smoking, crispy pile of shifter.

"A fiery one, I see," Rage said. "That should make things more fun."

Ky growled, sounding like his lion, and I injected every scrap of hate I had into my gaze. How dare this asshole kidnap my brother and me? How dare he intend to kill us just because he could? How dare he believe that his brother's power was more important than our lives? I narrowed my eyes and pictured the heat of my gaze searing through his face, his cranium, and into his head, where it'd make his brain sizzle.

Rage yelped and flinched, and rocketed to his feet while backpedaling from me. When he brought both palms to either side of his skull, I didn't manage to hide my shock. Had I actually managed to do what I'd thought? I scrambled not to let my shock show.

"What the...? What'd you do to me, bitch?"

I smiled sweetly. "I didn't do a thing, asswipe. How could I? My hands and feet are bound, and you put this pretty collar on me."

He wasn't fully buying my spiel. Whatever I'd managed to do to him had been tangible enough that he couldn't dismiss it. *Shit*. I didn't want to go revealing that I was possibly a dual mage-shifter.

"You did something to me," Rage accused. "What did you do? How'd you do it?"

"I don't know what you're talking about. I'm a

shifter, and you've blocked my powers. There's nothing I can do." I was big on honesty, but in circumstances like these I'd lie up a storm if it had any chance of freeing Ky and me. "Maybe you have a headache. You know, from all the stress of kidnapping and trying to kill us."

He snarled at me as Fury returned with a small entourage of big, burly, grisly men. No doubt, they were all shifters. "We're ready," Fury said, and I silently thanked him for the interruption. Rage was still squeezing his head, and Ky was studying me curiously. "You okay?" Fury asked his brother.

"Fine. But change of plans. I'm going to carry the girl. You get the boy."

Fury arched dark questioning eyebrows, but didn't ask, nodding instead. He appeared to be his brother's lackey, nearly as much as everyone else. I'd never met an alpha of a shifter pack before, but from what Boone had told me over the summer, no one questioned or talked back to their alphas, not even their seconds. I supposed with Rage and Fury it'd be no different. Even if they were brothers, pack hierarchy would still rule.

Rage stomped toward me, dropping his hands from his head to his waist … from where he pulled a sharp blade as long as my forearm.

I scooted back against the column and drew my legs to my chest, unconcerned that it meant I was giving every man in the room a crotch shot of my panties. Better to be a flasher than dead. I pressed my head against the painted concrete column and shot a look at Ky. His eyes were wider than I'd ever seen them, his head jerking left and right as he searched fruitlessly for an avenue of escape.

"Ky," I called out, thinking I should say goodbye before it was too late. "I ... I love you." I'd never told him that before; I'd never told anyone that before, not even Dad. "Tell Dad I love him too." Assuming Ky got out of here if I didn't.

"Don't say goodbye," Ky ground out. "Don't you do it."

"Neither of you two idiots do it. Enough with the melodrama," Rage grumbled. "I'm not going to kill anyone—yet. I need you alive for the spell."

He circled behind me and sliced through the zip tie binding me to the column. I pulled my hands to me, rubbing at my sore wrists. But when Rage appeared in front of me again, he already had a fresh tie in his hands. "Stand up," he ordered.

I debated whether I should fight him on this, but the other men in the room were huge. They could take me down in one blow. I wriggled awkwardly to my feet; the binding at the ankles was tight enough to prevent any wiggle room. But I managed it, of course, and the moment I did, Rage yanked one of my arms behind my back, and as he reached for the other, I passed it to him. My shoulders were already screaming at the angle he held them at. He fastened the zip tie around my wrists, and I swear the binding was even tighter than the first time.

"Just in case you get any fancy ideas," he murmured as he leaned next to my ear.

I shivered and wiped my ear against my bare shoulder. Yuck. The moist heat of his breath lingered.

He shoved me in front of him, and of course I pitched straight forward. He caught me and pressed me far too close to him.

"You bound my feet," I sneered. "Or have you forgotten? Maybe you treat all the ladies who come into your house this way."

"Rina," Ky warned as I sensed Rage go rigid behind me. Ky didn't have to say more. I needed to keep my mouth shut to keep things from escalating faster than necessary. I nodded my acquiescence to my brother and clamped my teeth shut. It was going to be tough not to tell this asshole exactly what I thought of him.

"That's a good girl," Rage said. "Listen to your brother. No girl can get the one-up on me, and I'll punish you for trying."

"Great. Thanks for the memo."

One of Rage's men bent behind Ky's hands, a glint of shiny blade marking his movements as he sliced through the zip tie that bound my brother to the column.

In a move that shouldn't have been possible with his ankles still bound, Ky shot to his feet, shaking his arms and hands out. "You'll take your hands off my sister right this second."

"Or what, Tough Stuff?" Rage asked.

"Or I'll make you."

Rage waved a bored hand at the man who'd cut Ky's ties. "Grab 'im."

The shifter sheathed his blade and circled around Ky's back, arms outstretched as he prepared to grab him from behind. But when the shifter's arms started to close around Ky's chest, Ky slammed his butt out, ramming into the other guy's crotch and shifting him a few steps back. Ky hopped to face the opposite direction and rammed the heel of his hand into the guy's chin, snapping his head back.

While the dude groaned and pinned murderous eyes on Ky, Fury and another of the hulky guys converged on my brother, who quickly punched the hulk in the temple, sending him tumbling like a towering tree. By the time the shifter crashed to the floor in an unconscious heap, the other two had formed a solid wall behind him and two more were coming at Ky from either side to attack from the front.

Ky hopped another time to face me, keeping his attackers in sight from both sides. But I could tell from the wild desperation that widened his eyes and how his brows converged that he realized he couldn't win this one. Not bound the way he was. Not outnumbered by so many huge guys.

When Fury lunged for him, my brother latched onto his arm and yanked him forward, pulling them both off balance. Rage rumbled and shoved me roughly behind him as he prepared to intervene.

But as I lost my balance and hurried to sit on the floor before I could fall, Fury proved he didn't need his brother's help. He yanked Ky back with as much ferocity as Ky had pulled him, snapped a lightning-fast hand to his belt, and emerged with a knife.

"No!" I screamed while my heart took off like a wild stallion making a getaway.

Fury spun the blade so he held it upside-down, and slammed the hilt into the base of Ky's skull with a thud that made my scream strangle to a stop in my throat.

I'd thought he was going to slit Ky's throat—but of course they still needed us alive. Thank God.

As Ky slumped to the ground next to the man he'd knocked out, I couldn't help but be grateful things weren't worse. Yes, my standards were appallingly low. However, the longer we remained alive, the longer Sadie or Damon or the trolls or someone else had the chance to find us. Damon's semi-automatic rifle sure would come in handy right about now.

Rage heaved me up and across his back like a sack of flour. With my ass in the air, he stomped across the room, barking orders as he went. In seconds, Fury had slung my newly zip-tied brother across his back and stalked out after his alpha. The entourage of muscled, enraged shifters marched through the house, which might have seemed ordinary, even pleasant looking, if not for the fact that it was the scene of a dual kidnapping.

❧ 17 ❧

RAGE DEPOSITED ME ON THE RED ROCK OF THUNDER Mountain without preamble or care, more or less tossing me from his shoulder to the ground. Given that he was taller than Ky, the ride down was far from fun, especially since I couldn't do a thing to brace myself for the fall beyond twist my head up so it wouldn't hit. The impact rocked through my body as my arms and legs whined in complaint at their poor positioning. I'd never take freedom of movement for granted again, assuming I lived through the night to do so. My arms and shoulders were one mass of painful tingles, and my legs weren't much better. I blinked away tears that pricked from the sudden jolts of discomfort.

"Are you sure we have to be out here to do this?" Rage asked Jevan, who was already unpacking a large leather satchel that he'd slung across his chest, removing a series of small leather pouches and spreading them out on the ground in front of him.

"I'm sure," Jevan said distractedly, greedily taking

in his pouches. "I told you, the magic will be strongest here because of all the spells being performed within the mountain. It'd be better to do this inside the mountain, where the levels of power will be even stronger, but I take it you'd prefer to be out here."

Fury joined us and tossed Ky from his back to the ground with a bit more care than his brother had thrown me, but not by much. I winced as Ky's unconscious body slammed against hard dirt, his head clunking against the rock beneath it.

"You guys are real assholes, you know that?" I bit out. "You've decided your lives are more important than ours, but do you have to go out of your way to hurt us without need? What if you gave my brother a concussion throwing him like that?"

Fury almost looked apologetic for a moment, the planes of his face scrunching up into a grimacing wince beneath the silver light of the moon, low in the sky. But Rage? He went in the opposite direction. He looked pissed, as if I were the one in the wrong here instead of them.

"Your life and your brother's are now forfeit," Rage said. "Accept it and stop your whining before I decide to gag you."

One look at his cold eyes had me pressing my lips shut. He wouldn't hesitate to gag me. He probably wouldn't hesitate to beat the crap out of me if I said much more. Because he was a lunatic—in a leadership role. The shifter world had really gone to shit.

"Your brother probably already has a concussion,"

he continued. "He got hit on the back of the head at the house, or did you forget?"

I waggled my jaw as I forced myself to swallow the biting remark swirling around in my head. I never imagined I'd be capable of killing anyone, but now … if I had the chance, I'd kill the bastard, and I wouldn't even feel bad about it.

"Oh good, she figured out how to keep her trap shut," he remarked to his audience of hulky shifters as they settled into a circle around us. When he crouched next to me, I flinched before wishing I'd had more control of my reaction. I was scared out of my mind, for Ky and me, but I didn't have to broadcast that. I needed to find a way to make things better for us, not worse.

"Do what I tell you and I'll make sure you don't suffer any more than the transference spell requires. Got it?"

I tried to stare a hole through his head, but I sensed his anger building like a tangible wave, and I finally nodded, the back of my head scraping against the rock beneath me, my long hair trapped uncomfortably under my back.

Rolling to my side, I winced as the shifting of my weight sharpened the pain in my arms, but I needed to better see what was happening. I was relatively certain that we were on a different side of the mountain than where we usually arrived to enter the school. Rage, Fury, Jevan, and the handful of oversized minions had crammed us into three SUVs to get here, but I hadn't recognized where they'd parked. It wasn't the usual trailhead.

The circumference of Thunder Mountain was vast enough that even if someone were looking for us, they very well could miss us if they looked in the wrong place. Assuming they had any reason to search for us here. If I were on the other end of this, at the school trying to figure out where my friends had been taken, the mountain was the last place I'd look. Most kidnappers avoid exposed areas, especially those in close proximity to the site of the disappearances.

I tried not to lose hope entirely. Sadie was scrappy, and if she'd woken from whatever that traitor Wendi had done to her, then surely she was out looking for me. She would have roused Damon to join her. Hell, she probably would've put up the alarm all over the school, which would mean that Sir Lancelot would be directing the small army at his control.

But this assumed that Sadie had woken up. I knew little of spells, but I understood enough to realize they were incredibly powerful, and when under the control of one, you were unable to operate in the usual ways. My stomach sank. Wendi would have been certain to knock everyone of importance out for long enough to ensure she wasn't discovered, and apparently she was working with the vampire students. Between Paige's crew and Anton's, there were enough of them to knock out everyone who might want to look for us. I couldn't be sure Anton was involved, but I'd bet big money on it. And even though the vamps and the shifter Wendi wouldn't have the magic of a magician, spells and magical objects could be purchased—for the right price. The magical black market was alive and thriving, from what Jas had told me.

Ky and I were well and truly screwed.

Rage paced across the flat patch of rock that was apart from any evident trail. No one would come across us here by accident. Though Sedona was known for its many amazing trails, and hikers flocked to the area, no one in their right mind would be hiking in the middle of the night, and off trail to boot.

As much as I wanted to hope we'd be discovered and saved, the odds were terrifyingly low. If Ky and I were to survive this, it was all on me. And I was the least qualified of everyone here to save a thing.

Shit.

"All right," Jevan said. "I'm ready to start."

My blood chilled. So soon?

Rage spun to face the sorcerer, and Fury advanced closer too, neither one of them paying attention to Ky or me for the moment. Rage's underlings stood at attention, waiting for a command, but none of them watched me either. This was my opportunity, but for what? My brain fired off in a dozen different directions, but my thoughts were scattered, latching on to nothing useful.

I was bound, useless, and cut off from my shifter magic.

My mage magic.

That was it. Our only possibility. A fickle, unstable power I'd only managed to access once before, totally by accident, and never since.

Our chances sucked, but at least now we had one. It was a long shot, but a shot nonetheless.

I'd do this or I'd die trying. There was no in between.

"I think the power transference will be more effective if we do it with a conscious shifter," Jevan was saying, and every man swung his focus onto me. I hurried to school my features into defeated terror—easy enough to do—before they suspected something was up, that I had a plan.

"You *think*?" Rage said, his eyes on me though he spoke to the sorcerer. "The boy is probably more powerful than she is."

"Yeah, I *think*. I've never done this before. It's rarely done, for obvious reasons. Most people don't want to lose their power."

But this wasn't just about Ky and I losing our power. These asshats had decided to steal our lives too, when it apparently wasn't necessary. That's just the kind of awesome dudes they were.

"You came to me because I'm one of the best dark sorcerers there is," Jevan said, and I struggled to match the scrawny man with the choppy haircut and creepy looks to the best of anything. "I can do this, I'm sure of it. So do you want me to or not? I'm ready. The only one wasting time now is you."

Rage's shoulders visibly tensed beneath his short-sleeved t-shirt. I was certain no one talked to the head honcho shifter like this. Maybe I'd get lucky and Rage would kill Jevan before he could complete the spell. The way his eyes vibrated with anger, his mouth curling in a vicious sneer, it was definitely possible.

It appeared that Jevan arrived at the identical conclusion. "I'll start with the girl," he said hurriedly. "I'll be able to feel her power as it streams through to Fury since she's awake. Maybe by then the brother will come to."

I shivered in the chill of the night. It wasn't quite spring, and the nights in the desert were still cold. The ground beneath me radiated the chill through every part of my body. But the shivers that racked me now had as much to do with the disinterest with which the sorcerer spoke of taking our lives as it did with the temperature.

"Where do you need 'er?" Rage asked.

"Let me set up my circle of energy first. I'll link the elements with my ingredients and build the base of the spell. But once I do, I won't be able to give you instructions. I'll be linked into the circle too. So watch for my nod. When I signal, roll her into the circle. Do *not* step inside it, or you'll screw everything up. Nothing else can touch the circle once I start."

"And Fury?"

"I'll nod again when I'm ready for Fury. He can step inside the circle and sit directly across from the girl." Though Fury was standing right there, Jevan addressed his alpha. "He'll need to walk in barefoot and place his palms against the earth. We need to be strongly connected to the earth element to pull on her strength."

It seemed wrong that someone preparing to

perform such foul magic should speak so reverently of the earth. He obviously respected the elements and his magic, he just didn't respect life. At least not ours.

Jevan kicked off his shoes, pulled off his socks, rolled them and neatly tucked them inside his shoes, which he set several feet behind him. His care for his effing socks and shoes pissed me the hell off, shaking me up and loosening the uncontrollable shivers that had hold of me. Surely the men had noticed my discomfort, but not one of them offered me a layer of warmth. To them, I was dead already.

Finally, the sorcerer faced Fury. "You don't have to do anything once you're in the circle other than keep your hands and feet against the earth at all times. The girl's power will go directly into you as I guide it. As long as you don't do anything to interfere with the transference, you'll get what you came here for."

Fury nodded with a glance at me, but he quickly looked away in the manner of someone struggling with his guilt. Still, he wasn't feeling badly enough to stop what was about to happen, so I'd still kill him if I got the chance. The world was messed up enough without creatures like these in it.

"Any final questions?" Jevan asked Rage and Fury. "Or should I get started?"

A rock slid somewhere in the distance, and Rage, Fury, and the rest of the posse whirled to check it out. I waited, my heart beating in my throat, hoping it was a rescue team.

But nothing but the deep silence of the night emerged from that direction, and finally Rage turned back to Jevan. "Must've been a wild animal. Start. We'll make sure nothing interferes."

"Good. Complete silence from here on out," Jevan said as he rose.

I grinned for a quick second. If all it took to throw off his spell was an interruption or two, that I could do. I'd wait until the spell was close to complete, and then yell out so that he'd either have to start all over again, or abandon it entirely. I had no idea how a transference spell worked, but if silence was important, I'd give him its opposite.

"Gag her," Rage ordered one of his men, and I whipped my gaze up to his. Triumph shone from his eyes as I realized I'd revealed my thoughts on my face.

How could I have been so stupid? Finally I'd had an advantage and I'd messed it up.

"No," I cried out as a small mountain of a man knelt beside me and reached across my face with a long piece of cloth. "No!" I thrashed my head every which way, but a second beast joined the first and held my head still with hands strong enough to crush my skull. The pressure of his fingertips against my cranium was powerful enough to freak me out. He was hurting me! I'd never felt more fragile in my life.

The other shifter dropped the cloth in my mouth, wrapped it around my head, tangling it in my hair, and cinched it tight, pulling clumps of my hair into the knot. My eyes watered and I gagged against the cloth, trying to cough and failing. I breathed heavily through my nose, pulling in the scent of old, dusty rag. Yuck.

But then Jevan started his spell and I couldn't tear my eyes from his slight frame as he laid his ingredients around him in a large circle, muttering under his breath so softly that I thought he must not want the shifters to hear. I caught snatches of words—magic, power, shifter, cost, and references to elements and ingredients.

I followed his movements as he placed each one of the small pouches on the ground with care, peering at them to make sure they were equidistant. If one of the pouches contained the bone marrow of a poor dwarf, what the hell did the others hold?

My breathing was coming too fast and too heavy over the gag when I felt power building within the circle a few feet away from me. *Get your act together, Rina. It's now or never.*

With a final look at Ky, who remained unmoving in the precise spot where Fury had unceremoniously deposited him, I closed my eyes and worked to push the hushed mutterings of the freaky sorcerer away. When that didn't work, I steeled my nerves and reached for the powers that had eluded me since last term.

Glowy, goopy mage magic, I need you now.

I reached deep within me, hoping to find it like I'd never hoped for anything before.

❧ 18 ❧

WHEN THE SORCERER CEASED HIS MUMBLING AND placed the final pouch on the ground, completing the circle, energy blasted outward in a wave strong enough to slide me back across the rock a few inches. It whisked across my prone body, temporarily warming my skin. But as it passed, it left behind a chill far worse than that caused by the bite in the late night air. The spell Jevan was building was powerful; I had no doubt it would accomplish what he said it would.

I threw a final frantic glance at our surroundings, twisting my head against the rough rock, my hair pulling with every desperate movement. But beyond the sage brush, Juniper trees, cactuses, and an array of other prickly plants, I spotted nothing that could help us.

Though it went against every one of my instincts, I closed my eyes. I wouldn't be able to focus with the stares of the sorcerer and nasty shifters, with the view of my brother's slumped body. Once I'd blocked them out, I immediately attempted to reach for my mage power. But when I searched, I struggled to move past the reality of my circumstances. They were too damning, too overwhelming, and devastatingly stacked against me. A seed of a defeated sob bounced around deep inside me a bit too much like a death rattle.

Tears burned behind my eyelids. I couldn't do this. What I was trying was freaking impossible! I was reaching for magic I wasn't even sure I had when that effer Jevan was minutes away from killing me just for funsies. Mages studied a lifetime to properly control their powers. The Magical Arts Academy was an entire school set up to teach mages how to do what I was trying to do on the fly.

I sucked in air around my gag, working to calm myself. It only seemed to accentuate my desperation. I was bound, gagged, and collared. I was fucked!

Huge, strong muscled arms swept under my body and I squeaked against the gag. My eyes flew open, and I stared up into the determined, furious planes of Rage's face. Far too soon, I was airborne. Instead of rolling me, he tossed me over the circle. I landed on my side with a loud snap that rang out into the otherwise silent night.

I winced against the onslaught of pain. My eyes watered, and I began to breathe too heavily through my nose. The mother-freaking-effer had broken my arm. I had no idea what part of it had snapped, since the entire damn appendage was blazing like the fires of hell, or wherever bastards like this went once they died—hopefully after a slow and pain-filled death.

With my arms bound behind my back, and torturous tingles racing everywhere, all I could determine for sure was that my body was broken.

And yet, the searing pain zoomed right past my frantic, harried thoughts to deliver pure, blessed clarity —or at least as much of it as I could access through the multiple avenues of pain. The asshole had just given me the edge I needed. I'd get us free and kill him. Twice.

Jevan's eyes were wide but he didn't stop. His mumbling resumed, and this time his attention was directed at me. He was working to link me into the foundation he'd laid for his spell.

I clenched my eyes shut and got to work. What had I done to bring about the glowy, goopy magic that first time? I hadn't understood much then, and any helpful memories of that day a semester ago were beyond my reach now. No matter. I'd find another way.

If my shifter magic was an inherent part of me, inherited from my mother along with the rest of her genetic coding, then my mage power should be the same. Passed on through my father's lineage, it should be an essential part of me in the same way my mountain lion was. The more I connected with my lion, the more I discovered that she was always with me. Even if I didn't reach for her, she was just beneath the surface of my human form. She was a part of me, as essential as my heart and lungs.

My mage magic should be the same, woven into

the fabric of my very being. All I had to do was identify it.

My breathing was ragged, condensation gathering on the rag, moistening it. The breath I sucked in didn't quite fill my lungs. My left arm throbbed from fingertips to shoulder, the pain radiating into my neck and clavicle. My legs were numb to the point of agony. And I'd never been colder in my life.

Yet I managed to push the physical sensations away. Mind over matter. The discomfort receded, not enough to afford me true relief, but enough that I could focus beyond the limitations of my body.

My mage magic was almost certainly linked to my body, but a greater part of it must be connected to my mind, heart, and spirit. I envisioned calmness settling across me, filling me, and I reached for whatever made me a witch: the ability to create a different reality from what would have otherwise existed without my magic. What within me allowed me to manipulate reality and shift it? Where would that power be?

Bare feet padded near me, followed by a faint shuffling as Fury claimed his seat in the circle and slapped the palms of his hands against the rock.

I swallowed my fear and pressed onward. Where did I feel my power? Where was the magic hiding from me?

I scanned my mind and quickly abandoned the search. Panic was all I encountered there. I reached for my heart and spirit, whatever it was that distinguished me from the rock beneath me and gave me life, able to interact with the world and adjust its outcome. My heart beat steadily at what was likely twice its average speed, but I didn't sense anything unusual there. I moved outward toward my essence, toward that feeling of true me-ness.

There.

My heart thudded and I gasped, though around the gag I suspected my captors wouldn't notice. I'd found it, or at least I thought I had. There, mingled with everything I identified with my true self—my dreams, passions, fears, and longings—was a spark of something so powerful and so alive that it had to be it. It had to be magic. It was alive, and though it was an innate, deep part of me, it also felt apart from me, as if it were something with its own essence and identity.

Hot tears burned behind my eyelids, this time from relief. Before I could think that I had no idea what to do with this magic now that I'd found it, I reached for it, extending my consciousness toward it. I pictured my essence, my energy, reaching for this intangible magic. I extended an invisible hold and enveloped the mage magic in my grateful embrace. I held it against my center like a treasure and sighed as its warmth spread from my core outward to my limbs.

Okay. Now all I had to do was use the magic to break the zip ties limiting my movements and break the collar around my neck that prevented my shift. With any luck, much of my broken arm would heal once I shifted, and I'd be able to free Ky and get us out of here.

I hesitated. Even whole and healed, I was no match for Rage or Fury, not to mention the dark sorcerer and the hulky minions. I couldn't rely on my newly discovered witchiness to fight them. They outnumbered and outpowered me a gazillion to one.

My better bet was Ky. He at least wasn't injured, and he was far stronger and more capable of fighting them off than I was. If I could manage to snap off his collar, then he might be able to shift and break free of the zip ties just by transforming. The proportions of our lions were so different than those of our human bodies, there was a chance the zip ties would simply slide off after his shift. Of course, Ky was unconscious, but maybe I could, you know, zap him awake.

Oh my God. My plan had holes in it the size of Texas. If I pulled this off, it'd be the biggest underdog win in all of history.

Jevan's mumbling rose in volume until I could make out some of the words—none of them encouraging—before they escalated into a crescendo that felt all too final as it rang out into the night.

I was out of time. I scrambled to clench the mage magic in my hold and aim it at Ky. In my mind's eye, I pictured the collar around his neck popping open. Just like that, *pop*. But just as I was about to fling my magic in his direction, Jevan's magic—dark and insidious—reached inside me to mingle with my own.

No! No, no, no.

Greedy claws raked through my etheric body, searching for my shifter power. I felt Jevan's spell land on my mage magic first, and I snatched away my father's ancestry, holding it with an iron will. I would *not* let Jevan take all of my magic, and since he wasn't aware that I was a dual mage-shifter—you know, since they weren't supposed to exist—I had a chance at keeping it. I clutched my witch power with the entirety of my determination ... leaving my shifter magic wholly exposed. I wasn't sure I could protect both, and I didn't dare release my focus from my mage powers to test my abilities.

I sensed the instant Jevan's spell alighted on my shifter power. My mountain lion reared inside me in protest, kicking and clawing from the start, fighting to overcome her invisible opponent. My heart wrenched when she roared, her protest reverberating inside me, shaking my core, though I doubted the sound extended beyond my being. It felt as if she looked to me for aid, and my heart broke as I accepted that I couldn't help her. I was abandoning her when she needed me most, and I was going to lose her because of it. I threatened to break entirely right then ... but no, I had to fight on.

She snarled and whipped her head around in a frenzy, but Jevan's magic was drawing her out, dragging her out from my being.

I'm so sorry, girl. I'm so incredibly sorry. If there's any way to get you back, I promise you I will. I'll fight for you with everything I have.

I was a hypocrite. I was choosing to play it safe and keep my mage magic rather than fight for her now and risk losing both. After this, there might never be another chance. In fact, it was pretty much guaranteed.

My lion was about to lose her fight. I had to seize

my chance. I had no idea what losing my lion might do to my mage magic, but surely it'd do something. My shifter and mage powers were deep parts of me; certainly the loss of one would spin the other into some sort of imbalance. I couldn't guarantee that I'd be able to use my mage magic at all after losing her.

I put the entirety of my witch powers behind my vision of Ky's collar snapping, the blast of magic waking him so he could fight our opponents. Then, before it was too late, I shoved every last bit of my mage magic into my intention … and released it like a loaded exhale, sending it out, aimed straight for my brother.

I lost my focus. I had no idea whether it had worked or not. My lion was mostly freed of my etheric body, hanging from her claws as if draped over an abyss. Without thinking, I lunged for her, directing tendrils of my mind to latch onto her, to give her a hand to hang on, to return to me, to win this fight with the dastardly sorcerer.

But as I reached for her, my desperation fueling me to grab her in time, she slipped. Her claws grasped thin air. Her golden copper eyes seared into my being until they faded away, along with the rest of her. I hoped the betrayal I'd felt from her had been a product of my guilty imagination, since this had all played out in my internal vision, but I wasn't so sure. I'd failed my lion, and chunks of my already broken heart flecked off as she vanished from my senses entirely.

My breath stuttered in my chest as I processed that

I couldn't feel her anymore. The familiar buzz of her energy was absent, as if it had never been a part of me.

I opened my eyes, and right away Fury captured my full attention. He sat in the circle across from me, knees bent, his feet flat against the ground, his hands next to them. His head tilted back while his mouth hung open … sucking in a golden-coppery stream of light.

My lion.

A whimper escaped me around the gag, but no one looked my way. The scene engulfing Fury was mesmerizing. His short hair rustled in every direction beneath the forces of an invisible wind, the fabric of his t-shirt flapping too. The beam of light originated from me and traveled directly into him … until the golden tendrils of magic shifted, traversing the space between us, and entered him all the way.

The light ceased, and he swallowed, his Adam's apple bobbing. When he snapped his mouth shut, he tilted his face forward, and I swallowed in abject fear. His eyes glowed with the same golden copper of my eyes—and Ky's. Fury had my lion. He'd stolen her, and she was beyond my reach.

Emptiness raced through my insides, like a raging river carving out a canyon. I experienced the loss of my lion as truly as if both my legs had been amputated. Though I'd still been working to understand her and our connection, she'd been one of the most important things to ever happen to me.

Now she was gone, lost to me forever.

I didn't bother trying to staunch the tears. These fuckers could stuff it.

I wrenched heavy, pained eyes toward my brother … and his eyes popped open and stared straight at me.

❧ 19 ❧

UNLIKE ME, KY DIDN'T WASTE PRECIOUS TIME. I WAS
trying to broadcast to him that I might have broken
the spell that controlled his collar, but around a gag
and with my hands tied, there was no good way to get
my meaning across. He stared at me for only a few
beats before snapping his gaze across the rocky ledge.
It took him mere seconds to take in the scene, illuminated by the light of a nearly full moon. I couldn't tell
if he realized that Jevan had already succeeded in
transferring my power to Fury, but either way, all that
mattered was that he shift and get us out of there.

Entranced by Fury's receipt of my power, none of
the shifters had noticed that my brother was awake.
Not even Jevan, who was positioned so that my
brother was directly behind Fury, appeared to pay
attention to his subtle movements.

When the edges of Ky's body began to blur, relief
flooded me. He'd understood my signals, or he'd realized on his own. Either way, once he shifted, at the

very least he should be able to escape before the others in their human forms could catch him.

I'd never seen him shift so quickly. One moment he was a human, tied up with nothing on but his boxers, and the next he was a glorious mountain lion, an apex predator, all fine-tuned muscle and lethal instincts. The zip ties had simply disappeared along with his underwear, as if they were just another accessory.

I did my best to ignore the pang of loss that arrived with my admiration of his animal, but I didn't succeed. I suspected I'd probably never stop mourning the loss of my shifter magic.

Ky took off the instant he landed on four strong paws. He raced past Fury, aiming for the sorcerer. Jevan squeaked, backpedaling across the rock as if he were a crab. He knocked into a couple of his precious pouches, breaking the circle of power. My brother lunged at him with open jaws, snapping them around his neck, piercing his jugular. Blood spurted across Ky's golden fur while the life drained from Jevan's eyes.

The entire process from shift to kill attack had probably lasted less than ten seconds. As Ky dropped the sorcerer's throat, the shifters around us jumped into action, including Fury, who shot to his feet. Blood pooled around the rock beneath Jevan's head, but no one paid him any mind.

Ky moved between me and the guys, lowering his head and growling, the fur around his mouth a bloody red. Rage and Fury squared off to face him, the other shifters lining up behind them. I was torn between wanting Ky to run away and save himself, and my terror at him abandoning me to a certain fate. Rage's brow was lowered in menace, and his lips twitched, baring teeth. He'd kill me the first chance he got after Ky had messed up the rest of his plan.

The crackling and snapping of bones, cartilage, and flesh punctuated the night. I would have recoiled, assuming the sounds accompanied pain, but I found a dark part of myself enjoying whatever suffering they might be enduring. While their bodies began to distort, each in different ways and at different speeds, Ky pounced on Fury. His teeth tore through the jeans the shifter wore, leaving a gaping hole. He snapped at his exposed calf, slicing through muscle until he clamped down on the bone. Fury howled, a sound halfway between human and beast, before he clenched his jaw and quieted. His eyes blazed, and he kicked his leg out, trying to dislodge Ky.

But Ky was a step ahead of him. He released his hold on Fury's leg and pierced his teeth into the shifter's bare forearm, crunching and grinding his teeth until he snapped the bone into shards. This time the shifter whimpered and collapsed to the ground, his shift temporarily halted, leaving him deformed, half man, half beast. Fur rippled along his forearm, trying to reach the site of injury, to accelerate healing, I imagined; it failed, as if his magic—*my* magic—were unable to prevail through the severity of the pain. He crumpled in a moaning heap, creating a second pool of blood, which appeared black beneath the moonlight.

By then, Rage's shift was complete, and a couple of the shifters behind him seemed as if they weren't far behind. Instead of running to his brother's aid, he sped toward me. I screamed against my gag. I would like to say it was because I was trying to alert Ky, but the reality was that the look in the eyes of Rage's lion chilled my blood. They promised vengeance and destruction, and I had no doubt he'd kill me as swiftly as Ky had ended Jevan.

Ky leapt at Rage and intercepted him, knocking the lion to the ground. Rage landed with a snarl and a whoosh of air, but claimed his paws immediately, turning his ire on Ky. The two lions circled each other, Ky being careful not to turn his back to the five other uninjured shifters, while also keeping them away from me. It was a losing proposition. All he could do was hold them off. Eventually, they'd corner him. There was no avoiding it, not when Ky and Rage were so evenly matched. Three of Rage's minions were large werewolves, and I couldn't tell what the other two were yet, slower to transform than the rest.

"Get out of here, Ky!" I screamed. Around my gag, it sounded like an impersonation of the teachers in Charlie Brown's *Peanuts*. Still, there was a good chance he'd get the gist. "Leave me!" I insisted.

He ignored me, continuing with his fruitless maneuvers.

A howl split the tension. A fresh wave of shivers raced across my skin.

The other shifters tensed, but not Ky. He bobbed his head forward and back, as if seeking an opening to attack Rage.

That's when I knew. If Ky wasn't worried, then that must mean he'd recognized the wolf howl. And if he'd recognized the wolf, it had to mean it was someone we knew.

My heart leapt in my chest as I indulged in a fresh wave of hope. Could it be that the troops had finally arrived to rescue us? The shivers began racking my body in earnest, the adrenaline, I assumed, catapulting the cold to another level. I scooted my body around the rock ledge, scraping myself along fragments of rock while trying to angle myself so I could see in the direction the howl had seemed to spring from.

A large shape flickered across the moon, blotting its silver light. I squeaked as I startled, blinking repeatedly as I tried to make sense of the image crystallizing in front of me, swooping closer.

A humongous bird, ten, maybe even twenty times the size of a regular bird of prey, flew directly at me. The moonlight glinted across its body, wings outstretched, casting it in a silver glow.

I squeaked again as the bird—no, not just any bird, an eagle—extended its monstrous talons toward me, even though by then I suspected who this might be. Still, I couldn't help it. The bird was ginormous, and those talons … well, they looked like they could slice right through me with as much efficiency as Ky's jaws.

In no more time than it took me to admire the

grace of his flight and the span of his wings, the eagle grazed across the ledge, gathering me in its talons. One wrapped around my bound legs, the other around my torso, their pointed ends slightly puncturing my flesh, though I didn't think Leander could help this. His talons were sharp as razors.

I lost sight of Ky and the seven shifters who faced off with him—more like six and a half, since Fury was severely injured—while the giant eagle rose to the top of Thunder Mountain. Though the mountain was more than six-thousand feet tall, Leander covered the distance in less than a minute. He set me against the prickly, harsh surface of stone with extreme gentleness, and I resisted the fresh wave of emotion that threatened to spring loose. That he should treat me with infinite care when Rage and his accomplices had mistreated me so...

I writhed on the loose rock that coated the mountain until I noticed the eagle shifting. A burst of silver light flashed around the eagle ... leaving the striking elfin prince in its stead.

"Rina," Leander breathed, rushing toward me while slipping a pocket knife into his hand. With two fast swipes, he freed me of the zip ties. He helped me to sit and worked carefully at the knot on the gag, untangling the hair from it before slipping it off.

I rubbed gingerly at my tender wrists while I shook out my legs. "Oh my God, thank you." I labored not to grimace against the fresh onslaught of discomfort as unhindered blood flow returned to my limbs, throbbing like a thumping bass beat along the length of my arm.

He sank to his knees by my side, his brows low with concern. "Are you all right?"

"Ky! We have to help Ky," I said.

"It's all right. I didn't come alone. The others are helping him now."

"Who? Who's helping him?"

He bent over me, and his brow creased even further at the urgency in my voice. "Boone and Marcy June came as their animals. Two of the vamp professors, Damante and Vabu. Quickfoot and McGinty. A bunch of the trolls and a few Enforcers that were manning the perimeter. Oh, and Damon and Sadie of course, and Wendi."

"Wendi," I said on a sharp inhale. "She's the one who betrayed us. Along with some vamp students."

He straightened his back. "Wendi? You're sure?"

"Totally sure."

"Then we need to get back down there and warn them." He stood, preparing to leave.

"Just leave me. I'll slow you down. Get there as fast as you can and warn them."

"Rina, I'm not leaving you ever again."

I was in the midst of puzzling out what the heck that might mean when wings burst from his back in a flash of silver magic. My mouth dropped open and I didn't even care. With his wings spread wide, moonlight illuminating his silver hair and coating his wings in the same tones, he was more beautiful than any man I'd ever seen—or supernatural creature, rather.

His chest was bare, and he wore nothing beyond thin pajama pants, which revealed the contours of his body that would undoubtedly visit my dreams later. He was the most splendid elfin prince eagle man I'd ever seen.

"Come on," he said, bringing my gawking to a swift end while he tucked my gag into a back pocket of his pajama pants.

I tried to stand, pushing up on my good arm, but fell back down. "Sorry, I was tied up for too long. My legs—oh!"

Leander swooped me up from the ground and cradled me in his arms, pressed against his bare, muscular chest. "Hold on," he said, and I nodded, unwilling to complain about the nature of my rescue. He ran toward the edge of the mountain and leapt off the side of it. I couldn't even manage a startled scream, my eyes were so wide, my heart thundering in my chest, as if bouncing against my aching ribcage. I wrapped my good arm around his neck, while cradling the injured one in my lap, and held on for dear life. We dropped into a dead fall for several hundred feet before he spread his wide wings and gentled our descent. I loosened the death grip I had on him, but only slightly.

"Don't worry. I've got you," he said. "I'll always protect you now."

Whatever that meant. He still had a king for a father, who wouldn't allow us to be together.

He set down on a neighboring ledge with the gentleness of experience. But he didn't release his grip on me as he moved across the rock, steps sure despite his bare feet.

"Are you going to put me down?" I asked.

"No, not any time soon."

Ooo-kay then.

He set off toward the others, the grunts, snarls, and whimpers of a full-out brawl leading the way. I exhaled in relief, the shivers finally ceasing completely as I took in the scene. Not only was Ky safe, but he had a small platoon at his back attacking the five shifters, though half were already disabled from severe injuries.

Bloody hell. Five shifters! "Where are Rage and Fury?" I called out.

Sadie whipped her head toward me. "Took off when Leander grabbed you. Fucking cowards." She smiled in that deranged way of hers as she sliced at a rust-colored wolf in front of her, or maybe it was all the blood making his coat seem that color. Her curved blade hacked through its side, and it fell, heaving against the cold rock.

Damon was at her side, his semi-automatic strapped to his back, but he wasn't using it. Fighting another wolf with his bare hands, he was punishing the creature. There was no way any of Rage's minions would walk away from here alive. The shifter world was merciless in more ways than one. The Enforcers were authorized to mete out appropriate punishment on the spot, though Sadie probably would have killed them all whether she had the authority or not.

Three trolls, with their bright fro-hawks pulled up into high knots atop their heads, were taking on a bear and a lion, like a king of the jungle kind of lion, with Quickfoot and McGinty getting their own punishment in alongside them. The two vamp professors stood over the incredibly still body of a wolf. Ky paced along the ledge, his muscles rippling with each taut movement while he peered into the night in search of unseen dangers.

"Where are Marcy June and Boone?" I asked.

"Off tracking Rage and Fury," Damon said.

"Fury was super injured," Sadie said. "They won't get far with Rage carrying him. And MJ and Boone have some trolls with them too."

"Good. And where's Wendi?"

Sadie straddled the wolf she was fighting and sliced clean across its throat. Blood spurted from the gaping wound, painting more of the rock ledge in crimson. "I don't know where she went," Sadie said, as if she really couldn't care less about Wendi.

"Well, we'd better find her. She betrayed all of us."

Every defender there turned to level a narrow-eyed gaze on me. I squirmed in Leander's strong arms, suddenly all too aware that I was practically naked. "Some vamp students too." I leveled a meaningful look on the two vamp professors.

"If that's the case, then we'll deal with them," Professor Damante said in an Arctic tone while Vabu gave an abrupt nod, his face a rigid mask of whoop-ass. Oh shit. The vamp professors were seriously pissed. "We'll talk once this"—Damante gestured toward the bloody brawl that was winding down—"is finalized."

I probably should have said something, but the cold stares of the two vamps had my tongue twisted in knots several times over. I gulped and nodded, then purposefully trained my gaze on Sadie.

If I thought the vamps were pissed, I hadn't seen Sadie yet. She looked positively murderous, thoughts of her revenge glinting in her eyes. "That fucking..." She trailed off and growled like a shifter, her nostrils flaring. "I'm going to kill her. I don't care that we're supposed to take Enforcers to Thane. I'm gonna kill her myself."

"Sadie..." Damon placed a calming hand on her shoulder, though his hand was covered in blood. "Think this through."

"No need. I already know what I'm going to do. Come on. We have a bitch to find."

Damon stared at her with a tight grimace, then finally nodded. Together, they stalked off in the opposite direction, then loped off in a run, Damon's gun bouncing against his back, until the night swallowed them whole.

Ky edged toward Leander and me, sniffing at my feet. He was trailing his nose across my legs when a deep sorrow shadowed his coppery lion eyes.

He'd scented the loss of my shifter magic. Every fear and every loss of the night bubbled inside me like a rushing tsunami.

I couldn't bear to meet the torment in my brother's gaze. I allowed my head to fall limply against Leander's chest. Every ounce of fight I had left evaporated all at once. "Please take me home." Only after I said it did I realize that I was nowhere near Iowa, and I wasn't really sure where home was anymore.

But Leander simply nodded, his eyes welling with understanding and compassion. He beat his gigantic wings as he leapt into the sky, leaving the bloody scene behind. If only I could have left the depth of my loss behind just as easily.

At least Ky and I had lived. I'd allow myself to focus on that amazing blessing. It was a small miracle that we'd survived the night.

Right away, my heart disobeyed my wishes; it gaped like a festering wound; silent tears trailed down my cheeks and onto Leander's chest. I closed my eyes and allowed his warmth to calm me. The night was all encompassing as we merged with it.

❧ 20 ❧

NEARLY TWO WEEKS PASSED, HALF OF WHICH I SPENT IN the healing ward under Melinda's care, recovering from a fractured arm and two cracked ribs. Sparring between shifters was a dangerous activity, and I'd witnessed the badger repairing physical injuries graver than mine in far less time. With the way Melinda fussed over me, I had the feeling she was more concerned about my non-physical trauma. The mother hen couldn't bear to let me go when my heart was so obviously broken.

In the school's century-long history, never before had a shifter lost her magic. Sir Lancelot had informed me that in his many ages of life, he'd never witnessed a power transference spell. It was magic so dark that few sorcerers dared attempt it. According to the headmaster, when a sorcerer used magic to create an imbalance, as happened when stealing another's power or taking their life, it tarnished their very soul, thus ensuring that few magicians were willing to engage in such practices.

Though Sir Lancelot had been seriously aggrieved by the situation, apologizing profusely for the invasion of the school's defenses as if he'd been the one to kidnap me himself, he'd told me that he didn't have the authority to override the school's decision if it should choose to kick me out. The Academy Spell, which governed everything about the Menagerie, including student attendance, would decide whether I was allowed to remain at the school. I imagined that, without shifter magic, I no longer belonged at an academy for magical creatures, and that the Academy Spell would give me the boot sooner or later. The owl's somber eyes didn't dispute my conclusion. I was playing a very un-fun game of wait and see.

With a rigid posture, the owl had proceeded to inform me that Professors Damante and Vabu had dealt with the offending vamp students. I'd been right about Anton's involvement, and he and his crew of three, who followed him everywhere, along with Paige and her three vampire tagalongs, would never bother me again. When I'd pressed the headmaster, he'd grudgingly revealed that the academy wasn't in the habit of executing its students, no matter how severe their crimes. Damante and Vabu had placed them in a stasis that would last a hundred years. For the next century, the immortal vampires would sleep while the world changed around them. After that, Damante and Vabu would wake them and evaluate whether additional punishment was required to ensure they learned their lessons. Apparently, Professor Vabu, who was actually Count Vladimir Vabu in title, had been around for several centuries already, and had been a part of the original Magical Arts Academy staff. Go figure. When dealing with supernaturals, assumptions were a risky proposition. Professor Lorenzo Damante seemed to be nearly as old as Vabu given the hints I garnered from the chatty owl, who seemed unable to remain tight-lipped even when he was trying to be discreet. His regular visits to my sickbed had been most informative.

But as forthcoming as Sir Lancelot had been, I was left with a lot of questions, along with the discovery that the loquacious owl was fond of tangents, and it wasn't always possible to guide him in the direction I wanted before Fianna or Nessa fetched him for "important business." I still had to find out what had happened to Wendi, Rage, and Fury. Sadie would have no problem telling me exactly what went down, but I hadn't seen my protector since that night, nor had I seen Damon either. Replacement Enforcers guarded Ky and me while the other two were off "dealing with things." Their stand-ins hadn't told Ky or me what Sadie and Damon were up to, but knowing Sadie, they were kicking ass.

Not even Leander or Boone, the usually well informed sons of kings and alphas, had the whole story, which was why I was supremely excited to make my way to the dining hall for the first time since the kidnapping. Ky, Leander, and Boone had swung by my room to pick me up, with news that Sadie and Damon were back and would meet us for lunch. Our temporary Enforcer bodyguards rotated out, and today two tall, lanky shifters, who might have been fraternal twins, followed several paces behind us, twitchy hands skimming across the hilts of the swords that hung from their belts.

Leander squeezed my hand as he walked alongside me. Though it'd seemed as if he'd smashed through the barriers between us on the night of my rescue, we hadn't had whatever talk he'd been planning before the kidnapping. He'd visited me plenty during my recovery, but we'd barely had a moment alone.

Wren, Jas, Dave, and Adalia had been constant fixtures nearly as much as Leander, and even Ky and Boone. They all seemed to rotate visits according to class schedules, as if they didn't want me to be left alone for long. I was the sole one exempt from classes. I suspected Melinda had convinced Sir Lancelot to excuse me from course requirements for the rest of the term to avoid additional stressors, or whatever her excuse might have been to cover for the true reason. I needed the time to mourn; my friends had barely given it to me, and even then only by accident, when none of them could be there with me, like when they all shared Defensive Creature Magic 101. Obviously I had no need of Marcy June's class now, as I was no longer a creature by definition. I was a lost, broken soul...

I was too numb to care sufficiently about the things that might have consumed me before. I simply wasn't the same Rina as I'd been before Jevan syphoned off my shifter magic. I feared the loss of my lion had somehow fractured my soul, but I didn't share that deep, dark secret fear with anyone. I privately worried that I might never recover.

"What are you thinking about?"

Leander's softly spoken question startled me. I'd barely noticed our surroundings as we meandered. I blinked rapidly, bringing my brain into focus. "We're on the other side of the quad. I thought we were going to the dining hall?"

"We are." He smiled tentatively. "We were giving you time to work through whatever you were thinking about."

"Oh. Uh, thanks, I guess." A couple of weeks ago I would have been shocked at their consideration. Not anymore. The whole lot of them treated me like I was made of porcelain.

I purposefully ignored his question about what I was thinking about. "We can head to the dining hall now. I really want to see Sadie."

"Me too," Ky said. "They'd better have caught Wendi." He kicked at the grass in front of him hard enough to tear it up in two angry divots. "I can't believe Rage and Fury got away." He growled, and hearing his lion so close to the surface made me miss mine with a physical pang through the chest.

"Don't worry. We'll get them," Boone said, his voice as fierce as Ky's. "The term is almost over. We can hunt them over the break. We'll find them."

"You can't be serious," I said.

"Of course we're serious," Ky said. "After what

they did to you, we're going to hunt them down and make them pay."

"That's the job of the Enforcers, not yours. What if they do the same thing to you as they did to me, huh? You can't put yourself at risk like that. Both of you."

"They have no need for another transference spell. They got what they wanted. Now they just need to die."

"Damn right," Boone encouraged. "My dad was furious when he found out. He's offered to send some of his wolves to help." Boone leaned in front of his friends to meet eyes with me. "You know the Enforcers are understaffed after the Attack, Rina. They don't have the manpower to track them when there's so much other shit going on."

"Well, then maybe they shouldn't spare the two Enforcers who guard Ky and me. If Rage and Fury got what they wanted, there's no need for them."

Leander growled fiercely, something I'd never heard the more composed shifter do. Startled, I spun to face him. "So long as Rage and Fury are out there, you need the protection," he said.

"I hope you're not going along with Ky and Boone on this hunting deal."

"No, I'm leaving tracking Rage and Fury to them. I'm not leaving your side until we're sure you're safe."

Ky nodded his agreement, delivering another shock. I narrowed eyes at him. "You're okay with this? With Leander and me spending time together?"

"I think he can keep you safe." Ky started leading us toward the dining hall in a clear evasive technique.

"You didn't answer my question."

His back muscles scrunched as he shrugged up ahead of me. "Boone and Marcy June should've been able to track them. Fury was dripping tons of blood, for fuck's sake. He should've left an obvious trail. That Boone and Marcy June didn't find them doesn't sit well with me."

"Agreed," Boone said. "The trolls didn't scent anything either, and they're decent trackers too."

Leander squeezed my hand again. "We're worried Rage and Fury might have had some help in getting away."

I swallowed thickly. "What kind of help? Like dark sorcerer help?"

"Maybe. We're not sure. We just know they shouldn't have been able to get away, not like they did. They vanished without a trace."

I brought my free hand up to rub at my forehead, grateful that Melinda was as skilled as she was. I felt no more than a twinge of discomfort from my broken arm and cracked ribs. Life shouldn't be this freaking complicated. I was a student, for goodness' sake. This was supposed to be a carefree time in my life. At this point, I wondered if I'd ever be carefree again.

Ky clapped a rough hand on my shoulder. "Don't worry, squirt. We'll deal with it."

"That's not particularly reassuring, Ky. You're my brother, and I don't want anything to happen to Boone either."

"Are you insulting our rugged manliness, saying we can't take care of ourselves?" Boone's smile made it obvious he was trying to make light of the situation, but the tension riding his shoulders canceled out his efforts.

I made my own attempt at a smile. "I'd never insult your rugged manliness, Boone. I'm not crazy." But I wasn't entirely certain I wasn't. The loss of my lion left me feeling off kilter, like something was terribly wrong with me.

"Rina! Hold up," Jas yelled as she, Wren, and Dave walked from the direction of Bundry Hall, from the shifter practice room, I'd bet. Leander, Ky, Boone, and I, along with the bodyguards, stopped to wait for them by the entrance of the dining hall.

"Hey, everyone," Jas said when they were close enough, though her attention was zeroed in on my brother, sweeping up and down his body before looking at me. "I can't believe you get out of Basic Shifting, Rina. You're so lucky." Jas continued toward the double doors to the dining hall, expecting us all to follow, totally oblivious to her insensitivity. At least some things never changed.

We traipsed inside behind her, taking up an entire table while our bodyguards claimed the one next to ours. "Where's Sadie?" I asked, scanning the large, crowded room.

"Here," she said, startling the crap out of me, and laughing uproariously when I jumped about a foot. She was with Adalia and Damon, neither of whom laughed along with her. As usual, Sadie didn't appear to mind singling herself out. Today she wore a tight *Kung Fu Panda* t-shirt, featuring Po front and center.

Before I could think it through, I flung my arms around her. Yeah, somewhere along the line since the kidnapping I'd become an emotional hugger. I guess there were worse things … maybe. I just couldn't quite seem to get my act together.

She stiffened at first, but then gave me a quick squeeze while awkwardly thumping my back, heedless of my recently healed ribs. "All right, girlie. That's enough of this mushy shit."

I pulled back and gave Damon a shy smile. "Hi, Damon. It's good to see you."

When he smiled, the gesture illuminated his eyes. "Glad to see you doing well, Rina." He bobbed his head a few times, thick dreads bouncing with the movement. "Hey, guys." Ky and Boone swooped in for some fist bumps and back thumping of their own while Leander resumed his place at my side like a sentinel.

"We have a ton of questions for you guys," I started, unable to wait a moment longer to find out what happened to Wendi, or if they knew more about Rage and Fury, or the vamp students. How had Wendi and the vamps even duped the school's defenses in the first place? "No one around here tells us much of anything." Not an entirely fair statement when Sir Lancelot couldn't help himself, but I didn't care. I needed to know everything. Maybe then I'd feel as if I had some control over my life.

Sadie laughed hoarsely, as if I were a riot all on

my own. "Hold your wild horses, girl. If you have tons of questions, then I need to fuel up first. Damon and I have hardly stopped since we last saw you. I've been dreaming of dining hall food."

"Well, that's not something you hear very often," Jas said.

"Why don't we all get some food and sit down for a civilized conversation?" Sadie suggested.

Damon grinned. "Are you sure you're capable of that?"

"Hey, there's always time for a first." Sadie gave the Enforcer who towered over her a saucy wink and strutted off toward the buffets. She put an extra sway into her hips, causing several of us to peer at Damon with great interest.

He noticed, but shrugged it off with the kind of cool I was incapable of imitating. In his torn jeans, casual t-shirt, worn boots, and waist-long dreads, he looked like he was ready to kick back with a fat joint and some Bob Marley tunes. Sounded like a far better way to spend the day than the torturous despair looping through my brain.

As if he'd read my thoughts, the Enforcer led me toward the food, clapping a large hand on the back of one of the seated Enforcers as we passed him and his maybe-brother. "Come on, Rina," he said. "Everything always looks better with a full plate of good food in front of you."

I wasn't sure he was right, but it was worth a try. I followed him toward the pygmy trolls manning their stations, not embarrassed at all to cower behind him.

❧ 21 ❧

ORANGESICLE HAD SHOCKED ME BY BEING ALMOST pleasant when preparing Damon's foot-long Italian submarine sandwich with extra salami, lots of hot peppers, and drenched in vinaigrette. He'd muttered only a couple of complaints while making my sandwich, a smaller version of Damon's, mostly because I didn't think well under pressure—when the troll pinned me in those black, beady eyes of his, I ordered the first thing that came to mind. But though Orangesicle had never been less scary, I was freaked the hell out to discover him slipping out from behind the counter he manned and following Damon back to our table. When he climbed onto the bench seat and claimed the seat next to mine, my entire body seized in panic. I worried I'd be too nervous to eat ... and then maybe Orangesicle would kill me for insulting his food preparation or some shit. I was so not cut out for this...

When Orangesicle turned to speak with Damon, I

tried really hard not to look, I really did, but my eyes drifted down toward the bench seat as if of their own accord, landing directly on two round little troll butt cheeks, peeking out from beneath the straps of his front-only apron and a loincloth that essentially amounted to a g-string. *Look away before he catches you looking,* my wise sense of self-preservation warned, but I couldn't seem to wrench my focus away. I finally looked up when I sensed someone's gaze crawling across me. Wren's doe eyes were wide as saucers as she took me in and then the troll and then me again. Yeah, Wren might have a heart attack before lunch was over. My gentle friend wasn't cut out for the stress of this life either.

Using the distraction of Wren as a crutch, I faced forward, steadfastly promising myself that I wouldn't look at the troll again. Not until he left the table. Still, I was hyper aware of his stubby arms that leaned onto the table and the way his ears and nose protruded from his head. I whisked a hand across my forehead, wondering how the hell I was going to keep my composure long enough to survive lunch.

When Leander settled at my other side, I knew there was no chance I wouldn't make a fool of myself in one way or another before this was over. The sexy elfin prince made me nervous all on his own, and he didn't even have to be mostly naked like the troll to cause the reaction. Though just the thought of Leander naked had me flushing and suddenly staring at my sub with extreme interest.

Leander's hand alighted on the small of my back,

and though his touch was brief, my cheeks flamed, and I shoved a bite of sub into my mouth, just to have something to do other than squirm with my many discomforts.

"Is something wrong, Rina?" he asked, but his voice was laced with amusement, which meant the fucker totally knew what was going on. I chewed my bite and pointed at my mouth. I wasn't going to answer with my mouth full … or at all. *Sucker.*

He grinned, his silver eyes glinting with mischief, and I wanted to throat punch him. Okay, not really, but I welcomed the badass thought. I'd been too much of a mushy pile of emotions lately.

Sadie slipped into the seat across the table from me as I swallowed. "Holy crap, Sadie," I said, taking in the plates of pepperoni pizza, two burritos drenched in Mexican sauce and melted cheese, and a huge bowl of spaghetti swimming in red sauce and meatballs. "I seriously don't get where you fit all that. You have enough food right there to feed the whole table."

The Enforcer opened her mouth to comment, but before she could, Orangesicle leaned forward, seeming to admire her dinner. "That's how women are supposed to eat," Orangesicle said in his sandpaper voice, and I met Wren's terrified stare as she settled next to Sadie. "You have to eat to be strong and meaty."

Jas giggled from Sadie's other side. "Meaty, that's funny."

"And why is that funny, girl?"

Dave, Adalia, Ky, and Boone took their seats then, and along with the rest of us they seemed to wait to see whether Jas would finally pay the price for her ill-timed comments. But Jas didn't appear concerned at all. "Because when I think of meaty, I think of hot guys and their *hot* parts." Worst of all, Jas flicked a hungry gaze at my brother further down the table.

Triple ew.

"Seriously, Jas," Wren said. "Do you ever think before you speak? The crap you say sometimes..."

"Is pretty hilarious," Sadie said happily, plowing into her spaghetti while her eyes rolled back at her first bite. "Oh my God. This is so damn good. Hmm." She moaned and spoke around a stuffed mouth, and Orangesicle grinned, as if this were his version of porn.

I scooted a couple of inches away from the freaky troll ... a couple of inches closer to Leander. Hmm. The length of my leg pressed against his, and I decided I wasn't going anywhere until someone made me. I could feel the muscles of his legs through his dark blue uniform pants. He reached beneath the table and squeezed my thigh beneath the hem of my skirt, and a rush of heat sizzled across every part of my body.

Until I sensed Ky glaring at me from the other side of the table. Yep, my brother definitely knew what was going on, or he had an idea. Maybe he had a worse idea of what Leander was doing to me since all he'd be able to see was Leander's hand disappear beneath the table and reach in the direction of my skirt. I plastered extreme innocence on my face for his benefit and trained my focus back on my sandwich.

"Before things have a chance to … digress … any further," Dave said, and I sent him a wave of silent gratitude, "we're dying for updates, Sadie and Damon. Fill us in."

"Yeah," Boone said. "Did you get Wendi?"

Sadie's mouth was stuffed so full she couldn't speak even if she tried, but the way she grimaced around her food had my stomach sinking even before Damon answered for them. "Wendi's in the wind."

"What!" Ky blurted as Leander's body went rigid beside me, tension rolling off him and into me. "She got away?"

"Yeah. Trust me, dude, we're far from happy about it. But by the time we found out she'd been the one to betray all of you—"

"All of *us*," Sadie interjected. "She fucked over every single one of the Enforcers as much as she fucked Rina and Ky."

"I love a fierce woman," Orangesicle grumbled seductively, snapping his hair net off and running a hand up his tall fro-hawk, his apron hitching up his thighs while he did so.

I ignored him entirely, I had to. "How'd she get away? She definitely didn't seem more competent than either of you."

"She isn't," Sadie growled, stabbing at her burritos before switching to twirling more spaghetti around her fork. "We have no idea how she got away like this, without a trace."

"We think she had some help," Damon added, and I looked between my brother and his best friends. That was too close for comfort to what they'd said about Rage and Fury. "It doesn't make sense otherwise. There's no sign of her anywhere. None of the other Enforcers have seen or heard anything about her. And supernaturals always talk."

"Yeah, she took her mother and ran, I guess." Sadie scowled. "The fucking coward."

Orangesicle licked a finger on each of his stubby four-fingered hands and wiped them across his bushy eyebrows, gaze pinned on Sadie as her movements became sharper and more violent, her food her convenient victim of her frustration.

"Well, we assume she got her mother back, anyway," Sadie said. "We don't even have proof of that, other than that her mom has dropped off the map too. And she has no more family to interrogate."

"To question, you mean," Damon interjected.

Orangesicle tsked. "Don't go correcting the fierce woman. She's got it right. Creatures respond to force and violence."

I scooted another inch toward Leander, capturing the loose fabric of his pants under my leg ... and stilled when Jas, Wren, Adalia, and Dave suddenly stared at something behind me.

Did I want to see what captivated their attention so? I was pretty sure I didn't, but I spun anyway.

Stacy stood several feet behind us, her mouth hanging slightly open in an uncouth look most unlike her. Even her usually bouncy red hair drooped like the rest of her. Her gaze went from my face, to the closeness between Leander and me, and blazed with anger when she followed his hand onto my leg, which was fully exposed since I'd turned.

After all the times she'd been nasty to me or draped all over Leander, I wished I could say something biting to her now. But I didn't have it in me. She looked defeated, and I knew a bit too much about that feeling. I wouldn't make it worse for her.

As Tracy and Swan swept around their friend, each taking an arm to lead her away, Jas smirked. "Karma's a bitch, isn't it, Cat Pack?"

Leave it to Jas... She couldn't keep her mouth shut if you paid her a fortune to do it, despite the fact that I didn't think this fully qualified as karmic payback.

Tracy and Swan sneered full-on in defense of their friend, and Sadie rocketed to her feet and let rip a snarl that sent the hairs across my arms standing on end. When the trio scampered away, Sadie laughed and reclaimed her seat, digging into her pizza with over-the-top ferocity.

"Be still my thumping heart," Orangesicle crooned, pulling at the top of his apron to fan himself. "Now that's one feisty woman." He leaned across the table, shoving aside plates and glasses, and giving me a full shot of his round, bare behind. "Where've you been all my life, sweetheart?"

"Feed me more like this, and maybe I'll tell ya."

Sadie was nonplussed, but I couldn't stop ogling the troll's ass while silently hating myself for it. Obviously the world of supernaturals didn't overly concern itself with health codes.

"Rina," Leander whispered into my ear, sending shivers through me and drawing me back to him—thankfully. I was all over the place, a freaking mess. He squeezed the hand that hadn't moved from my thigh.

I cleared my throat and plowed on: "I overheard Wendi saying that Rage had taken her mother, so it makes sense that the two of them would be gone once she turned Ky and me over." Too many concerned gazes settled across me, but I pretended not to notice. "I get that she did something to put Sadie and Wren to sleep, but how'd she get connected to the vamps? And how'd they knock Damon, Ky, Leander, and Boone out?"

"The dark sorcerer Jevan must have given her a spell to use," Damon said. "We assume Rage connected Wendi with the vamp students, and either he, Jevan, or Wendi handed out the spells for the vamps to use since Wendi wouldn't have been able to get into the boys' dorm after curfew."

"Right," Sadie said. "The Academy Spell would've kicked her right the fuck out. And if it wasn't a spell, which would've been simple enough once she got the drop on us"—she growled—"she and that Anton fucker must've had some sort of magical object or something."

I'd never heard Sadie let the F-bomb fly so freely. She was seriously pissed.

Boone leaned onto his forearms, giving Sadie his full attention. "Wouldn't you guys have found the magical object once you woke up if they used that?"

"Probably, I guess, but there are some out there that are so powerful that just a swipe from them is enough to knock you out cold."

"Really?" I blurted.

"Oh yeah," she said animatedly. "Magical objects are more powerful than most supes realize. I think Sir Lancelot and others like him work to keep the power of the objects secret so more supes don't go chasing them." Sadie stuffed an entire large meatball in her mouth, but that didn't stop her from continuing. "You should see the talismans. They're even crazier than the objects. They're..."—she shook her head in amazement—"just super insane. That's why there's a whole secret academy dedicated to teaching those with the gift to craft them."

Damon groaned. "Emphasis on the word *secret*, Sade."

She looked up. "Oops." But she didn't seem overly concerned by her indiscretion. She was like a more grown-up Jas.

"So what happened when you woke up?" Boone encouraged Sadie to get back on topic.

"Well, the second I woke up, I knew something was wrong. I had a killer hangover without the fun of getting stupid drunk. When I didn't find Rina, I figured that fucker Rage had taken her. Of course I didn't realize then that Wendi was the biggest fuck-head of them all. I 'woke' her up, thinking she'd been hit with the same sleep stuff. I assumed they'd done the same to Wren, but left her sleeping it off, and I ran to the boys' dorm while Wendi was supposed to go for help in another direction.

"Of course, the stupid curfew alarm went off the second I stepped foot inside the building, but we needed the alarm anyway. When I got to Ky's room, I found Damon and the rest of the boys out cold. And Ky was gone. I woke up Damon—"

"By pouring a bucket of water on my head," he interjected.

"Hey, whatever gets the job done, right?"

"Absolutely." And he meant it. Though he wasn't quite as colorful as Sadie, he was every bit as furious that their wards had been stolen from under their noses.

"Leo and Boone woke up quickly enough," she said, "and by then Fianna had arrived to find out who was breaking curfew. We told her what we thought was going on, and she took it from there. She went straight to Sir Lancelot."

I hung on her every word as she filled in the gaps of my assumptions.

"By the time Damon and I and the guys reached the gate, the rabbits were out cold. By the way," she said to Ky and Boone as if she somehow already knew of their plans to track Rage and Fury over the summer, "the rabbits seriously have a hate-on for Rage and Fury. They want to help find them."

Boone and Ky nodded. "We'll take the help," Ky said, and I decided my brother had lost his damn mind. They were killer rabbits as big as him and with a serious attitude problem.

"I've never seen any of the rabbits so angry," Orangesicle added, his moony eyes unmoving from the object of his affection across from him. "If they get their paws on those shifters, they'll slice them to shreds."

Maybe having the rabbits along to guard Ky and Boone's backs wouldn't be so bad after all. A thought popped into my head: "Hey, what about Jacinda?"

"What about her?" Sadie grumbled grumpily.

"Well, she and her, uh, men, I guess, attacked us when we arrived at the start of term, right? Maybe that was Rage's doing."

"Probably," Damon said, "but she won't be bothering you ever again."

"She won't be doing anything ever again." Sadie's face split into a deranged grin, only making her admirer sigh like a love-struck boy. "Thane took care of her."

It seemed every one of us more or less sane people at the table decided we didn't want to know. Whatever had happened to her and the others, she was no longer a threat.

"And we'll take care of Wendi," Sadie said. "Damon and I won't stop looking till we find her, isn't that right, Damon?"

"For sure. We'll get her. She can't evade us forever."

"Especially not when she has her mom with her. Her mom isn't trained and eventually she'll slip up."

"And the dead bodies from the mountain?" I asked, needing to know despite not really wanting to know.

Sadie waved her hand across the table in a dismissive gesture. "Nancy took care of them."

"Nancy as in Nancy the staff witch?" Dave asked, sounding as shocked as I was.

"Oh yeah, don't let the sweet little old lady act fool ya. She's tough as nails, that one. She incinerated the bodies with a flick of her hand. There isn't even a bloodstain left."

I swallowed hard. The Menagerie revealed itself to be more terrifying with each new disclosure.

"You know, Rina," she continued on as she cut into what was left of her burritos, "it's actually pretty damn lucky that you overheard Wendi talking, and that you fought those vamp bitches."

"Wait," I said. "How'd you hear about that?"

Her lips curved in a wicked smile. "You'd be surprised by the stuff I know."

I wouldn't doubt it.

"If you hadn't figured out that Wendi was a traitor and which vamp students had taken you guys, we might've never figured it out. I really believed Wendi had been asleep in the room next to me the whole time." Her chest rumbled. "That *bitch*."

"Breathe, Sade," Damon said. She nodded, her ever-present ponytail bouncing behind her while he picked up where she left off. "The vamp students obviously messed up if they let Rina figure out their identity. Wendi has to have been the one who took out the rabbits."

"She has to have had some object or something that would've allowed her to take them down quickly," Sadie said. "There's no way she could've outmaneuvered all three of them if not."

"Agreed," Orangesicle said. "Those rabbits are the best at what they do, behind us pygmy trolls of course."

"Of course," Damon agreed diplomatically.

"Anyway, however it all went down," Sadie said with her usual gruffness, "we'll find them all and make sure they're punished for their bad choices." Then her shoulders slumped in defeat and her gaze zeroed in on me like a missile. "I'm sorry I let you down, Rina. I'll never forgive myself for it."

"And she has heart too," Orangesicle whispered under his breath.

I blinked away sudden stupid tears and nodded jerkily. "It's not your fault." My voice hitched, and Leander removed his hand from my thigh to wrap it around my shoulders.

"It's totally my fault," she protested. "I was supposed to protect you so they couldn't get at you. Now you've lost your magic, all because of me."

I shook my head vehemently, trying to reassure

her, but I couldn't get my words to move past the gigantic lump in my throat. I hated being such a wuss.

"I know it's too little, too late, but I got your back, girl. And even if the powers that be decide to remove your protective detail, I'll still watch out for you."

My gaze flashed to the maybe-brothers Enforcers, only to discover them gone. Wren followed my thoughts and asked for me. "Where'd they go?"

"Now that Sadie and I are back," Damon said, "they left since we're so understaffed. But there's been some discussion that Rina no longer needs protection..." He trailed off while everyone at the table must have filled in what I was thinking: *Because I no longer have shifter magic.* I was no longer valuable or important.

Damon shrugged by way of apology. "They don't think Rage will come after Rina anymore now that he's gotten what he wanted."

"Makes sense," I said weakly. But the truth was that little made sense in my world anymore. I didn't have the heart to ask any additional questions, and my friends, who'd been so sensitive not to say the wrong thing since I'd returned to the academy—well, all except Jas of course—let the topic fall, filling the silence with mundane conversation about classes and the weather, though the weather varied little in the protected bubble within Thunder Mountain.

But even within the mountain, it wasn't safe. Not safe enough at least.

I allowed Leander to pull me against his chest, not even checking if this bothered Ky. I'd barely begun to be a part of the supernatural world, I was nowhere near ready to give it up yet.

Somewhere deep within me, hope rekindled, reminding me that I still had my mage magic. But I snuffed its subtle messages. I wasn't ready to pull myself back into the saddle just yet.

❧ 22 ❧

THE WARM SUNSHINE ACROSS MY BARE LEGS AND ARMS was pleasant enough to allow me to put aside all my worries. I was fed up with concerning myself about things I couldn't change. I was ready to move on with my life—whatever that looked like. I tilted my head back, my long hair snaking across the grass of the quad behind me, and let the sun beat against my face, pretending the heat could reach deep inside to warm that part of me that had remained frigid and empty since I'd lost my lion. Sadie had taken a seat on the grass far enough away that she wouldn't intrude on my moment while she kept an eye on me. For now at least, she continued to fulfill the role of my protector.

The spark of my mage magic had grown stronger since it no longer competed with my shifter powers. I could now find it whenever I looked for it. But I didn't yet have the heart to explore it, though I'd have to soon. It was nowhere near as potent as my shifter magic had been, but perhaps it could eventually fill some of the gaping pit within.

I peered up at the wily willow behind me. Its branches hung low, nearly skirting the ground, swaying in the slight magical breeze that seemed to continually waft across campus. As if the tree relished my sudden attention, it danced its long, flowing branches in my direction, brushing against my skin and uniform. I giggled before realizing what I'd done.

"See, there's hope for you yet," Boone said as he, Leander, and Ky plopped down next to me, Damon taking a seat next to Sadie across the way.

I caressed the wily willow's branch, covered in long, tendrils of leaves, before turning my attention to the guys. "Did you just get out of class?"

"Yeah." Ky peered at me in that calculating way he'd developed lately, as if he were taking my emotional temperature. "You skipped classes again?"

"Yep. I just wasn't feeling it today." I'd finally started attending classes again this week. "There doesn't seem much point to going to shifting class or Defensive Creature Magic when what's being taught no longer applies to me." I could've gone to Beginning Creature History more often than I did, since whatever I learned there might still be potentially relevant, but it was hard to care, especially when Professor Whittle was a walking, talking sleeping pill.

Ky scowled in disapproval, wrapping his arms around his knees and staring at me to make sure I got his point. I smiled like being the only one who no longer belonged didn't get to me, though none of the guys there would believe my act. "Besides," I said, "it's the last day of classes. I think you can cut me some slack."

"All you've had is slack lately."

I waggled my jaw, refusing to fall for his bait. I knew what he was doing. He was trying to rile me up.

"Come on, Rina, snap out of this funk. You can't keep wallowing."

I sucked in a harsh breath. "I am *not* wallowing. I'm recovering." But shit, what if he was right?

Leander scooted closer to me so that he sat beside me instead of facing me. "Back off a bit, Ky. It's reasonable that she should need a lot of time to come back from ... what happened."

Ky's scowl deepened. "Maybe." I no longer could tell if his frustration was directed at me or the situation.

More than ready to change the subject, I asked Ky the question I'd been dreading: "So... What are we going to be doing for winter break? Are we going home to Dad?" I hadn't forgotten that he'd planned to chase after Rage and Fury, but I was hoping he had.

He was already shaking his head before I finished. "I'm going to stay with Boone. His dad's sending a bunch of his wolves to help us track Rage and Fury."

"What about me, then? You're sending me home to Dad alone?" I gulped nervously. Though I'd texted Dad a few times since the kidnapping, I hadn't actually spoken with him. Unless Ky told him what happened, he didn't know. Which meant I'd have to relive it all over again when I told him the story. And

I'd be stuck in the house alone with him for an entire month.

Leander placed a hand on my knee. Ky's gaze shifted to where his skin touched mine like a laser beam, but Leander ignored him. "I'd like you to come home with me."

I blinked in surprise. Ky, Boone, and I had spent last summer in the fae's Golden Forest, but I'd thought that was a one-time thing. "But … but why? Your dad offered Ky and me asylum last summer, but that's when Rage and Fury were actively hunting us. Now that they got what they wanted, why would he extend a repeat invitation?"

"Because I asked him to."

"Oh. And he's okay with me coming there alone? With you? He didn't exactly seem pleased to have me around last summer."

"He'll live."

"Does that mean he's going to keep you so busy all break that you won't have the chance to spend any time with me again?"

"I won't let him. My father is a powerful, stubborn, hard-headed elf. But so am I, and he knows it."

I bit my lip. "He's still the king."

"And I'm his son. I choose what fights to wage with him, because it's a headache to take him on. I fought him on this, and I won."

"Just like that?"

"Just like that. For now, anyway."

Whatever that meant. No matter what Leander

said, I'd met his father and felt all the angry glares he'd leveled my way. There was no way that man would allow Leander and I to be together. But if Leander was willing to take his father on, maybe we could at least get to know each other better. It was about time. Despite the nature of my preoccupied thoughts as of late, I hadn't forgotten the way he'd kissed me on the night of the party. In fact, I'd taken to reliving the kiss and the feel of his hands on my body.

"Leo has already promised me that he'll be a proper gentleman with you," Ky said, his words tumbling out in a moody grumble.

I barked out a laugh before I could think better of it. "A proper gentleman? What, you mean like you are with girls?"

Ky grunted. "I'm plenty nice to girls."

"Yeah, to all dozen of them you cycle through at once, unless you've changed and I don't know about it."

He scowled, the gesture on repeat. "My best friend here has promised to treat you like he would his own sister in my absence."

"Oh dear God, I hope not."

"Those weren't my exact words," Leander said, an amused air to him. Boone waggled his eyebrows at the handsome prince. Obviously the werewolf wasn't opposed to our coupling as Ky was.

"Hey, hey, hey," Jas called from thirty feet away, oblivious to the moment she was interrupting, as usual. For once, I welcomed the intrusion as she,

Wren, Dave, and Adalia cut across the grass toward us from the direction of Irele Hall.

The skunk shifter plopped down between Boone and Ky, and sidled closer to Ky, seemingly uncaring that he hadn't done anything to return her blatant interest. She flipped the white streak in her hair back from her face, pulled her legs—clad in knee-high Minnie Mouse socks—under her, and shot my brother a saucy look. Her dangling nose ring swung as she batted heavily mascaraed eyelashes at him.

I waited for the inevitable brush-off … but it didn't come. He smiled at her instead.

Shit. *Double shit.*

Wren claimed the seat on the other side of Boone and shot him timid looks when she thought no one was looking. From her other side, Dave watched the interaction with interest, and I wondered if he might not have a thing for my roommate. He and Wren would be sweet together.

"I can't believe you skipped the last day of classes," Jas was saying to me across our haphazard circle of bodies. "You're my hero, girl. I thought I was going to have to jab my eyeballs with my pen just to keep myself from dying of boredom in Whittle's class. I hoped the guy would give us a break since, you know, it's the last day of classes and all. But nope. He just droned on and on like he always does. I don't even have a clue what he was talking about."

"He was talking about the history of the fae," Adalia said from her place between Ky and Leander. She gazed reverently at her prince.

"Was he really?" Jas asked while I kicked myself for not attending the class. I could've used more information about the people I'd be sharing winter break with. I was going to read as much of Dad's *Compendium* over the break as I could; I'd barely made it halfway through volume two so far with all the distractions. But Jas didn't seem to care about the information she'd missed, fiddling with the clasp of her Doc Martens. "Well, whatever he was talking about, I'm so freaking glad I won't have to hear his voice for the next month. Shit, I hope it doesn't haunt my dreams. That would suck."

"You're so dramatic," Wren commented.

"You can't seriously be such a goody-two-shoes that you're going to argue with me about how terrible his class is. You must struggle to stay awake in there, or else, I don't know what … you're like a god or something."

Wren smiled timidly, allowing her long brown hair to sweep around her face to partially conceal it. "I do fight to stay awake."

Jas clapped, startling all of us. "See! I knew it. The man is like the Sandman or something. Shit, maybe he is." Her light blue eyes widened at the idea. "Is the Sandman real?"

"Probably," Dave said. "We're all real, and according to humans, none of us exists."

"That's an excellent point, Davey Wavy."

Experience suggested that Jas would continue monopolizing the conversation so long as we let her, while the topics of conversation quickly digressed.

Several of us started to speak at once, probably with the same idea of cutting her off, when Sir Lancelot zoomed across the quad from the direction of the library. I stopped what I was saying to watch his flight, graceful and swift as ever.

He landed with enviable grace in the midst of our circle, Fianna and Nessa arriving several moments later, slightly out of breath from keeping up with the larger owl.

I stiffened at their arrival, wondering if he was here to scold me for my absence in classes today, or much of the days before. But when he pinned those wide, yellow eyes on me, I relaxed. They brimmed with compassion, and I found myself smiling at the headmaster.

"Good afternoon, Lady Rina," he said, before giving a slight nod toward Leander. "Prince Leander Verion, good day." As if unable to disobey etiquette despite the ridiculousness of addressing each one of us individually, he turned his head to take all of us in while his body remained stationary. "Lady Adalia, Lord Kylan, Lady Jasmine, Heir Boone, Lady Wren, and Lord Dave, good afternoon to you all."

The crimson fairy Fianna tapped her tiny foot impatiently while she hovered just above the grass—probably because its blades, though relatively short, would rise beyond her waist. When Sir Lancelot circled his head back around to me, she immediately ceased tapping her foot and plastered a patient smile on her face. It didn't suit her at all; I almost burst out laughing, but the thought of the fiery fairy's vengeance was enough to encourage restraint.

The sapphire fairy Nessa flew closer to me, flanking Sir Lancelot, looking at me with tiny, doleful cerulean eyes. Uh-oh.

Sir Lancelot brought his wings in front of him in a plaintive gesture. "I wanted to stop by before you departed, Lady Rina, to tell you that I sincerely hope the Academy Spell chooses to allow you to remain as a student of the school. I'm uplifted by the fact that it hasn't dismissed you yet. Perhaps you yet hold secrets we haven't anticipated."

I nodded mutely, not trusting myself to say anything.

He stared into my eyes as if he were staring into my very soul. "I'll be very pleased to see you at the beginning of next term. I hope that will be the case. Until then, be well, Lady Rina. I leave you in Prince Leander Verion's capable hands."

"Thank you, Sir Lancelot," I said, grateful that I managed to get it all out without a hitch. My insides rolled like molten lava. Not even the mention of Leander's capable hands was enough to distract me from the uncertainty of my fate.

He stared at me for longer than etiquette warranted as if memorizing my face, then dipped his head to me, flapped his wings, and rose into the sky.

"We'll catch ya later, Rina," Fianna said while she tugged at her short red skirt. "Hang in there."

"Thanks, Fianna."

The fairy with the scarlet hair flew off after her

boss, and Nessa appeared ready to do the same before she zoomed straight at me at alarming speeds. I jerked backward ... and she placed a kiss so small and so light on my cheek that I barely felt her lips alight on my skin. But her kiss warmed my heart as if she were a thousand times her size.

Clutching my cheek with diminutive hands, her wings a blur of movement behind her, she whispered. "I'm rooting for you. Make sure you come back."

"I'll do my best. Thanks, Nessa." And then my voice did crack.

She patted my cheek with one hand before rising to follow the others.

I swallowed thickly. "All of you, if I don't come back ... I mean, if I'm not allowed back, promise me you'll keep in touch. Text or call me or something. I'll miss you all tons."

Wren's eyes watered, and even Dave blinked faster than usual before Leander jumped to his feet and extended a hand to me. I allowed him to pull me to my feet while arching my eyebrows at him. "What?" I asked suspiciously.

"I can't take you being sad anymore. I'm making it my mission to cheer you up."

"Oh yeah? What makes you think you can?" I couldn't restrain the coquettish smile as it turned up the corners of my mouth.

"Because I'm about to unleash the entirety of my irresistible charm on you. You won't stand a chance."

I chortled. "Full of yourself much?"

"You tell me." In a swirl of silver light, his wings

burst from his back in a ripple of magic strong enough for me to sense it. His wings were pure white, tipped in silver, their feathers perfect. I couldn't help but stare at them as he spread them wide.

"Ready?" he asked.

"Uh … ready for what?"

He chuckled, the mirth lighting up his silver eyes that rolled like liquid mercury, pulling me into them with a magnetism I couldn't resist, didn't want to resist. If his plan was to distract me from the loss of my mountain lion by immersing me in him, then as far as plans went it was a damn fine one.

I yelped as he swept me into his arms and pressed me against his shirt front. Before I could say or do a thing, like make sure I wasn't flashing my brother with a view right up my short skirt, he pivoted, took a few running steps in the other direction, and leapt into the sky.

Sadie and Damon were scrambling to their feet, but they couldn't reach us up here. Nothing and no one could touch us.

He looked down at me while ascending past the wily willow that had caressed me minutes before. "I'll make it better, Rina, I promise. I'll distract you so hard that you'll forget you were ever sad."

I wasn't sure he could deliver on that promise, but I sure as hell would let him try. I grinned. "You've got yourself a deal. Fly me away, miracle man."

"You got it, beautiful." And as he soared toward what appeared to be infinite sky, but surely couldn't be within the enclosure of Thunder Mountain, I focused on nothing but the rush of air against my face, the steady beating of his heart beneath my ear, and the way my flesh tingled with heat everywhere he touched me.

If he wanted to distract me until I thought of nothing but him, I'd let him rise to the challenge— pun intended. A month alone with the prince might be just the medicine my broken heart needed. Right then I decided I was finished playing it safe. I had nothing to lose, everything to gain. I was through holding back with Leander. In fact, I was through holding back with life. I might have lost my lion, but there was plenty more to live for. I'd find every good thing in my life and celebrate the heck out of it.

The winter break promised to be sinfully pleasurable. Just the thing to turn my life around.

MAGE SHIFTER

Magical Creatures Academy: **Book Three**

Continue Rina's adventures in *Mage Shifter*!

ACKNOWLEDGMENTS

I'd write no matter what, because telling stories is a passion, but the following people make creating worlds (and life) a joy. I'm eternally grateful for the support of my beloved, James, my mother, Elsa, and my three daughters, Catia, Sonia, and Nadia. They've always believed in me, even before I published a single word. They help me see the magic in the world around me, and more importantly, within.

I'm thankful for every single one of you who've reached out to tell me that one of my stories touched you in one way or another, made you smile or cry, or kept you up long past your bedtime. You've given me reason to keep writing.

Lucía Ashta is the Amazon top 100 bestselling author of young adult and new adult paranormal and urban fantasy books, including the series *Magical Creatures Academy*, *Sirangel*, *Magical Arts Academy*, *Witching World*, *Dragon Force*, and *Supernatural Bounty Hunter*.

When Lucía isn't writing, she's reading, painting, or adventuring. Magical fantasy is her favorite, but the action, romance, and quirky characters are what keep her hooked on books.

A former attorney and architect, she's an Argentinian-American author who lives in Sedona with her beloved and three daughters. She published her first story (about an unusual Cockatoo) at the age of eight, and she's been at it ever since.

Sign up for Lucía's newsletter:
https://www.subscribepage.com/luciaashta

Connect with her online:
LuciaAshta.com
AuthorLuciaAshta@gmail.com

Hang out with her:
https://www.facebook.com/groups/LuciaAshta

facebook.com/authorluciaashta

bookbub.com/authors/lucia-ashta

amazon.com/author/luciaashta

instagram.com/luciaashta

Made in the USA
Middletown, DE
13 October 2020

21913836R10182